THE SACRIFICIAL DAUGHTER

THE
SACRIFICIAL
DAUGHTER

Mary Anne Kalonas Slack

White River Press
Amherst, Massachusetts

First published by White River Press, Amherst, Massachusetts
whiteriverpress.com

ISBN: 979-8-88545-002-7

Book interior and cover design by Douglas Lufkin,
Lufkin Graphic Designs, Norwich, Vermont • www.LufkinGraphics.com

Library of Congress Cataloging-in-Publication Data

Names: Slack, Mary Anne Kalonas, 1956- author.
Title: The sacrificial daughter / Mary Anne Kalonas Slack.
Description: Amherst, Massachusetts : White River Press, 2024.
Identifiers: LCCN 2023035960 | ISBN 9798885450027 (trade paperback)
Subjects: LCSH: Mothers and daughters--Fiction. | Parent and adult
   child--Fiction. | Self-realization--Fiction. | LCGFT: Novels.
Classification: LCC PS3619.L3283 S23 2024 | DDC 813/.6--dc23/
eng/20230919
LC record available at https://lccn.loc.gov/2023035960

In memory of my parents,
Frank and Elizabeth (Daley) Kalonas

One

As Mary Ellen finished reading Kate's email for the fifth time, the phrase *take a slow boat to China* came to mind. It was something her mother, Agnes, used to say occasionally about people she didn't like—"I wish Mrs. Sullivan would take a slow boat to China"—that sort of thing. When Mary Ellen was a little girl and questioned her mother, she'd told her that it meant taking the longest journey you could possibly imagine. "Like to Boston?" she'd asked. "Longer," her mother replied. "One that takes you away from home for months."

She smiled now at the thought. That's what I want—to take a slow boat to China.

Her mother's voice called from the kitchen, breaking into her reverie. She sighed. It was time to return to reality. She avoided a heap of dirty laundry on the floor as she made her way to the door. Her room was a mess, but at least her desk was clean, with a new laptop sitting in the center. Corrected math tests were stacked up neatly, waiting to be put into the grubby little hands of her third-grade students tomorrow.

"Mary Ellen, can you hear me?" Agnes was shouting.

"Loud and clear," her daughter said as she entered the kitchen. "Is something wrong?"

"Look at this." She handed over a section of the Sunday paper and pointed to an article at the bottom of the page.

"March Madness or March Mayhem? Are you suddenly interested in college basketball?"

"Sit down and read it," Agnes said, nodding at the chair across from her.

"In the college town of Worcester," Mary Ellen read aloud, "local college basketball games attract a big following. For the residents of the College Hill neighborhood, this has created problems.

"'Drunken kids on the sidewalk, vomit on my front lawn, noise until all hours of the night,' complained Betty Murphy, a College Hill resident. 'This used to be a beautiful neighborhood, and Holy Cross was an asset. Not anymore.'"

She looked over at her mother. "Betty Murphy? Your friend?"

"Yup. She told me about this. She said, 'Agnes, you're lucky you live on Vernon Hill.' She said she was going to call the police next time she heard the kids out on the street and ask them to clear them out."

"Sounds like that's what happened." Mary Ellen read further. "'Police swept through the area Friday night, taking eighty-five students from Holy Cross and Boston College, many of them minors, into custody.'" She looked up, wide-eyed. "Shit. Wasn't Lou going to that game?"

"Watch your language, Mary Ellen."

"Sorry. Did you speak to Frank yesterday?"

Lou was Mary Ellen's nephew, a freshman at Boston College, her brother Frank's son.

"Lou would never get caught up in something like that. He's too smart."

Sometimes her mother's naïveté amazed her, but she held her tongue. She heard her cellphone ringing. "Hang on, someone's calling me," she said, dashing to her room. When she located her phone under a pile of books and magazines on her nightstand, she saw a missed call from Frank. She called him back.

"What's up?"

"Listen, we're not going to be able to come for dinner."

"Are you serious? The corned beef's almost done, and Ma's decorated the dining room with every bit of shamrock-themed kitsch we've got in the house. Why aren't you coming?"

Frank hesitated. "Well, Lou got in trouble."

"Oh, no. At the Holy Cross game?"

"After the game. Did you see the article in the paper?"

"Yeah, Ma showed it to me. I wondered if Lou was one of the eighty-five, but she said he's way too smart for that."

"Huh. Apparently not. Anyway, he's home and there's been a lot of drama since we picked him up at the police station. He feels really bad, and we're just not good enough actors to plant smiles on our faces and sing 'When Irish Eyes Are Smiling,' as if everything's fine. I'm not sure what you should tell Ma."

"How about the truth? And how about *you* tell her?"

"She'll take it better from you. Break it to her gently. I'll call her later. I've got to go. Thanks, Sis."

She started to speak before realizing he'd ended the call. *Coward.* She took a deep breath and went back to the kitchen where Agnes was poking a fork into the corned beef.

"Is Maureen here yet?" she asked.

"Not yet. Listen, that was Frank. He and Rosie can't come for dinner."

"What? I don't believe this. It's Rosie. She doesn't really like coming to our family home and celebrating our Irish traditions. No, she'd rather be off dancing the tarantella with her own family."

Mary Ellen stifled a laugh. "Sit down, Ma. I have something to tell you. This doesn't have anything to do with Rosie. It's Lou."

Agnes put down the fork and sat. She pressed a hand against her chest. "Oh, no. Please don't tell me he was one of the eighty-five."

"I'm afraid so. He's home with them now, but they're all pretty upset, and they don't want to spoil the party."

"How could he be so foolish? How could he ruin his life at nineteen? What was he thinking?" She covered her face with her ruffled apron.

"I really doubt this will ruin his life, Ma. He'll probably just get a slap on the wrist. He's a good kid with a clean record up to now. Let's have a nice dinner with Maureen and Joe and the kids and—"

"Cancel dinner." Agnes's dark brown eyes peered over the edge of the apron. "Call Maureen and tell them not to come. I need to lie down."

"Oh, Ma, is that necessary? The food is cooked, and you worked so hard decorating the place. The kids will be so disappointed."

"Tell them I'm sorry. This is too much for me. Pack up the food and bring it to them if you want. You'll have to deal with it, Mary Ellen. I'm going to lie down."

Mary Ellen sat at the kitchen table, shoved her hands into her curly hair, and clenched her fists. She wanted to scream. Her mother was famous for this—falling apart in any crisis, whether real or invented. Mary Ellen should be used to it by now. Usually, she just took a deep breath and carried on, but she'd reached the end of her quiet tolerance. It had been ten years since her father's death, and Agnes had become more and more dysfunctional—controlling, unable to deal with anything that threatened the status quo. Mary Ellen muttered a string of expletives as she found containers for the hot food. When she'd assembled them on the table, she took a belated deep breath and called her sister.

"Dinner at our house is off. I'm delivering the food to you. I'll be there in about fifteen minutes. It's hot and ready to eat, so set the table while I drive over."

"What? Why? Where's Ma?"

"In bed, after having her usual overreaction to bad news. I'll explain it when I get there. Maybe you can meet me at my car and help me carry the food in. There's a lot of it."

Maureen was waiting outside, wrapped in an oversized sweater, her long brown hair pulled back in a low ponytail.

"Tell me what's going on," she began as soon as Mary Ellen got out of the car and headed for the trunk. "I'd like to hear what would make Ma cancel her annual St. Patrick's Day dinner."

In as few words as possible, Mary Ellen told her about the newspaper article, Frank's phone call, and their mother's over-the-top response.

"Poor Lou," Maureen said. "He's such a good kid. Nothing like his father. I hope Frank isn't being too hard on him, considering what a two-faced juvenile delinquent he was at that age. Ma was the only one who didn't see the stuff he got up to."

"Maybe she only pretended not to see, and now she's afraid that Lou is just like him. At any rate, she's in bed, probably waiting for me to sit beside her with the smelling salts."

"Well, come in and eat with us first. Let's tell the kids that Ma feels sick all of a sudden and doesn't want to infect anyone."

Mary Ellen was so tired of her mother's little games that she didn't say a word while Maureen explained to the kids.

Twelve-year-old Joanna accepted without question, but six-year-old Teddy continued to ask throughout the meal what exactly was wrong with his grandmother. Yesterday, she'd told him she was decorating the dining room so it would look like a leprechaun's lair, whatever that was, and he couldn't believe he wasn't going to be able to see it.

His father finally promised Teddy an extra scoop of vanilla ice cream with green sprinkles for dessert if he gave it a rest. The boy seemed to consider whether it would be worth it or not, then nodded his curly, blonde head and ate his meal quietly.

Maureen and Mary Ellen headed to the kitchen to wrap up leftovers and wash the empty bowls after lunch. Mary Ellen knew that Maureen sometimes felt guilty when she thought of how she'd escaped through marriage to Joe while her little sister was stuck with their mother.

"I'm sorry you have to put up with this, Mary Ellen. Is Ma getting more difficult as she gets older, or does it just seem that way?"

"Yes, and I'm sick and tired of it." She dried a bowl and placed it on the counter. "If you promise not to tell I'll share a secret with you."

"You're planning to kill her?"

"Not funny, Maureen. No, my friend Kate and her husband, Danny, are taking their adopted daughter, Mariah, back to China to show her the country where she was born. They want me to come with them. Kate told me all about it at lunch the other day. The trip is planned for July. Kate mentioned Beijing, the Great Wall, Shanghai, and some other places. I think it might be just what I need."

"You really have a desire to go to China?" Maureen asked.

"I love to travel—you know that. I love to go to places that amaze me, and I can't imagine China would disappoint."

"Ma's not going to be thrilled about this," her sister reminded her.

"Ma would like me sitting in the front room with her every evening watching *Jeopardy* and stupid sitcoms before giving me a lecture about how I should get out more. How will I ever meet a man if I'm sitting at home watching TV?"

"Have you ever pointed out to her that she contradicts herself?"

"No. That would require an honest conversation. Have you ever had one with her?" Mary Ellen challenged.

"Once or twice. Like when Joe and I got engaged. Ma threw a fit because he wasn't Irish. I called her on that one. She finally backed down and apologized. Most of the time I just let things go, but if there's something you really want, you've got to fight for it. She seems to cling to the illusion that she's in charge of her children's lives, and when reality sets in, it really throws her."

"You know, I'm going to be thirty-five in a couple of weeks," Mary Ellen said, tucking a few blonde-streaked strands behind one ear. Her normally pale skin was flushed, and her blue eyes flashed with frustration. "Thirty-five, and still living with my mother. Something's got to change. Maybe a trip to the other side of the world would do the trick."

She left the kitchen to say goodbye to Joe and the kids.

"Don't you want ice cream with green sprinkles, Aunt Mary Ellen?" Teddy asked.

"No, I've got to go check on Grandma. I'm sure she'll make this up to you. You can come over this week to check out the leprechaun's lair."

Maureen walked her to the front door and gave her a hug. "Good luck with Ma. I'll call her tonight and try to talk her out of being so upset about Lou. And you sign up for that trip to China, if that's what you really want."

When Mary Ellen got home, she took the leftovers to the kitchen and listened at her mother's door. Agnes was snoring softly. She went to her room and logged onto her email, reading Kate's message about the trip again. Then she googled some of the cities Kate had mentioned and read about The

Forbidden City and the Summer Palace in Beijing, and the panda bears in Chengdu. The house phone rang; she got up to get it but heard her mother speaking in the kitchen. She went to the door and listened.

"I can't help being disappointed, Frank. He's always been such a good kid. Yes, I know we have to forgive him. I already have. I said a rosary for him, so I know he'll be okay. You're a good father, and I know you'll help him through it. Can I count on you and Rose for dinner next Sunday? I'll just leave the decorations up and we'll pretend that St. Patrick's Day hasn't come and gone."

Mary Ellen heard her end the call and waited a minute outside the door before going in. "How are you feeling, Ma?"

"A little better after talking to your brother. Frank thinks Lou's going to be on probation at school for the rest of the semester, but that's probably the extent of it. Did you take the food over to Maureen's?"

"Yes. Teddy was a little disappointed. He wanted to see the leprechaun's lair."

Her mother chuckled. "I'll have Maureen bring the kids over one day after school, and I'll make cupcakes with green frosting to make it up to them."

"That's sweet of you, Ma." Despite her mother's irrational response to things, Mary Ellen knew she was a deeply caring person who would do anything for her family. "Are you hungry?"

"Is there any food left?"

"Of course. Want me to heat some up for you?"

"Sure. I think I can eat now that I know everything will be all right."

Silently, Mary Ellen heated the food. Then she put a plate of hot corned beef, cabbage, and potatoes in front of Agnes and watched her dig in.

"Not bad," Agnes said. "Is there any soda bread left?"

"Lots of it. The kids don't seem to like caraway seeds."

"I'm sorry you had to take the meal to Maureen's. I didn't mean to give you so much extra work. Something just comes over me when I hear bad news about my family. I can't describe it. I just get weak and I have to lie down."

"And when you get up again everything's fine, isn't it?"

Agnes hesitated. "Well . . . most of the time it is, I guess. But there could always be a time when it's not."

"But your family would be here to support you and to deal with whatever is needed. Whether you take to your bed or not doesn't change the outcome. Why not just stay with whatever's happening?"

"I don't know, Mary Ellen," Agnes said with a hint of defensiveness. "I remember my mother and my grandmother having the same reaction. Someday, you'll probably do it too."

"I don't think so, Ma."

"Why not?" She straightened her spine. Mary Ellen was reminded of a cobra preparing to strike.

"Because I don't like it when you do it, and I think I'll choose not to repeat the behavior."

"Well, don't you sound like a guest on the *Oprah* show?"

Mary Ellen could feel the shift toward dangerous waters. It was time to end this conversation. "Back to school tomorrow. I'd better pack my briefcase and get things organized for the morning." She stood up. "Would you like me to wash those dishes?"

"No, I'll do it. Go do what you need to do. Thanks for being such a big help today."

Mary Ellen kissed her mother goodnight and went to her room. After she gathered her school things, she returned to Kate's email and replied: *Kate, I want to go on the trip to China more than anything. Let's get together this week to discuss.*

Two

MARY ELLEN WORKED LONG DAYS all week. When Friday afternoon rolled around, in spite of having plans to go to Kate and Danny's, she fantasized about spending the evening in her room watching *Braveheart*. When she got home, she found her mother in the kitchen arranging crackers and cheese on a platter. Cocktail glasses had been set out next to a pile of green napkins and a bottle of Jameson's whiskey. Bags of chips were ready to be poured into serving bowls.

"I guess you're hosting the card party tonight."

"I told you that twice. You said you'd help me get ready."

"Did I?" Reaching across the table, she took two crackers and a piece of cheese.

"That's not for you," her mother scolded.

Mary Ellen pretended to be hurt. "Remember back when you had milk and cookies ready when I got home from school? All my friends were jealous. I guess those days are over."

"Oh, sit down," Agnes said with a smile, pulling out a chair for her daughter. She went to the refrigerator, got two homemade whoopie pies, and poured a glass of milk.

"Thank you," Mary Ellen said. "This is nice after the week I had. I'm exhausted."

"When I was your age, I had two kids, worked two nights a week at Jordan Marsh, kept the house clean, kept my family fed, washed, and ironed," Agnes said, taking a seat. "I don't see why you're so tired."

Mary Ellen made an effort to keep the irritation out of her voice. "Well, let's start with eighteen nine-year-olds from eight-thirty in the morning until two forty-five every day. Add in progress reports, testing, recess duties, a conference with a student's parents—who think I'm picking on their precious baby boy—and the night custodian out on medical leave with no one to fill in for him, so I end every day sweeping the floor."

"Yeah, I guess that's a lot. Well, you've got the weekend to take it easy. I only need you to take me grocery shopping tomorrow."

"Did I tell you that I'm going to Kate and Danny's tonight?"

"What time?"

"Six. I'm going to chill out for a while."

"You do that. Everything's ready for my party, so I guess I'm going to put my feet up for a little while, too, before my bevy of Irish beauties arrive."

Agnes was referring to Betty, Nora, and Ellie, old friends Agnes had gone to school with at Sacred Heart for twelve years. Every Wednesday the four of them went out to lunch, followed by Bingo at the parish center; every Friday night they played cards together, alternating as hosts. This troupe of women had always been part of the backdrop of Mary Ellen's life, and she mostly liked them, even though they seemed entirely too interested in her personal life. She was pretty sure her mother kept them apprised of her love life, or lack of it.

Mary Ellen sank into her well-worn recliner and watched *Braveheart* until it was time to get ready. She dressed in jeans and a deep blue sweater that reflected the color of her eyes. She was planning to forgo makeup until she heard her mother's friends' voices coming from the kitchen. She figured she might as well try to look nice, so she applied mascara, lip gloss, and a dash of blush to her pale cheeks. A little mousse dabbed into her hair gave her natural curls some bounce. She snapped off her bedroom light, and then remembered her cellphone, turning back into the dark room to retrieve it just as the ladies entered the adjacent dining room, highballs in hand. Her mother's voice stopped her in her tracks.

"Mary Ellen's having dinner with Kate and her family tonight."

"That doesn't sound very exciting," Betty said, putting down her highball and pulling out a chair.

"I wonder if that girl will ever get married. What do you think, Agnes?" Nora asked.

"She's got her students and her niece and nephews. She doesn't seem to want kids of her own. She's a homebody," Agnes replied with an air of resignation.

"You just don't want her to get married and leave," Ellie challenged.

"Oh, Ellie, nobody would be happier than me if she met Mr. Right, but I don't think it's going to happen."

Mary Ellen banged her shin on the bedpost and swore softly.

"Oh, Mary Ellen. You're still here?" Agnes laughed nervously.

"I'm leaving."

"Don't be too late."

Mary Ellen nodded, noticing that they at least had the decency to blush.

Bevy of old bitches, she thought as she headed out.

The Chinese food had already arrived by the time Mary Ellen came through Kate and Danny O'Day's front door. Kate was wearing jeans, a WPI sweatshirt, and a pair of slippers. Her long blonde hair was pulled up in a topknot away from her pretty face.

"We're not being fancy tonight, Mary Ellen," she said. "We'll serve right from the takeout boxes."

"Fine with me. Sorry I'm late." She sat at the dining room table.

"You look very nice, although a little tense. Everything okay?"

Mary Ellen shrugged.

"Danny, fetch this woman a glass of wine," Kate ordered.

"A big one," Mary Ellen insisted. "Maybe one for each hand."

"Behavioral issues again?" Kate asked, thinking of Mary Ellen's classroom.

"Yes. My mother and her friends."

Kate laughed. "What happened?"

"Let's eat first. I'm starving."

Danny entered with a cloth over one arm, carrying a bottle of chardonnay. He'd tied a dishtowel around his waist and hunched his lanky, six-foot-four frame toward their guest.

"Your wine, Ms. Kelleher," he said as he poured with a flourish. "And the menu for this evening is beef and peapods, Peking ravioli, chicken and cashews, beef teriyaki, and chicken fingers."

"Thanks," Mary Ellen said, raising her glass to him. "It sounds great. But please don't call me Ms. Kelleher. I get that all day from my students."

"Got it," he said, and then called to his daughter. "Mariah, get in here, please."

The ten-year-old slid into an empty chair and grabbed a chicken finger. "Do they have these in China?"

"Something similar. They eat all kinds of things," her dad replied.

Mariah wrinkled her nose. "I know. Like turtles, frogs, birds, fish, even dogs. Disgusting."

"I remember liking the food when we went to China to get you," her mother said. "There was never dog on the menu, so I don't think you need to worry about that."

"I don't think we liked everything," Danny countered. "But there's always rice or noodles, so you can fill up on that. And if worse comes to worst, there's always McDonald's or KFC."

"Seems insane to me to go to China and eat American fast food," Mary Ellen said, as she bit off a piece of beef teriyaki.

"For adults, yes," Danny agreed. "For a ten-year-old? Whatever works."

After dinner, Danny volunteered himself and Mariah to clean up. Kate suggested that she and Mary Ellen take their wine out to the back deck. They put on their coats and sat down, looking up at the night sky.

"Are you ready for this?" Mary Ellen asked. "As I was leaving tonight, I heard my mother and her friends discussing my boring plans for a Friday night, and how I don't want any kids of my own. That I'm just a homebody, happy to stay single."

"Wait. I thought you liked your mom's friends. I thought they were a bunch of sweet old ladies. Why would they say that?"

"I guess it was mostly my mother. She has a whole practiced speech about the status of her single daughter. She fits me neatly into a little cubby and hopes I'll stay there."

"And are you comfortable in that cubby?" Kate asked.

Mary Ellen thought for a moment. "Too comfortable, maybe. I've been in it so long that my limbs have conformed to the shape of the space. For some reason, it's now starting to feel really confining. I need to stretch these limbs." She reached her arms up toward the stars. "I want to go far,

far away and get a break from all of them—my mother, my siblings, our apartment, even this city."

"Is China far enough?"

"Yes, I think China is perfect. A slow boat to China."

"Except it will be a fast plane. Though it does take a long time to get there."

Mary Ellen laughed and tipped back the rest of her wine. "Truthfully, China was never on my list, but I can't say no to this opportunity. It'll blow my little cubby to bits." She laughed again, picturing her mother staring at the blown-up cubbyhole, a bit of soot on her unhappy face.

After a few minutes, they went back to the house, where it was warm and bright, and the dishwasher was humming. From his usual spot on the recliner, with Mariah wrapped in her favorite blanket at her father's feet, Danny suggested they watch a DVD about China.

"I don't think I need any persuading," Mary Ellen said.

"Yay," Mariah cheered.

"I need to make sure I can afford it, but I really want to go." She sat on the sofa next to the recliner; Kate sat beside her.

Danny picked up a pile of papers off the coffee table and shuffled through them. "I think I've got everything here. I printed out a proposed itinerary with the costs I've been given so far. The first deposit of $300 is due in about three weeks." He handed the papers to Mary Ellen. "I just talked to Lily this morning. She's the travel agent the adoption agency deals with. Since we're such a small group, she suggested that we travel with another family from Boston. Bishop is their name. I'm pretty sure she said it was a husband and wife, an adopted Chinese daughter, and an older biological kid. It's a way to cut costs. We don't need to do the same activities, but we can share some of the local guides and transportation. Lily gave me the guy's number so we can arrange a meeting to make sure it's a good fit. I'll need your decision by April tenth."

"I've already decided. I'm going." She flipped through the paperwork. "I can do this. Do you want the check now?" She pulled her checkbook out of her bag. Kate and Danny watched as she signed and handed it over.

"Wow. I thought you'd be a tougher sell than this. We're thrilled, aren't we, guys?" Danny asked.

"Absolutely," Kate agreed. "When we went to pick up baby Mariah, I wished every day that you were with us. You would've fallen in love with those little ones in the orphanage."

Mary Ellen leaned down and put her hand on Mariah's shoulder. "Instead, I fell in love with the one you brought home." She kissed the top of her silky head.

"I won't send the deposit until April tenth, so if something comes up, I can shred it," Danny said.

"Nothing is going to stop me," Mary Ellen replied confidently. She took a deep breath and pushed a vision out of her head of her mother taking to her bed in shock when she told her she was going. "I'm going to start learning Mandarin this weekend."

"Great," Kate said. "We only know 'hello' and 'thank you.' Somehow that seemed to be enough when we were there ten years ago."

They hugged goodbye, and Mary Ellen drove home feeling excited for the first time in a long while. This was what she needed. Something completely out of the ordinary.

Three

SATURDAY MORNINGS always included a trip to the grocery store. Mary Ellen wished her mother would drive herself, but she'd given up her license five years ago at seventy because she said driving made her anxious. Mary Ellen would rather sleep in, but this was her life. And on the morning after her dinner with the O'Day family, she actually found herself humming as she pulled out of the supermarket parking lot.

"You're in a good mood today," her mother noted. "What's making you so happy?"

"It's a lovely sunny morning, and spring is finally here. What other stops do you need to make? Anything at the dry cleaners?"

"Nope. Remember, I got ice cream. We've got to get that into the freezer."

"Is everybody coming tomorrow?"

"Yes. I just talked to your brother. Even Lou is coming."

"Lou?" Mary Ellen was surprised. "Is he home for the weekend?"

"Frank is making him come home on weekends. I guess that's his way of grounding him."

"And how does Lou feel about that?"

"We'll find out tomorrow."

She and her mother carried their groceries up to their third-floor apartment, then worked together like a well-practiced team, Agnes putting the cold food away while Mary Ellen stocked the pantry.

"How does grilled cheese and tomato soup sound for lunch?" Agnes asked.

"Perfect. Need any help?"

"No, thanks. Go correct papers. I'll call you when it's ready."

Instead of correcting spelling tests, Mary Ellen rehearsed her speech about the China trip.

When Agnes called her for lunch, she took a deep breath and went to the kitchen. She grabbed a bowl of soup and put it on a red plastic placemat next to the grilled cheese sandwich, which was done just the way she liked—brown on the outside with cheese melting over the edges.

"This looks great."

Agnes nodded, seeming preoccupied.

Mary Ellen hesitated to ask what was on her mind. After they'd finished eating, Mary Ellen put on the kettle for tea.

"Ma, there's something I need to talk to you about."

"Yeah, I need to talk to you about a few things, too."

"Oh? Do you want to go first?"

"We need to advertise for the first-floor apartment." Agnes owned the triple-decker where she and her daughter occupied the third floor. "Yesterday Jill Jackman told me they're going to close on their new house July twelfth. Can you put an ad on Craigslist that it'll be available August first?"

"Sure. I can do that today."

"Good. And Betty's son, Kevin, has invited the girls to spend a week at his house on the Cape in July. Everybody wants to go, but nobody wants to drive. I said maybe you'd come with us for the week and you can do the driving. What do you think?"

"The girls," of course, meant the troupe of Betty, Nora, Ellie, and Agnes.

"Actually," Mary Ellen said, the words now forcing themselves from her mouth, "I'm making some travel plans."

"Where are you going now? To the Brimfield Fair?" Agnes laughed as she said it. After all, Mary Ellen hadn't traveled far from home in a long time. Agnes got up and grabbed two cups and put them on the table. "Black tea or herbal?"

"Black is good."

The whistle on the kettle pierced the silence and Agnes poured.

"Milk?"

"Sure." Mary Ellen dunked her tea bag in her cup.

Agnes placed the milk in the center of the table and sat back down. "What were we saying?"

"I was starting to tell you about a trip I'm planning to take. Do you remember me telling you a while ago that Kate and Danny wanted to take Mariah back to China this summer?"

Agnes narrowed her eyes.

"They've invited me to come along. Isn't that great?"

"Oh, dear God! Do you have to do everything Kate wants? Don't you have a mind of your own?"

"What's that supposed to mean?"

"You two are attached at the hip." She slapped the table for emphasis.

"We are not. Our lives are completely different."

"But you do everything she wants you to do!"

Exasperated, Mary Ellen pushed herself away from the table. "I don't want to go to China because Kate wants me to go. I want to go because right now I need something completely different. This will make me a better teacher. It will be good for me!"

"And how will it be for me? Have you thought about that? How long will you be gone? What am I supposed to do while you're on the other side of the world?"

"You'll play cards and Bingo with your friends, make Sunday dinner for Frank and Maureen and the kids. You'll do what you always do. And now you've got an invitation to go to the Cape. That will make the time I'm gone go even faster."

"Well, I can't go to the Cape now," Agnes huffed. "We need somebody to drive. If you won't come, we won't be able to go at all."

"That's just silly. I'm not the only person who knows how to drive. If Kevin really wants you all to come, he can make arrangements."

"But I told the girls you could do it," Agnes said, crossing her arms across her ample breasts.

"That's not exactly fair, is it? Don't you think you could have asked me first?"

"You have the whole summer off. And you love the Cape. I thought you'd want to go. And why China, of all places? Aren't you afraid to fly that far?"

"It is a long flight. Two, actually. One to San Francisco, and a second to Beijing. And no, I'm not afraid. I know that the thought of it scares you, but I'm okay with it." She leaned forward, allowing herself a hint of a smile. "Once we're there, it will be amazing. There's so much history. We'll start in Beijing and see the Forbidden City where the emperors lived. Remember when we saw *The Last Emperor*? It was filmed there. We'll see a bunch of sights and then go north to see the Great Wall of China. We'll get to climb this huge structure that's been . . ."

"I can't believe you're doing this to me. I have to lie down," her mother interrupted, heading toward her room, which was off the kitchen.

"Ma, really. I'm only going on vacation," Mary Ellen called after her.

Agnes dismissed her with a sharp, backhanded wave. "Don't talk to me. You will be the death of me." She slammed her bedroom door.

Mary Ellen's head sank to her hands just as the phone rang.

"Hi, is Ma there?"

Frank. Great timing.

She took the conversation out to the dining room. "She's here, but she can't talk right now. She's in bed. I might have killed her this time."

"What are you talking about?"

"I want to take a trip with Kate and her family to China in July. I just broke the news, and now I can hear Ma sobbing. It's like I've broken her heart or something. Maybe she's just too frail now."

"Frail? Ma? Are you kidding? She's as strong as an ox. She's playing you, kid."

"What do you mean?"

"If you want to go to China on vacation—although frankly I can't understand why you'd want to—then go. Don't let her stop you from living your life. And pull it together."

Mary Ellen swatted at a tear. "That's easy for you to say. I have to live with her. June is still three months away. I can't look at her depressed, martyred face for that long. She'll break me, I know she will."

"I'll come over and talk to her. June, huh? You know what? Lou can live with her while you're gone. That'll be his penance for screwing up. She'll love that."

"Would he do that?"

"He might not like it, but I won't give him a choice. He'll probably have a job for the summer, so it's not like he'll be with her all day. I'll bet when she hears this, she'll forget all about you abandoning her."

"Nice, Frank."

"Should I come over now?"

"I can't tell you how much I appreciate this. Honestly, I thought you'd be on her side."

"Are you kidding? This is win-win. I was trying to think of some way to make Lou suffer. This is perfect. I'll be over in a half hour."

Mary Ellen hung up the phone. She could hear Agnes sniffling. She moved toward her mother's bedroom door but changed her mind. *She's all yours, Frank. Good luck.*

Tuesday, March 30, 2010

*It's been an interesting day. My thirty-fifth birthday.
I'm still wrapping my head around the fact that I'm
now halfway to seventy. Ugh.*

*On Sunday Ma decided to start speaking to me
again. For a week and a half, she pretty much ignored
me, which was actually a relief. I went to yoga class
a couple of times, went over to Kate's to hang out and
watch videos about places we'll go in China, kept myself
busy outside the house. On Sunday, Ma told me she'd
like to have a little party at dinnertime on my birthday.
I'd already made plans to go out with Ben after school.
Ben is the music teacher, new this year. He's twenty-
eight, really cute and fun, and gay. I just love him, and
we make each other laugh. I told her I'd made plans
but that I could be home by six for cake, so she invited
Maureen and the kids over and I brought Ben home
with me. Ma seemed pretty excited that I brought a
guy home, but the longer he stayed, it seemed like she
figured out that we would never be a couple. She kept
quiet about it, though, which is something in itself.*

*Ma gave me a hat you'd wear on safari—tan,
lightweight, tons of UV protection. She said she looked
up the climate in China in the summer and she's
worried about my fair skin burning. Looks like I don't
have to worry about that now, as long as I don't care
what I look like. I guess she's coming to terms with me
going on this trip. Maureen gave me this journal so I
can record every detail of my trip. Until then, I'll write
a page a day to get in the habit.*

Four

AT LAST, JUNE TWENTY-SIXTH ARRIVED. Mary Ellen got up well before dawn and said goodbye to her mother, who'd come downstairs to see her off.

"You be careful, Mary Ellen. Please don't do anything foolish."

"Ma, I'm always careful when I travel. And I won't be alone."

"Still, it's a dangerous world out there. Promise me you'll come back in one piece."

"I promise," she said, hugging her close, kissing her damp, wrinkled cheek. "I love you. Please don't worry. I'll see you in seventeen days."

Mary Ellen slid into the van that was waiting to take them to the airport, while Agnes stood in the doorway, looking small and alone. Mary Ellen blew her a kiss and closed the door.

A large cup of Dunkin' Donuts coffee pre-flight made Mary Ellen jittery during takeoff. She watched the Great Lakes appear, the checkerboard fields of the Midwest. The sky was clear as they soared over the Rockies. She pointed out the snowcapped Sierras to Mariah, and they both cheered when they finally cleared the bay and landed in San Francisco.

After a brief layover, they boarded the plane to Beijing. Mary Ellen's seat was next to a Chinese woman with a croupy-sounding cough.

"I'm glad my vaccines are up to date," Mary Ellen whispered to Kate, who was seated on the aisle across from her.

"Is she at least covering her mouth?"

"Not yet," Mary Ellen replied, angling her body toward the aisle.

"You could hold your breath for twelve hours," Kate said with a grin.

It was seven-fifty a.m. Beijing time. That would be three-fifty p.m. San Francisco time, six-fifty p.m. in Worcester. At least Mary Ellen thought that was right. She changed her watch to China time, so she'd adjust before the plane landed. She pulled her journal out of her bag and placed it in the seat pocket for later. She closed her eyes, hoping she'd be able to sleep. Her mind was still racing from a whirlwind of preparations since school had ended the previous week. At least her mother was happy that she'd have her precious grandson with her while Mary Ellen was gone. Agnes would enjoy pampering him, and Lou would take it in stride. Mary Ellen breathed deeply, exhaling three months' worth of stress, and dozed off.

Nearly twelve hours later, the plane touched down, and the passengers made their way to the terminal. Perhaps it was because she'd only slept in short naps, but to Mary Ellen it seemed that there was a hush over everything. The ceilings were vaulted, and Chinese music echoed softly as they passed stands of potted bamboo. It was clean and peaceful, nothing like the churning chaos in Boston and San Francisco. Their luggage scrolled off the conveyor belt in the first fifteen minutes. They followed signs to customs, joined the line marked "Foreigners," and were checked through with impressive speed and efficiency.

Danny, who was heads taller than everyone else, spotted a slender Chinese woman holding a sign: "O'Day!" He pointed in her direction, and everyone followed him through the crowd.

The young woman introduced herself as Dorothy Chang. She asked them to stay close as she guided them onto a packed elevator. When they reached ground level, a white van was at the curb. The driver jumped out and took their bags, tossing them into the back. Dorothy introduced him as Leo *shi fu*, explaining that shi fu meant "master."

Then they were off, the van plunging into traffic. Mary Ellen said a silent prayer of thanks for Leo, who was indeed masterful, dodging cars and avoiding the thick throngs of pedestrians, bicycles, and rickshaws that edged into the road, trying to cross. She decided to look up at the skyscrapers instead, some of them barely visible through the smog.

When they arrived at the President Hotel, a turbaned Indian man wearing a red coat welcomed them, and then loaded their luggage onto a cart. Dorothy collected their passports, checking them in. As they waited, she told them that the Bishop family had arrived the day before and were anxious to meet them for sightseeing the next day. A few minutes later Larry Bishop, his wife Erica, and their two daughters came through the revolving door; the females were carrying shopping bags. Mary Ellen and the O'Days had met them for coffee at Starbucks back in April to make sure they seemed like good traveling companions. Though their older daughter hadn't been with them, it had felt like it would be a good fit.

Larry, a good-looking man in his forties who carried himself with confidence, extended his hand to Danny. "You made it! Quite the flight, isn't it?"

Erica was petite and very attractive, with green eyes and a short, blond-streaked haircut. She gave Mariah's shoulders a quick squeeze as she greeted the women. "You're exhausted, aren't you?"

Mary Ellen and Kate nodded.

"We felt the same way. We were lucky to have a day to rest. We went out around one o'clock for lunch, hitting the shops, but other than that we've been lying low."

"I just feel so grungy," Mary Ellen said. "I can't wait to shower and brush my teeth."

"You'll feel better after a nap," Erica advised, "but don't sleep too long. We should make plans to meet for dinner. Don't you think, Larry?"

Larry turned away from his conversation with Danny. "Don't I think what?"

"We should plan to meet for dinner. Maybe around seven? We can eat someplace around here."

Larry looked at the new arrivals. "That's entirely up to you folks."

"I just want to get to the room and clean up and rest for a while," Kate said. "I think a late dinner would be fine. We'd better call you in case we need more time. Okay with you, Mary Ellen?"

She nodded, anxious to end the conversation and get to her room.

Dorothy stepped forward with their room keys. "I'll take you up and make sure you have everything you need."

Mary Ellen made sure she knew where to find everyone, and then slid the keycard into her door and turned on the lights. The room was furnished with a double bed, writing table, chair, and dresser. Nothing about it seemed particularly Chinese; it could have been anywhere in the world. She turned on the bathroom light and checked out the shower and separate bathtub, noticing the clothesline above.

After brushing her teeth, she stripped off her clothes, and got in the shower, savoring the feel of the hot water. She rinsed her hair, wrapped it in a towel, and lay down on the bed. Within seconds, she was asleep.

She woke up an hour later and called Kate's room to tell her she was going to head down to the lobby to check out the hotel's offerings.

Across from the main desk, Larry Bishop and his youngest daughter sat at a table, engaged in conversation. Mary Ellen hesitated, but Larry looked up with a smile and invited her to pull up a chair.

"You remember Anna-Mei, don't you?" he asked, gesturing to his daughter, a pretty young teen with shoulder-length black hair. She wore black-framed eyeglasses and was dressed in shorts and a t-shirt.

"Of course. It's nice to meet you again. Remind me. Is this your first trip to China since you were adopted?"

"Yes. I was a year old and that was thirteen years ago." She smiled shyly.

"Are you excited to be back?"

She nodded. "It's kind of unbelievable to think I'm from here, but I have no memory of it."

"And your other daughter . . ." Mary Ellen looked back at Larry.

"Dakota. I guess you folks didn't meet her, did you? She was at school when we had our coffee date."

"And I was too dazed to introduce myself earlier in the lobby. How old is she?"

"She's twenty," Anna-Mei answered. "She goes to Northeastern. She's going to be a physical therapist."

The elevator door opened, and Dakota and her mother emerged. The twenty-year-old was tanned and long-limbed, while Erica now looked pale and tired, her face pinched.

Erica forced a smile when she approached Mary Ellen. "You look refreshed."

"I do feel much better," she said, "although I'm running on little sleep. It'll have to be an early night for me, I'm afraid."

"How's your migraine?" Larry asked his wife.

Erica frowned. "I agree with Kate. Definitely an early night."

"Actually, I'm Mary Ellen. Kate is Mariah's mother." She reached a hand out to Dakota. "You're Dakota, of course."

Dakota flashed a beautiful smile as she shook Mary Ellen's hand. "Is Kate your sister?"

"No, just a very good friend. We both teach third grade in the same school. Our classrooms are next to each other."

Then Danny, Kate, and Mariah joined the group.

"We checked out the local restaurants this afternoon," Larry said. "There's a Japanese restaurant, of all things, around the corner, two or three Chinese restaurants, and even a pizza joint."

Mariah's eyes lit up. "Pizza! Please?"

The rest of the group chuckled and looked at each other hesitantly.

"Pizza our first night in China, Mariah?" her father said. "Are you sure about that?"

Anna-Mei smiled sweetly at Mariah and said, "I think that's a great idea. Pizza is my favorite, too. Let's go—I remember how to get there."

Without waiting for the others, the two girls headed for the door.

"Wait up, Mariah," her mother called, running across the marble floor.

"I'm sorry," Danny said to the others. "Are you okay with pizza?"

Larry laughed. "Sure. Our daughters are natural-born leaders, I see."

"That's one way to put it," Danny replied.

Conversation ceased as the group hurried to keep up with the girls.

"Good Lord," Erica panted. "It's too hot for this." She put her hands on her temples and rubbed.

"Oh, no. This isn't good for your head, is it?" Mary Ellen said and mouthed "migraine" to Kate.

Erica looked as if she might be sick. "I need to go back to the hotel."

"We'll walk you back," Mary Ellen offered.

Erica shook her head. "Dakota can come with me."

"But, Mom, I need to eat."

"Would you tell Larry to bring some pizza back for Dakota, please?"

"What about you?" Kate asked. "Can we bring you something?"

"Nothing," she replied, taking her daughter's arm and turning around.

Dakota pointed toward a pedestrian bridge. "Go across that and you'll see the restaurant down on the ground level. It's called Roma, I think." They walked away.

"Poor Erica," Kate said.

Mary Ellen nodded and glanced around anxiously. "Where did the rest of them go?"

"Don't worry, the hotel's just around the corner. We're not lost." They climbed the stairs leading to the bridge. "I can't believe this is your first night in China and you have to eat pizza."

"Ironic, isn't it?" Mary Ellen replied, her eyes darting around, in search of the restaurant. "Is that it down there?" she said, pointing to a storefront with a photo of Roman columns in the window.

"Must be."

Mary Ellen caught Kate's arm. "Kate, I'm in Beijing, China, on a busy street at night. This morning I was in Worcester."

"Actually, that was yesterday morning, which is why it all seems surreal. Stick with me. I won't lose you."

They entered the restaurant and found Larry waiting. "We're upstairs," he informed them with a smile. Halfway up the staircase, he stopped. "Where are Erica and Dakota?"

"They went back to the hotel," Kate explained. "Your wife wasn't feeling well. Dakota went with her. She said to tell you to bring back some pizza."

"She really didn't look good," Mary Ellen added.

"I see," Larry replied as they reached the table. Danny and the girls were poring over the menus, which were written in Mandarin and English.

"Where's Mom and Dakota?" Anna-Mei asked.

"They went back to the hotel. Mom's headache, I guess," Larry answered. "What looks good to you girls? Is there any sweet and sour pizza? Or noodle pizza?"

"We don't want Chinese food, Dad," Anna-Mei whispered, conscious of the waitstaff hovering nearby. "Let's get a cheese pizza and a pepperoni."

"They have pepperoni in China?" Mary Ellen asked. "I wonder if it's imported, or if it's a local concoction that looks like pepperoni."

Mariah wrinkled her nose. "I'll have cheese pizza, no pepperoni."

"You don't like pepperoni?" Anna-Mei asked.

"Only the imported kind," she answered. Her parents laughed.

The pizza arrived and they all dug in. Mariah and Anna-Mei seemed quite happy with it and continued their lively chatter through dinner while the adults quietly ate. Mary Ellen wanted to engage Larry in conversation but couldn't think of a thing to say. She glanced at him discreetly, noticing his handsome, clean-shaven face, his strong, well-kept hands, the touch of gray at his temples.

"Why is nobody talking except Anna-Mei and me?" Mariah asked.

Larry unfolded his arms and smiled. "You two are more entertaining. Why compete?"

"That's not true," Anna-Mei replied.

"Frankly, I think we're all a little brain-dead. Here we are in China eating pizza under a mural that says, 'Roma.'

31

Our bodies think it's eight o'clock in the morning, and I don't know about the rest of you, but I feel like I've been run over by a rickshaw," Larry offered.

Mary Ellen erupted with laughter. Kate looked at her as if she were insane, then suddenly joined in. When she felt on the verge of hysterical tears, Mary Ellen grabbed a napkin and dabbed her flushed face. "I'm sorry. It's becoming clearer every minute that I need to get to bed."

Larry eyed the leftover pizza. "I wonder if they'll give us a doggy bag."

Mary Ellen started to laugh again. She shook her head. "Just ignore me."

His face broke into a grin. "We'd better get you back to the hotel before they lock you up."

"Come on, Mary Ellen," Mariah said, taking her by the hand. "Pull yourself together."

Mary Ellen kept laughing. "Don't anyone talk to me."

Anna-Mei started to laugh and then everyone joined in as they made their way outside, getting puzzled looks from the Chinese diners along the way. Larry paid the bill and followed.

"I'm not sure what we did for Chinese American relations in there, but I'm sure it had some effect," he said.

"To bed, Larry," Danny replied. "As quickly as possible, please. And nobody says a word to Mary Ellen."

When they got back, Larry handed the leftover pizza box to Anna-Mei and walked down to say goodnight to the others. "We're meeting Dorothy downstairs at nine o'clock. Breakfast starts at seven. I expect we'll all be up early."

The O'Days wished him goodnight and closed the door to their room. Mary Ellen was still groping for her card-key, trying to control an attack of the hiccups, when Larry stepped up.

"Take a really deep breath and hold it down in your stomach," he said. "Then swallow and release the breath slowly. That always works for me."

Mary Ellen pulled the card from the pocket of her pants and tried to open the door while following his directions. She hiccupped again, feeling a little uncomfortable at how close Larry was, the gaze from his grayish blue eyes intent on her face.

"May I?" he asked, taking the card from her and turning it over, successfully unlocking the door. He pushed it open and slid the card into the light switch. "You'll probably have to do it a few times before they'll stop."

Mary Ellen nodded. "Thank you," she hiccupped.

Larry smiled. "Thanks for a good laugh, Mary Ellen." He walked away, calling over his shoulder, "I was overdue for one. Sleep well."

Mary Ellen waved, then closed and locked her door. She smiled as she got ready for bed, thinking of the laughter and camaraderie of the evening. She liked Larry. Maybe they'd become friends. She concentrated on his instructions, which worked after the third time. And then she fell into a deep sleep.

Five

I T WAS A HOT AND HUMID MORNING, the sky an unrelenting white due to the air pollution. The travelers stood at the edge of the vast Tiananmen Square. Stretched around the perimeter of the square, a long line of Chinese people waited patiently to see the body of their dead ruler, Chairman Mao. A huge portrait of the chairman appeared to keep watch from above. Mary Ellen didn't see any Westerners in the line, and Dorothy, who carried a pale pink parasol so they could see her in the crowd, didn't offer to stop. Instead, she pointed out the monument to fallen revolutionaries where tall, rifle-carrying soldiers looked to be goose-stepping in front of the Chinese flag.

Mary Ellen offered to take a photo of Larry and his daughters. They posed with the face of Mao over Dakota's left shoulder.

"I'm sorry Erica's feeling lousy. I would be furious if I came all this way and couldn't leave my room," Mary Ellen said.

Dakota and her father shared a look.

"It's nothing serious, is it?" Mary Ellen asked.

"No, it's just that it happens a lot. After a while it's like the boy who cried wolf, if you know what I mean," Dakota said.

Larry frowned. "Your mother has a migraine. She has to get past it before she can handle all this light and heat, not to mention the crowds."

"Okay, Dad. Whatever."

Larry looked at Mary Ellen and started to speak just as Dorothy called out to them. "If you feel you've had enough time here, I'd like to take you to the Forbidden City. Okay with everybody?"

"How will we get there?" Dakota asked, looking at the lanes of traffic between them and the distant structures of the ancient city.

"Follow me," she said with a smile. "We go through an underground pedestrian walk." They followed her to a staircase that led to a wide tunnel underneath the busy street. "The Chinese really know how to move people, don't they?" Danny said, stopping in the middle of the tunnel to look around and take a photo. "Impressive engineering."

"I read somewhere that while the U.S. is run by lawyers, China is governed by engineers," Kate offered. "Being married to an engineer," she said more quietly to Mary Ellen, "I'm not sure which is worse."

They emerged from the tunnel into the brightness. Ahead of them at the ticket counter, they saw Dorothy's pink parasol.

"I can't believe I'm standing here," Mary Ellen marveled. "I think this is where the young emperor tries to leave the city on his bicycle."

Larry looked at her, puzzled. "I'm sorry . . . ?"

"Oh, I'm referring to the movie *The Last Emperor*. I just watched it last week. Have you seen it?"

"Yes, a few weeks ago. Amazing cinematography."

"That's for sure. It's the only film ever made here. I can't wait to go in."

"I'll bet your students love you, Mary Ellen. Your enthusiasm is contagious."

She felt herself blush. "Thank you." She looked away from Larry and spotted the girls, who were having their photo taken, holding a fan that Mariah had talked her parents into buying her in the square.

"Look at how beautiful they are," she said, nodding in their direction. People in the crowd had turned to watch the girls, smiling at the scene—a tall, American beauty with a killer smile and two equally beautiful Chinese girls. Larry and Mary Ellen moved closer as a thin, Chinese girl of twelve or thirteen tapped Dakota's shoulder.

"Please," she said, "may I take photo? You are very pretty."

"Oh," Dakota said, surprised. "Sure."

Dakota smiled as the young girl beamed with delight and aimed her camera. Behind her, Chinese tourists of all ages and genders quickly snapped photo after photo of Dakota.

Dorothy returned with tickets in hand and glanced at Larry. "Your daughter looks like a movie star."

"She's certainly getting a lot of attention," he replied. "Is it because she's Western?"

"Some of these people have never seen a foreigner before except in the movies. Depends where in China they come from." Dorothy moved toward Dakota and spoke in Mandarin to the crowd, which dispersed in a flurry of smiles and waves.

Dakota turned to her father. "Wow. That was freaky. I felt like I was on *Entertainment Tonight* or something."

Back in step behind Dorothy, they squeezed into the crowd that was moving through the first gate of the Forbidden City. The gate created a deep shadow in contrast to the intense sunshine; Mary Ellen felt Mariah take her hand as they shuffled through the darkness. Once on the other side, they entered an enormous courtyard that seemed to stretch for a mile before it reached the first building. Stone fences and stairways sectioned off different areas. Beyond the Forbidden City they could see the skyscrapers of modern Beijing, many with cranes on top.

Dorothy waited until they'd all stopped taking pictures of this juxtaposition of ancient and modern before beginning her speech. "The Forbidden City was the home of emperors for hundreds of years. It was built in the 1400s, burned down, and was rebuilt. It contains 9,999 rooms."

"That's a lot of rooms," Mariah noted. "Where are they?"

"It is not the way we think of rooms," Dorothy replied. "Each one is simply the area between four pillars. I will show you when we get to the first building."

As they walked, Mary Ellen aimed her camera at the glazed tile roof of the building, its curling edges holding carvings of dragons, carts, and horses.

Dorothy narrated, giving dates, dynasties, and the significance of every statue.

"I will never remember all this information," Mary Ellen complained to Kate.

"That's what guidebooks are for. Just take pictures of what attracts you; you can fill in the blanks later. This is only the beginning. You'd have to have a mind like a steel trap to retain all the details," Kate reassured her.

Mary Ellen decided to take Kate's advice and moved silently through the space, asking an occasional question.

Two hours later, they left the last building and found their way to the Imperial Gardens at the back of the Forbidden City. Strange-looking rock formations and gnarly old trees and shrubs lined the walks. The younger girls had begun to wilt.

"I'm so hot," Mariah said. "And hungry and thirsty."

"Good," Dorothy said, "because it is time to leave here and meet our driver."

Mary Ellen kept turning around and stealing final glances as they headed away from the Forbidden City.

Danny nudged her. "I don't think Beijing is the best place to be walking backward on the sidewalk. You need to pay attention."

"Sorry," she conceded. "I just know I'll never be here again."

"Mr. Bishop, do you wish to call your wife to see if she is okay?" Dorothy asked once they'd safely reached the sidewalk.

"Where's our next stop?" he asked.

"We are going to a restaurant for lunch. It is quite far from the hotel . . . unless you want me to cancel the reservation and take you somewhere closer?"

"I guess I should see what she wants to do. Would you call for me?"

Dorothy called the front desk from her cellphone and handed it to Larry once she connected to the room. He walked a few yards away. Mary Ellen watched him out of the corner of her eye. He was frowning as he listened, then he turned his back to them. Mary Ellen noticed that his daughters watched him, too. After a few minutes, he returned and handed the phone to Dorothy.

"Thank you," he said. "She's resting and will see us later at the hotel."

"Is she better, Dad?" Anna-Mei asked.

"Seems to be. Hopefully she'll be back in the saddle tomorrow."

Dorothy looked puzzled, but their driver pulled up then and they boarded the van.

It seemed to take a long time to get to the restaurant. Between traffic, some driving moves on the part of Leo that were worthy of Mario Andretti, and the size of the city, all travel in Beijing seemed to be a lesson in patience.

At last they arrived, pulling into an alleyway. They got out and walked toward the main street, passing a bicycle on which several cages of birds were perched.

"I hope that's not lunch," Danny whispered.

Kate shushed him, nodding in Mariah's direction.

The restaurant was large and crowded. The waiters wore silk jackets and little caps and shouted loudly to each other across the room. The heat and noise of the place would have normally annoyed Mary Ellen, but this felt exotic and fun, and the food smelled wonderful. After some effort on Dorothy's part, they were all seated together on skinny benches at a long table. Dorothy asked them what they liked to eat, and after some discussion, she took the menu over to a bar and gave their order.

Larry had suggested they each order cold beer, soft drinks for the younger girls. Mary Ellen laughed when she saw the waiter headed toward their table with five very tall beers on the tray.

"Look at the size of them. I'll be staggering after this!"

"That's the hope," Kate retorted.

"Let me know if I can be of any assistance," Danny offered.

Larry spoke to his oldest daughter, who was pouring beer into a glass. "You'd better take it easy there, Dakota. You're not used to drinking that much beer, are you?"

"Don't worry, Dad. I'm a college student." She lifted her glass. "Sláinte!"

"Wrong country," her father said, shaking his head and chuckling. He turned to the others. "This is going to be a very educational trip, I think."

The food came quickly—fried rice, broccoli and garlic, chicken with peanuts in a savory brown sauce, beef and onions with sesame seeds.

Mary Ellen was thrilled at her success at getting every morsel into her mouth with chopsticks. "This is the best Chinese food I've ever eaten," she said.

Kate sat across from her, her face bright red, dripping with sweat.

"Are you okay?" Mary Ellen asked.

Kate mopped her face with napkins. "I feel like Albert Brooks in *Broadcast News*." Larry and Mary Ellen laughed, remembering the scene with the profusely sweating anchorman.

"What do you think is causing it?" Larry asked.

"Probably a combination of the heat, the food, the beer, the fact that I need to lose ten pounds . . . "

"Maybe the food will go right through you and help with that," Danny joked.

After lunch, everyone, including Kate, was ready for the adventure to continue.

Leo drove them to the Temple of Heaven, another ancient place where the emperors once went to pray for a good harvest. On the grounds surrounding the temple, local people had gathered to socialize. A man played some sort of traditional Chinese instrument that was two-stringed, with a bow, and created a hauntingly beautiful sound. Along a walkway lined with benches, groups of people played Mahjong.

"What a great sense of community," Danny observed. "Don't you wish we had more places like this in the States?"

Mary Ellen heard singing in the distance. "Yes, I love it. Let's check out the singing."

They walked over to where a large group of people stood together, singing in full, robust voices. Smack dab in the middle, a man was conducting them. Dorothy said they were singing Chinese patriotic songs.

Mary Ellen noted how much pride they seemed to be taking in their music.

Larry agreed. "And this isn't a formal event. This is people just getting together."

Dorothy pointed ahead and they followed her toward an open, paved area that had a tree in the center; women's handbags were tied to it with rope. Around the tree, women were line dancing to Chinese music that blared from a boom box on the ground.

Mary Ellen laughed and took a photo. "What a great idea. They can dance without worrying about getting their bags stolen."

Then she spotted a man with a large, pink-trimmed fan dancing gracefully in his own space, across from a woman in a white cotton hat who inscribed shapes in the air with a long rainbow streamer. They appeared uninhibited, not the least bit interested in the people who were watching.

Mary Ellen was enchanted. "Don't you love this?" she asked Kate, who had wandered over. "I can't imagine going to a park and just . . . dancing."

"Now Mariah wants me to buy her one of those rainbow streamers," she replied. "Can you tell we're raising her to be a true American consumer?"

"Have you used the public restroom yet?" Mary Ellen asked.

Kate shook her head. "I took Mariah in, but there are only squat toilets, so she decided to hold it."

"Well, I've got to go. How bad can it be?"

Kate smiled and said, "You go first and let us know."

Inside the bathroom, a row of raised stalls made it look much like a regular restroom. However, there was a pungent smell. Mary Ellen opened a door and saw an oblong hole in the floor with footprints on either side. Here goes, she thought, as she maneuvered into position. She felt awkward and uncomfortable, but she managed. She realized there was no toilet paper, so she rummaged in her purse and found a crumpled tissue. Behind her stood an open trash bin for the paper. She wrinkled her nose. No wonder it reeked. She washed her hands in cold water. There was no soap, so she used hand sanitizer when she was done.

The girls were waiting outside. "How was it?"

"An adventure," she answered without a smile.

"What kind of adventure?" Dakota asked. "Scary? Disgusting?"

"Unsanitary by our standards, but as long as you bring some tissues and hand sanitizer, you'll survive."

"I'll wait," Dakota decided.

"Me, too," her sister agreed.

"Mariah?" Kate asked.

"I don't have to go that bad."

"I'm pretty sure squat toilets are unavoidable in China, girls," Kate said. "You'll have to use one sooner or later."

"Let's go take a peek," Dakota said, leading the way.

They came back wearing looks of disgust.

"No way," Mariah said. "It stinks in there and how do you pee without getting it on yourself?"

"Practice, I guess," Kate laughed.

They joined Dorothy and the men and found Leo waiting patiently in the van, reading a newspaper. He put it down, giving them his routine smile. Dorothy explained that he would take them back to the hotel where they could rest, and that they would be on their own until tomorrow morning.

Dakota sat next to Mary Ellen. "So, we're just going to hang around the hotel for the rest of the afternoon?" she whispered.

Mary Ellen checked her watch. "It's almost four. I could use a rest, couldn't you?"

"It's just that it's kind of cramped and stressful in our room. And my mother needs it quiet and dark when she's got a migraine."

"If you'd like, get your things and come to my room. I'm planning to shower and write in my journal. You're welcome to shower and hang out until dinner."

"That's so nice of you. I'd love that. Thank you."

Mary Ellen was glad for the company. Dakota brought bottled water and snacks, and read a book while Mary Ellen wrote. The two of them spent the time getting to know each other better. Dakota carefully steered the conversation clear of her family. At first, Mary Ellen honored the fact that the girl needed a break, but finally she decided to broach the subject.

"So, you're finding your room situation difficult?"

"It's way too cozy in there. I've been away at school all year and now I'm sharing one room with three other people. My sister is fine. But my parents bicker all the time, and my mom is miserable. It's hell."

"And it's only your third day here."

"Don't remind me. I'm going to blow a fuse before we even leave Beijing."

Mary Ellen hesitated. Should she offer to share her room? Dakota seemed mature and poised, pleasant and intelligent, but Mary Ellen valued her own space.

"Mary Ellen," Dakota said nervously, her dark eyes showing just a hint of pleading. "Would you ever consider letting me room with you? I mean, I'd talk to my dad. We could reimburse you for half your room costs. I'd be so quiet you'd hardly know I was here."

Mary Ellen laughed.

"I'm not laughing at your idea, Dakota," she assured her. "To be honest, I was going back and forth on whether to offer it."

"Really?" Her eyes widened. "So, why'd you laugh?"

"Because I'd never want you to be so quiet that I wouldn't know you were here. I like having your company. And I think we'd get along fine."

This time Dakota laughed, showing a dimple in her right cheek that Mary Ellen hadn't noticed before. "Oh, my God. You've saved my life. You don't even know. Can I use your phone to call my dad and tell him?"

Did I just say yes? Mary Ellen could see the stress evaporate from Dakota's face. "Of course," she said, aware that she was committing herself to a very different vacation from the one that she'd expected.

"Dad, Mary Ellen has invited me to room with her. I told her you'd reimburse her for half. Is that okay?" She listened, then held out the receiver. "He wants to talk to you."

Mary Ellen took the phone. "Hi, Larry."

"Are you being railroaded into this?" he asked.

"No, not at all. You folks are a little crowded, and I'm by myself. I'm fine with it."

"But you've paid for a single room and I'm not sure I can reimburse you for half your costs."

"Don't worry about that. We'll need to get a cot in here because I've only got one bed. And if we're going to do this throughout the trip, we'll probably need someone to adjust our hotel reservations."

"If you're absolutely sure, I'll talk to Dorothy and see what we can do. But I don't want you to get conned into anything."

"Why don't we consider Beijing our trial run? Would that be okay?" She looked at Dakota, who nodded. "Maybe we can keep one reservation ahead of ourselves, and we'll discuss things in each city. As long as we're both happy, we'll go with it."

"You're a life saver," Larry said. "Thank you very much. Are you two ready for dinner?"

"We'll meet you in the lobby in ten minutes. I'll call Kate."

"Are you crazy?! Rooming with a twenty-year-old?" Kate said over the phone.

Dakota was in the bathroom, but even so, Mary Ellen lowered her voice. "I like her. She's a nice girl and she's stressed out."

"Yeah, tell me about it," Kate said. "By the time we get to Chengdu, I'll probably be ready to join you. Still, I wonder if Erica is Dakota's problem. Do you think she'll show?"

"I have no idea. I'll be interested to see what she thinks of the new arrangement."

Dakota emerged from the bathroom looking fresh and beautiful in a long, cotton skirt and a light blue tee. She'd pulled her long, dark hair back from her face with a headband. There was a knock on the door. Dakota opened it to find Mariah, who wore a sundress and a crossbody purse.

"Nice dress. You look pretty," Dakota said.

"Thanks. You, too." She entered the room and trained her black eyes on Mary Ellen. "Why didn't you pick me to be your roommate, Mary Ellen?"

"Oh, sweetheart, I'm sorry." She put an arm around Mariah's shoulders. "Your mom and dad wanted you with them and Dakota's room is crowded. We just decided this today."

"This will be the cool room, Mariah. Anytime you want to get away from your family, come over here," Dakota said brightly.

Mariah smiled. "Awesome! I'll tell Anna-Mei, too!"

Mary Ellen looked at Dakota. "What are you getting me into?"

Dakota laughed as they exited the room. Her smile faded as she looked down the corridor. Mary Ellen followed her gaze to see the Bishop family waiting by the elevator. Erica was listening to Larry; her arms were folded across her chest.

"Let me do the talking," Dakota said quietly. "I'm used to handling my mother."

Kate and Danny stepped out into the corridor and followed.

"Feeling better, Mom?" Dakota asked when they reached the elevator.

"Yes," she answered, giving her daughter a look that Mary Ellen couldn't decipher.

The elevator door opened, and they all got in and rode silently to the lobby. When the doors opened again and they stepped out, Dakota asked if anyone knew where they were going. They stopped and looked at each other.

"You mentioned a Japanese restaurant around the block. Does that interest anyone?" Kate asked. "It's close by. I'm not up for a marathon after this afternoon."

"And tomorrow, we're climbing the Great Wall," Danny added.

"Good point. I'm willing to try the Japanese place," Larry said.

Anna-Mei walked arm in arm with her mother, while Dakota was paired with Mariah and Kate with Danny. That left Mary Ellen and Larry to bring up the rear.

"Is Erica okay with Dakota's . . . defection?" she asked Larry.

He was silent for a moment. "She'll adjust. She and Dakota have a somewhat volatile relationship. The boat rocks for a while, and then it settles. I think it's a great solution for both of them. Thank you again. You're very generous."

"It's nothing, really. She's a lovely girl."

"Yes," he replied, "she's a sweetheart." He held the door open for her.

A hostess dressed as a Japanese geisha seated the group in a dining room made private with sliding doors. The waitresses spoke no English, so they ordered by pointing at photos in the menu.

The easy camaraderie of the day had been lost. Mary Ellen suspected that was due to Erica. Her rigid body and unsmiling face gave off negative energy. Mary Ellen knew how hard she had to work to change the energy in her classroom when a student came in feeling irritable and ready for a fight, or sometimes, just ready to be hurt. She couldn't tell which category Erica fell into and didn't look forward to finding out. Anna-Mei was solicitous of her mother, only engaging minimally with Mariah, who looked crestfallen. They'd been best buddies that afternoon. Kate and Danny tried to steer her into conversation with them, but she was quiet as she watched her friend.

The food arrived and to their relief, everything was recognizable. Erica ate nothing but a plate of noodles and drank bottled water. By the end of the meal, her color had improved. Mary Ellen could feel the energy shift again.

"Mom?"

Erica pursed her lips. "Yes, Dakota?"

"Did Dad tell you I'm going to room with Mary Ellen?"

Erica didn't answer but held her daughter's gaze.

Dakota continued, undaunted. "We get along really well and when we were hanging out, the idea just sort of came to us, right, Mary Ellen?"

She nodded. "I don't mind sharing. We do get along well, and I imagine it's a little cramped in your room. Are you okay with this?"

"Why, thank you for asking," she said. "You're the very first one to do so. Up until this point, I've only been told."

Larry's jaw tightened, and Mary Ellen feared she'd just stepped into something she shouldn't have.

Dakota rolled up her napkin and threw it on the table. "Mother, I am almost twenty-one years old. This was my idea. I don't think it's wise for the four of us to share a room. I'll go crazy. Between your illnesses and you and Dad's . . . ."

"That's enough, Dakota," Larry said softly.

Dakota stopped and took a deep breath. She looked like she was going to cry.

Danny stood up. "Kate, Mariah, let's go and give these folks a little space, shall we?" His wife and daughter rose from the table. "Mary Ellen, are you coming?"

"I think Mary Ellen should stay," Erica said smoothly. "After all, she's involved."

Mary Ellen stood. "I'd be happy to discuss it with you later, but this seems like a family discussion. Goodnight."

Dakota burst into tears. "Does this mean you don't want me to room with you?"

"No, not at all. But please work things out with your parents, okay? Let me know your decision so I can make arrangements."

The O'Days were waiting for her on the sidewalk. Kate raised her eyebrows in unspoken sympathy.

"I was only trying to be helpful," Mary Ellen said. The air was warm and heavy. Cars and buses rumbled by on the street. Neon lights winked on storefronts, Chinese characters describing the wares that were housed inside. Mary Ellen wasn't in a rush to return to the room. "Let's take a walk."

"Let's go to that mall," Mariah suggested, pointing to a brightly lit building with mannequins in the windows.

"Why not?" Danny shrugged, following his daughter's lead. "We're not buying, Mariah, just looking. Got that?"

They crossed the same pedestrian bridge they'd traversed the night before. The streets were filled with shoppers. Inside the mall were the same high-end retail shops one could find in the U.S. Mariah led them to the girls' department upstairs. There were racks of summer dresses in cottons, taffetas, silks, and satins.

"This is incredible," Kate observed. "You can barely find a decent dress back home. Do little girls in China wear dresses all the time?"

"Maybe we should buy one for me," Mariah suggested, heading toward a rack.

"Uh . . . hello, Mariah. What did I just say?" Danny reminded.

"Oh, Danny. It doesn't hurt to look," his wife said, joining her daughter.

"Ah, the old it-doesn't-hurt-to-look trick. Mary Ellen, do you know that one? It usually costs me fifty to a hundred bucks. Or yuan, in this case."

"So, it does hurt to look. Is that what you're saying?"

"What is it with you women? It's like my wife and daughter have a primal attraction to anything in a well-lit store. Are you like that?"

"I'm not a big shopper, although I do like to browse when I travel."

"This place doesn't seem much different from Massachusetts."

"I guess that's globalization for you." Suddenly Mary Ellen thought of Dakota. "I think I should go back to the hotel and check with the Bishops to see if Dakota will move in with me tonight."

"I guess we'll just have to get going then, won't we?" Danny said with a smile. "Okay you two, Mary Ellen wants to get back for Dakota. Have you satisfied your browsing urge?"

"Yes, Daddy. But not our buying urge."

Kate laughed. "There'll be other chances, honey. China is filled with opportunities."

When they arrived at the hotel they found Larry at the front desk trying to work out the room change. He hadn't gotten far because he needed Mary Ellen's approval. Luckily, the young woman behind the desk spoke English very well and made the arrangements easily. Mary Ellen and Larry decided to settle up the room costs once they returned to the States. Mary Ellen suspected that Kate and Danny would think she was insane, but somehow, she trusted Larry.

By the time Larry and Dakota arrived at her door with a suitcase and several tote bags, a bellhop had delivered a cot and a set of towels.

"This isn't a big space," Larry observed. "You're sure you want to do this?"

Dakota sighed loudly.

"Please don't give it another thought. We'll be fine. If there are any problems I'll deal with them, but I don't anticipate any." Mary Ellen squeezed Dakota's shoulder and smiled. "I'll give you a few minutes to get settled. Let me in when I get back, okay?"

She opened the door and stepped out. Larry followed.

"Should I speak to Erica? I don't want this to cause tension. I think it's important we all get along."

"I think it's okay now. They do love each other, but boy, do they push each other's buttons. Anna-Mei has such a different temperament, and this kind of stuff really bothers her."

"Family dynamics," Mary Ellen commented. "Challenging enough at home, but on a trip like this. . . ."

"Do you live alone?"

She hesitated. "No, I live with my mother."

"Seriously?"

Mary Ellen felt her cheeks redden.

"I mean, that's great," he quickly added. "You don't see that very often anymore. Can I ask you how old you are?"

"Thirty-five," she answered, feeling an edge creep into her voice. "And you?"

"Forty-three."

She did the math.

"Wow. You and Erica were quite young when you had Dakota, weren't you?"

"Yes. Erica was still in college when she got pregnant. I had just graduated. When I look at my daughter and imagine her as a parent at this age, it horrifies me. But somehow, we did it."

"Quite successfully. Your girls are great."

The door to Mary Ellen's room opened and Dakota poked her head out. "Dad, Mom just called to see where you are."

Larry smiled apologetically at Mary Ellen. "We'll continue this conversation another time, I hope. Thanks again for taking in my daughter. Sleep well, both of you."

"Thanks, Dad. 'Night."

Mary Ellen watched him for a minute. His usually confident stride looked slightly deflated as he walked away.

Dakota opened the door. "Um . . . is everything okay?"

"Everything's great. Let's get ready for another big adventure tomorrow."

Six

A FULL MOON WAS SHINING DOWN, lighting up the landscape as the overnight train to Xi'An sped along. Mary Ellen was lying in a low berth across from Kate. Danny and Mariah snored softly from above. She'd never slept on a train before, and she couldn't help feeling as if she were a character in a movie from the 1930s. She peered out the window just as the train glided onto a slender track over some silent body of water. Hearing Mary Ellen's soft intake of breath, Kate pulled herself up to see what she was looking at.

"Beautiful, isn't it?" Mary Ellen whispered. "Look at the reflection of the moon on the water."

Kate looked out the window for a few minutes before drawing back to look over at her friend.

"You're loving this, aren't you?"

"How can I not?" Mary Ellen whispered. "What about you? Are you enjoying yourself?"

"The last time we were here we were focused on the baby we came to adopt. Now that the baby is ten and needs cajoling into trying new foods, using squat toilets, opening her Americanized mind to the wonders of her birth country, it feels more like a job than a vacation."

"Vacation is sitting on the beach doing nothing. This is an adventure. It requires more."

"What were we thinking when we agreed to travel with the Bishops? Didn't they seem like a tight family, or is my memory failing?"

"Well, Anna-Mei couldn't be sweeter. And I really love Dakota. It's just Erica who's a little prickly. The family dynamics are . . . ."

"Tense? I'll say." Kate paused. "You and Larry seem to get along."

Mary Ellen turned over on her back and stared at the upper berth. "He's a nice guy. Much nicer than she is. Do you think their marriage is on the rocks?"

"I don't know. Are you attracted to him?"

"He's a married man with two daughters."

"So?"

"What do you mean, so? I'm not going to let myself go there."

"Can you really control that? Can anyone? Hell, I think he's very attractive, but I get this feeling he's into you. That if Erica weren't around . . . "

Mary Ellen sat up and faced her friend. "Why would you say that?"

"Yesterday at the Great Wall, you and Larry and Dakota were the only ones who made it to the seventh tower. Then Dakota came down alone, telling us about the incredible view. Erica was peeved when she saw you and Larry strolling down together. The girls were waving from our table in the café, but you guys were caught up in conversation. I mean, it's perfectly fine with me if you fall in love with him, but you might want to watch it a little on this trip. We've still got twelve days to go, and I'd like to see the group dynamics improve, not blow up in our faces."

"Falling in love with him? Really, Kate. I wanted to climb the Great Wall, not look at it from a table below. Dakota started talking to some gorgeous guy from New Zealand at the top and headed down with him. That's how Larry and I ended up together."

"I'm not accusing you of anything. I know you're just being your honest, lovely self. But be discreet."

"I'm not doing anything wrong," she protested. "But, okay, I guess I should keep my distance. Erica seems like she could be a loose cannon, and I don't want to give her any ammunition."

Kate dozed off while Mary Ellen stayed awake for another hour, feeling guilty. She tried to tell herself she liked Larry's personality and sense of adventure, but she knew it was more than that. She couldn't deny the slight increase in her heart rate when he was around. Why couldn't she meet a quality guy who was single and straight?

The rhythm of the car finally lulled her to sleep.

When she woke up the next morning, Mary Ellen found herself alone. She lay there a few minutes thinking about her midnight conversation with Kate. She knew she wasn't being inappropriate with Larry; she liked him, that was all. On their walk down the steep steps of the Great Wall, she'd learned that he was the editor of several small-town newspapers in the Boston suburbs. He was interesting and easy to be with. Erica had been pleasant at first, but now she was either bitchy or curt to everyone except Anna-Mei.

Mary Ellen got up, opened the door and stuck her head out to the corridor. Across from their sleeping compartment, Kate was sitting on a jump seat attached to the wall; she was watching the green, mountainous scenery speed by as she sipped from a paper cup. She turned to her friend.

"Good morning. Want some green tea?" She passed the cup to Mary Ellen. "Don't you love it?" she gestured toward the label. Mary Ellen glanced down to read it: *Can you tell me how to get to Sesame Street?*

She laughed and passed it back. "No thanks. How long have you guys been up?"

"I slept until about six when Mariah informed me it was time to wake up. You didn't hear her?"

Mary Ellen shook her head. "How long until we get to Xi'an?"

"A couple of hours, I think. Do you want me to find one of the guys and see if they'll get you tea?"

"Don't go to any trouble. I'm going to change my clothes and hit the bathroom to freshen up. I must look like a total wreck."

"From what I've seen so far, the only people winning beauty contests on this train are the girls. Youth is very forgiving."

When Mary Ellen returned from the restroom, she found a small crowd outside the sleeping compartment. Dakota was leaning against the window, talking with Kate. Danny was sprawled in the seat behind his wife, conversing with Larry. Mary Ellen ducked into the compartment and found Mariah and Anna-Mei playing cat's cradle on Kate's berth.

"Hi, girls," she said as she rummaged through her bag for a hairbrush and mirror. "Do I look as scary as I feel?"

"Your hair is a little messy. Want me to brush it?" Mariah asked.

Mary Ellen smiled. "That's very sweet of you but go on with your game. I'll fix it."

Danny came in and grabbed a guidebook out of his bag, just as a waiter poked his head in to ask if anyone wanted tea or coffee.

"I'll have tea, please," Mary Ellen answered. "Do I have to order the *Sesame Street* cup or does that come automatically?" she asked Danny.

"Luck of the draw, my dear. We'll see if you're worthy."

After she'd brushed her hair, Mary Ellen joined the others in the corridor. Erica was standing near her husband; when she saw Mary Ellen, she moved closer to him, tucking a finger into his belt loop, and looking pointedly at her. Mary Ellen turned and looked out the window, feeling her face get hot. She hated her tendency to blush. It made her look guilty even when she wasn't.

Kate handed her a paper cup of hot tea. "They must be out of *Sesame Street* cups."

"Thanks," she said softly, taking a sip. Big green leaves were floating around and it was an effort to keep them out of her mouth. "How authentic," she observed. "It's good, though."

As Mariah and Anna-Mei came out of the sleeping compartment, Kate pushed her friend inside. "Did I just see what I thought I saw? It looked like a 'keep your paws off my man' move if I've ever seen one."

"I feel terrible," Mary Ellen whispered. "I'm not interested in taking her man. But I do think she should be nicer to him if she wants to keep him, don't you?" They laughed, ducking their heads. Mary Ellen pressed a hand to her mouth just as Danny came in to tell them that the latest arrival time was now thirty minutes away.

"Thirty minutes? Some guy told me we had two hours to go," Kate objected.

"What language was he speaking?" he asked.

"I could have sworn it was English, but I wasn't fully awake. Would you find Mariah and tell her to climb up there and check to be sure she gets all her stuff?"

Following Kate's suggestion, Mary Ellen grabbed her bag and scanned the lower berth to make sure she had her things. She looked outside to see if the coast was clear, wanting to make room so the others could comfortably move around, but not wanting to run into Erica—or Larry, for that matter. The corridor was empty. She moved toward the nearest exit door and watched the city go by while waiting for the train to stop.

"There you are!" Dakota exclaimed, her duffel bag slung over one shoulder. "Boy, did I miss rooming with you last night. I felt like I was six years old again, sleeping in a bunk bed, listening to my dad snore."

Mary Ellen smiled. "Did you sleep at all?"

"Eventually. I'm starving. Please tell me we can get breakfast at our hotel. I can't go all day on a Clif Bar and green tea."

Mary Ellen opened her mouth to speak, but Dakota continued.

"I was reading the guidebook this morning. Xi'an sounds like a great city. I think we'll have fun there. I love cities, although, truthfully, I prefer American ones."

When the college girl stopped to take a breath, Mary Ellen pointed to the sky. A patch of blue was emerging from the clouds. "Look. I think we'll see blue skies in Xi'an."

Dakota ducked her head to get a better view. "Oh, my God. Dad, look!" she shouted down the corridor. "You'll love this."

Larry walked up to them, smiling.

"See?" His daughter pointed out the window.

He shook his head. "What are you pointing to, Dakota?"

"Look *up*, Dad."

He leaned forward. "The buildings? What am I missing?"

Mary Ellen laughed.

Larry looked at her expectantly. "What?"

"What haven't we seen since the morning we left Boston?"

"Don't tell me they have Dunkin' Donuts in China!" He scanned the horizon.

The laughter was cut off by the sound of Erica's strident tone.

"Larry, where are you?" She dropped two heavy suitcases to the floor and glared at her husband. "Thanks a lot for your help."

"Oh, chill, Mom. We were trying to get Dad to pick up on something we haven't seen since we left Boston."

Erica bent down to peek. "Well, look at that. Amazing. I guess we've left the smog of Beijing behind."

"Is that what you two were trying to get me to see? Wow. My brain must be slow from lack of sleep."

"Lack of sleep? Give me a break. I listened to you snore all night." Dakota hip-checked her father playfully. He put his arm around her and kissed her on the head.

Mariah and Anna-Mei arrived, followed by Danny and Kate. Larry counted to make sure everyone was there.

"Okay, we're going to be looking for a fellow named Qiu."

"Choo?" Mariah said with a giggle.

"I think that's how to pronounce it. He'll be holding a sign with one of our last names, I'm not sure which. Everybody stay together."

As the train came to a stop, Anna-Mei spotted a tall, young man standing by a concrete pillar only twenty yards away. He held a sign that read: "Mr. Bishop." Qiu shook hands with each of them as they exited the train and instructed them to follow. They joined the stream of people crossing a parking lot, which was rutted with foul-smelling puddles. Men in shabby clothes stood around, watching the group pass.

"This is gross," Dakota whispered. "I thought Xi'an was going to be a nice city."

"One should never judge a city by its train station parking lot, Dakota," her father advised.

Qiu led them to a minibus and introduced them to Mr. Lee, the driver, who loaded their luggage and got behind the wheel. As soon as they were on their way, Qiu pulled a binder out of his bag and opened it to a page with a map of China.

"You have just come from Beijing, the financial capital of China. Now you are in the beautiful city of Xi'an—the cultural center." He showed them photos of traditional Chinese paintings and explained that Xi'an was the birthplace of this art form. Mary Ellen hoped they'd get to see some artists at work, and that the pace would be slower here than in Beijing.

By the time they pulled up in front of their hotel, Mary Ellen's stomach was rumbling. Qiu took each of their passports and went to the registration desk. A uniformed man stood in their path in the lobby; he was holding a tray with what looked like damp towels on it.

Unsure of what to do, Mary Ellen hesitated.

Larry took the lead. He plucked one of the towels and washed his hands and face.

Mary Ellen and the others followed suit.

"What a nice amenity," she said to Erica.

Erica reached past her and deposited her used towel in a basket.

"Yes," Erica said, not looking at her. "Very civilized."

Well, Mary Ellen thought, at least Erica had acknowledged her. Perhaps it was a start.

Qiu returned their passports and gestured toward the patio. "Here is where *tai chi* master gives class in the morning. Is anyone interested in taking a class tomorrow?"

"Oh, yes," Mary Ellen said. "I've always wanted to try tai chi."

"If you're going to, I will, too," Dakota said eagerly. "How about you, Mom? Dad? Want to try it?

"What time is the class?" Erica asked.

When Qiu told them it was at six a.m., Dakota and her mother declined.

"I'd like to go," Anna-Mei said. "I tried it once at school, and I liked it."

"Then I'll try, too," Larry said, avoiding his wife's glare.

Erica turned to their guide. "Can I decide in the morning?"

"Of course."

They dispersed to their rooms. Qiu had suggested that they freshen up and meet him in the dining room, where breakfast was still being served. Mary Ellen and Dakota took turns in the small bathroom, showering and dressing.

When they arrived in the hotel dining room, Kate invited Mary Ellen to take the fourth place at their table, but Dakota squeezed her arm and whispered, "Let's get a table for two. My mother is driving me crazy again. Do you mind?"

Mary Ellen looked over at the Bishops' table, where there was one empty place. Erica looked at her daughter, one eyebrow raised. Dakota ignored her, taking a seat by the window. Mary Ellen sat across from her.

"Are you sure you don't want to sit with your family?"

"Positive." Dakota smiled radiantly at the young waiter and asked for tea. Then she turned back to Mary Ellen. "Just when I think this trip is going to be okay, she does something to totally piss me off."

Please don't tell me.

"She is such an asshole to my dad," Dakota continued.

Mary Ellen stood. "I'm starving, aren't you? Let's get some food."

Dakota wasted no time grabbing her hand. "I'm sorry to complain. Sometimes I just need to vent, you know?"

"I understand, but I really don't feel comfortable hearing about your parents' conflicts. I barely know them. We'll be traveling together for another ten days. It's not that I'm not sympathetic, I just don't want to know about things that should be private. Do you understand?"

Dakota gave her a sheepish smile. "I'm sorry. You're right. I won't do it anymore."

Mary Ellen smiled back and headed for the buffet.

"Thank God you're on this trip," her young friend whispered as she followed.

Qiu's uncle worked at the Terracotta Warrior Museum, and so they were able to enter through a restricted road and park the bus under a tree. Qiu led the way to the entrance as the hot sun beat down under a perfect blue sky. Luckily, a domed metal ceiling protected the enormous excavation pit, and cool air and shade welcomed them inside. A fenced walkway separated visitors from an array of six thousand statues of soldiers and horses. Mary Ellen marveled at the scope of the excavation and the beauty of the individual statues. Their guide told them that the site had been discovered in 1975 when a farmer began digging a well and found shards of terracotta. He contacted the authorities and, eventually, the place became a huge excavation site and museum.

Mary Ellen walked around the perimeter, keeping her distance from the others. She considered asking Dakota to room with her parents in the next city so she could have some space, but Dakota's disclosure about her parents' relationship made that difficult.

Strolling to the far side of the pit, she gazed across the expanse. On the other side, Danny was explaining something to his daughter while Kate took photos. A little farther on, Dakota and Anna-Mei leaned their elbows on the white metal guardrail, looking bored. She wondered where Larry and Erica were but forced herself to push those thoughts out of her head.

"Mind-boggling, isn't it?" Larry stepped up beside her.

She was startled. "It's amazing," she managed to say.

"To think that these guys have been standing here, underground, since before the first century, and that they were only discovered forty years ago. Qiu told us that the farmer who discovered them is often in the gift shop, signing autographs."

"Really? How old is he?"

"Must be in his eighties. Erica went over to try and meet him."

"Ah."

"And, actually, I wanted to catch you alone."

Mary Ellen kept her eyes on the statues. "Oh?"

"Yes. Two things: First, I wanted to make sure that everything is okay with Dakota and you. Any regrets?"

"None. Other than wishing I had a bit more alone time, it's fine."

"I'm with you on that. I'm ready to take a solo cruise down the Yangtze right about now."

"What's the second thing?" she asked, hoping to end the conversation.

"Excuse me?"

"You said you had two things to talk to me about."

"Right. I want to apologize for my wife's behavior. She and I have been . . . I don't know, out of sync, I guess, for a few months. And now she seems to think I've been paying too much attention to you. She's jealous, to put it bluntly, which is silly."

Again, Mary Ellen felt herself blush. "I'm sorry to hear that. I've enjoyed our conversations. Erica and I never really got on the right foot, but I don't know how to fix it. Do you?"

"It's not just you. I've seen her be this way with just about everybody on this trip. She's miserable for some reason and seems hell-bent on making everybody else miserable too. It's frustrating."

"So should we just stay away from each other?"

He shook his head. "You know, I've been married to her for twenty-one years. I can handle this. I just don't want you to feel hurt. You've been so generous and kind. You don't deserve to be treated badly."

"I can take care of myself. I'll keep my distance, and we'll see if anything improves. Thanks for talking to me about it, though." She walked away. "If anyone asks, I'm heading over to Pit 2."

Kate and Mariah were waving furiously, calling her over. She noticed that a tall Chinese man was standing with them, so she headed there.

Larry followed.

Kate was smiling broadly. "Mary Ellen, Larry, this is Michael Wong."

He reached out to shake their hands. "It's great to meet you." His accent was American.

"Michael came over to introduce himself and ask about Mariah, and we discovered we're from the same state. Isn't that cool?" Kate said.

"Incredible," Mary Ellen said. "Do you have family here?"

"My grandmother lives in Chengdu," he answered.

"Well, it's nice to meet you. I was just heading over to Pit 2. Does anybody want to join me?" Mary Ellen asked.

"Let me get Danny," Kate said. "He's still taking pictures. And Larry, where's your wife?"

Larry hesitated, then nodded toward the gift shop, and went off in that direction.

"I'd love to tag along if you don't mind," Michael said, walking alongside Mary Ellen. "What do you think of China?"

"It's amazing," she answered. "Everywhere I turn, I find something to astound me." She led the way across the bright courtyard to the second pit.

Anna-Mei and Dakota came in with the O'Days and were introduced.

"This is just like the other pit," Mariah complained. "I don't see what the big deal is."

Danny launched into a speech, pointing out how long the warriors had been underground, and how those in Pit 2 were archers, sculpted on one knee, bows drawn and ready.

"I noticed a sign for a teahouse that pointed up there somewhere. I think we should go have tea," Mariah said.

Kate and Danny exchanged a glance of mutual irritation.

"I think that's a great idea," Dakota said. "I've got some yuan in my purse, and I'd be happy to take Mariah. The rest of you can come there when you're ready. Want tea, Anna-Mei?"

Danny protested, pointing out that they were standing in the middle of one of the greatest excavation sites in history, but Kate gently put a hand on his arm.

"They can come back after their tea. Right, girls?"

"Okay, sure," Dakota agreed. "Unless you're finished looking around."

As the girls exited one side of the pit, Larry and Erica entered through the other. Erica was carrying a copy of a book on the warriors. She showed them the farmer's signature—big, black Chinese calligraphy on the title page.

"He's quite a celebrity," Erica said. "There was a long line of visitors waiting to get their books autographed. He's sort of cute. No smile, though. All business."

"Do you think he gets a percentage of every book that's sold?" Danny asked.

"If that's the case he would have been smiling, don't you think?" Erica said.

Mary Ellen introduced Michael to Erica, explaining that the Bishops were part of their traveling party and lived just outside Boston.

"Westwood," Erica clarified. "And you?"

"Originally from Brockton. I live in Chelmsford currently." He shook her hand and released it.

"What exactly brings you to China, Michael?" Erica asked.

"I came to see my grandmother in Chengdu and to do some research for a book I hope to write."

"How exciting! What's the book going to be about?"

Mary Ellen and Kate exchanged a glance. This was the most animated they'd seen Erica since they'd arrived in China.

"My family. My grandparents immigrated to the U.S. and had their children there, but after my grandfather died, my grandmother returned to Chengdu."

"How fascinating," Erica drawled. "Did anyone tell you that Chengdu is our next stop?"

"Oh? When are you going?"

"We fly out tomorrow afternoon," Larry answered. "Have you already visited your grandmother?"

"Not yet. I'm heading there early tomorrow morning."

Mary Ellen drifted away from the group as the discussion turned to pandas, feeling a strong need to get away from everyone. Kate caught up to her and led the way to the museum exhibits while Danny headed up to the tea shop to check on the girls.

"I can't believe we just met a guy from the Boston area who's going to Chengdu tomorrow," Kate said. "Erica seems quite taken with him, don't you think?"

Mary Ellen laughed.

"What's funny?"

"The whole situation. Larry just told me that Erica is jealous of the attention he's been paying me."

"Are you serious? When did he tell you that?"

"Around the time you ran into the handsome Michael Wong. Is that his name?"

"Yes. And now Erica's turned her charm, which was previously hidden from everyone, on the poor guy. Actually, I think he'd be perfect for you. He seems to like you."

"Oh please, Kate. We've barely met. And you seem to think everyone's interested in me. You have a vivid imagination."

"And you, my dear, have your head up your ass."

She turned to Kate, open-mouthed, not knowing whether to rage or laugh. She was spared the decision by Qiu, who tapped on her shoulder and said they needed to round up everyone to meet their driver by two o'clock.

They found Danny seated at a round table with the girls, watching a pretty hostess preparing tea for them and laughing at one of Danny's jokes. Wrappers and remnants of cookies lay on the table. The girls seemed to be mesmerized by the hostess's capable hands. She asked Kate and Mary Ellen if they would also like a cup. They declined, pointing out that it was time to leave. Danny took charge, thanking the hostess and paying the bill, while the rest of the group finished their tea and gathered their things.

Then Qiu came in, scanning the scene and counting heads.

"Did you find Larry and Erica?" Mary Ellen asked.

"Yes. They'll be waiting by the bus. Mr. Wong asked me to give you this."

It was his business card. She turned it over.

> *Mary Ellen—So nice to meet you today. I'm sorry we didn't get to speak for long. Would you like to join me for the fountain show in the square tonight? Please call me when you return to your hotel. Thank you.*

He had included the phone number and his room number.

Mary Ellen realized all eyes were on her. Could Kate be right? How did he know she was single? Was Kate playing matchmaker? She'd have to find out, but for now, she slid the card into the pocket of her shirt and led the way out of the teahouse.

Seven

MARY ELLEN SAT ON THE EDGE OF THE BED, rubbing lotion onto her aching feet. She was wrapped in a towel, her wet hair curling on her shoulders. Should she call Michael? It seemed like an intriguing opportunity, and she certainly could use a break from the group. And though she'd only met him briefly, he seemed like a decent guy. Before she could change her mind, she grabbed his card, took a deep breath, and dialed the number.

"*Wei*?" the hotel clerk answered.

"Michael Wong, room 2-1-2, please."

After a moment, the phone began to ring.

"Yes?"

"Michael, it's Mary Ellen."

"Hey there." He sounded relieved. "I thought maybe you didn't get my note."

"I'm sorry. This is the first time I've had any privacy to make the call."

"Well, it's great to hear from you," he said. "Do you have any plans for the evening?"

"I'm not sure what the group is doing, but I'd be happy to meet you. You mentioned the fountain show?"

"Yes. It's supposed to be quite an experience, but I've been reading my guidebook, and now I'm also intrigued by the idea of going to the Muslim Quarter. There's a mosque and an open-air market with all sorts of traditional foods. What if I picked you up in a taxi in a half hour? We can explore that first, grab something to eat, and get back to the Big Goose Pagoda in time to catch some of the fountain show. What do you think?"

"Sounds wonderful. I'm not sure I can be ready in a half hour, though. What time is it now?"

"Six o'clock."

"Oh, wow. How about if I meet you in front of my hotel in forty-five minutes?"

"Perfect. You're at The Garden Hotel, right?"

"Yes. See you soon."

She rummaged through her suitcase, looking for something decent to wear. Nothing seemed right—too casual or too wrinkled. When Dakota came out of the bathroom, Mary Ellen was tossing things on the floor, swearing under her breath.

"What's wrong? Did something happen?"

"I can't find anything to wear." Mary Ellen sat down on the end of the bed. "Can I swear you to secrecy?"

Dakota nodded.

"I'm going out with Michael Wong tonight."

"Who?"

"The guy from Massachusetts who we met at the museum today."

"He asked you out on a date? Already?"

"I don't know if it's a date. We're going to the Muslim Quarter and the fountain show."

"Sounds like a date to me. Here, I'll help you find something. Where are those black pants you wore in Beijing?"

Mary Ellen dug down in her suitcase. "Here," she said, pulling them out from the bottom.

"Okay. How about the green paisley top you had on the other night?"

"I haven't washed it yet."

"Does it smell?"

Mary Ellen sniffed it. "Not really. What do you think?"

She handed it to Dakota, who took a whiff. "Not bad. Nothing a little perfume won't cover up. Now get dressed, and I'll help you with your hair and makeup. You'll look gorgeous when I'm done with you."

By six thirty, Mary Ellen was dressed. Her hair was pulled back in a chignon, with wispy curls framing her face. Her makeup was natural and subtle—a contrast to the gold hoops adorning her ears.

"What do you think?" Dakota asked with a satisfied smile.

"I may just have to keep you. You could probably change my life in a major way."

"If you want to change your life, you don't need me. Now go out there and knock him dead."

Mary Ellen grabbed her purse and headed for the door.

"Have a fabulous time. Wait—what do you want me to tell Kate and my parents?"

Mary Ellen paused. "I'd better write Kate a quick note." She scribbled a brief explanation on the hotel stationery and handed it to Dakota. "Please give this to her. And as for your parents, tell them I had other plans."

"What kind of food would you like to try?" Michael gestured to the stalls in the open-air market.

"I wouldn't know where to begin. I'll trust you to lead me to the good stuff."

"I'll do my best," he said with a grin. "I just read up on noodles. Come this way."

"Noodles?" Mary Ellen hurried to keep up with his long stride. Michael stopped in front of a glass counter. Behind it stood a man who was twirling hundreds of strands of noodles on a big wooden spool. They watched as he showed off his skill to the tourists.

Mary Ellen took his picture. "I've got to show this to my mother," she said. "She loves to cook. I'll bet she's never seen anything like it before."

They continued along the narrow street, pausing to admire dumplings made in the shapes of chickens, swans, dogs, and birds. Mary Ellen found the smell intoxicating and realized that she was famished. Just as she was going to suggest that they stop, Michael pointed to some strange-looking creatures behind a glass case.

"I'm not positive, but I think those are blackened rabbit heads," he said. "Why don't you take a picture of those for your mother?"

"No thanks," she said, grimacing.

They finally decided on a stir-fry of dumplings, noodles, and vegetables to share. Michael led the way to a wooden plank balanced on two cinderblocks. The man who had cooked their food came over with a wooden crate and placed it in front of them, indicating that they should use it as a table. The two men conversed in Mandarin, and then the cook returned to his stove, leaving them alone.

"May I ask what the conversation was about?" Mary Ellen asked as she unsuccessfully tried to hook a few noodles with her chopsticks.

"Here. Allow me to teach the teacher," Michael said, showing her how to position the chopsticks. "Start off slowly. Before long, it will be second nature."

She laughed. "Sure. About the same time I return to the States." She was able to bring some food to her mouth without dropping it as Michael watched, smiling. "If you don't mind, I think I'd do much better if you don't watch me.

But thank you for the tip. I think it helped. And you didn't answer my question."

"Oh, yes. He wanted to know where I was from and what I was doing with the white lady. He wanted to know if you were my wife."

"I see." She focused her eyes on her food.

"I told him I don't know you well enough to marry you, but that I planned to ask you some questions over dinner."

She looked up, giving him a shy smile. "What do you want to know about me?"

"You mentioned your mother. Tell me about her."

"My mother? Why?"

"Why not?"

"Okay," she began. "Her name is Agnes. She's seventy-five. She was a homemaker all her married life. My father didn't want her to work, but she took a job at a local department store two nights a week. She also raised three children. I'm the youngest."

"Does she live near you?"

"She lives with . . . no, I live with her. She owns a triple-decker in Worcester. Nice big apartments. We're on the third floor, where I've lived my entire life."

Michael looked neither surprised nor appalled. "And your siblings?"

"I have an older brother who's married and has a son. My older sister is also married and has two young kids. They both live in Worcester, and they all come to dinner every Sunday. My mother insists."

He nodded, then asked, "And you've never been married?"

She shook her head. "I had a serious boyfriend once, but he decided to become a monk."

"Wow. I'm sorry. Hard to compete with that. I thought maybe you were the sacrificial daughter."

She was taken aback. "What do you mean?"

"I don't mean to offend you. It's just that I've noticed that in some families, one child, usually a female, stays home and takes care of her parents, sometimes giving up her own dreams in order to serve the needs of her family. It was very common in the past, not so much anymore, at least not in the U.S."

Mary Ellen ate silently for a few minutes. "I've never heard it put like that, but I suppose in some ways I am, as you say, the sacrificial daughter. But I manage to escape. For example, right now no one in my Irish Catholic family knows I'm in the Muslim Quarter of a city in China eating dinner off a crate with a handsome Chinese American man."

Michael laughed.

"And now I have a question," she said, putting her chopsticks down and blotting her lips with a paper napkin. "How old are you?"

"Thirty-three. And you?"

"I'm thirty-five."

He nodded as he sipped his tea, his eyes never leaving hers.

What was he looking for? Companionship? Someone to speak English with? A girlfriend? He certainly was attractive. Smart, handsome, curious about the world, educated, and a good sense of humor to boot. So far, she hadn't seen anything she didn't like.

"You don't have a Chinese wife, do you?" she blurted. She blushed, appalled at her nerve.

Michael threw back his head and laughed. "No wife, Chinese or otherwise, much to my grandmother's disappointment. I've been focused on my education, and now on my work. I haven't really felt the need or desire to get married."

"Does your grandmother want you to marry a Chinese woman?"

"Of course. She'll probably have them lined up in front of her apartment building when I get to Chengdu. I love to visit her, but that part is trying. I don't want to bring a Chinese bride back to America, but she doesn't understand that. She thinks it's a crime that I do my own laundry and cooking. If I so much as pick up a dish after a meal, she starts shrieking. That is women's work and there's no arguing. It used to make me very uncomfortable because I strongly believe in equality between the sexes."

"And now it doesn't?"

"Now I see that she's steeped in centuries of Chinese culture, and I will never change that. I just try to accept gratefully. And she loves to wait on me."

Mary Ellen laughed. "Such a problem to have."

"I'd like to invite you to come visit us when you're in Chengdu, but I'm afraid the experience wouldn't be fun. She'd probably put you to work making dumplings just to see how capable you are. And I doubt she'd be happy regardless of the outcome. No one is good enough for her beloved grandson, I'm afraid."

"What's your grandmother's name?"

"Li Hua," he answered. "It means Beautiful Pear Blossom."

"That's lovely. There's so much charm in traditional Chinese culture, isn't there?"

"I'm glad you can see that. So much of it is getting lost in the building boom. And with computers and cellphones young people aren't learning to write Chinese characters anymore. That's an art form in itself. I wonder if your guide will take you to the museum tomorrow to see the paintings and calligraphy. Do you know what's on your agenda?"

"I've got it here, I think," she said, reaching into her purse. She pulled out several pieces of paper that were folded together. "Let's see . . . is today our second day in Xi'an? Oh, my gosh." She looked up at Michael. "We arrived here at eight o'clock this morning. It's been a long day."

"An enjoyable one, I hope."

"Oh, of course," she said. "It's just that I've experienced so much here, it seems impossible that it all happened in one day." She looked back at her itinerary. "Yes, we spend the morning with our guide. We'll be going to the Big Goose

Pagoda and gardens and museums before leaving for the airport around one. What time does your flight leave?"

"Nine o'clock, so it will be an early day for me."

"Should we be getting back?" She folded the papers and tucked them into her bag. "You'll need to get some sleep."

Michael glanced at his watch. "Well, if we head back now, we can still make part of the fountain show. Shall we?"

She smiled at Michael and fell in step with him as they navigated the crowded sidewalks of Xi'an, feeling more alive than she'd felt in years.

Eight

MARY ELLEN RETURNED TO THE HOTEL at midnight, bursting with energy. The red-carpeted corridors were empty and quiet. She unlocked the door to her room and stopped short when she saw two heads on the pillows of one of the beds. For a horrified second, she thought Dakota had brought a man into their room. Then she realized it was the Bishop sisters. They'd left a lamp on, which worked to Mary Ellen's advantage as she changed into pajamas and brushed her teeth. She secretly wished Dakota was awake so she could divulge everything.

She turned out the light and slid into bed, sighing deeply.

"Mary Ellen?" Dakota whispered.

"Did I wake you? I'm sorry."

"I'm glad you're back. I hate to admit it, but I was starting to get worried. How was it?"

"Would I sound melodramatic if I said it was the most exciting, lovely, enchanting night of my life?"

"Seriously?" Dakota sat up in bed. "I'm so jealous. But I'm happy for you."

"What did you guys do?"

"Oh, Anna-Mei and I spent the evening with the O'Days. We had dinner and went to the fountain show. It was pretty cool, I guess."

"Michael and I saw some of it, too. I loved it."

"It ended a while ago. What did you do after that? Or should I mind my own business?"

Mary Ellen chuckled. "I honestly don't know where the time went. We sat and talked, we walked a little, then we sat in the hotel lobby and talked some more. By the way, why is Anna-Mei sleeping with you?"

"Long story. I'll tell you in the morning."

"Tell me now."

Dakota sighed, turning onto her side and moving closer to Mary Ellen. "Okay. After you left, I went down to meet everyone in the lobby. I gave Kate your note and she told everyone that you were going out with Michael. My mom made a bitchy remark . . . "

"What did she say?"

"Something like 'that was fast work.' I blew up and told her I didn't want to spend any more time with my family, that I was sick of them. I defended you. Of course, I didn't mean to target Anna-Mei, but she thought I did, and she started crying, and then Mariah got upset because Anna-Mei was crying. I asked my parents to please go back to their room and get their act together, so my dad asked Danny to take us with them. We left Mom and Dad in the foyer, looking terrible. We went out to eat, then shopped and watched the fountain show. Anna-Mei was sad, but everybody was really nice to her. Your friends are good people."

"Yes, they are. I'm sorry you had such a rough night. But you didn't need to defend me to your mom."

"Where does she get off judging you? Why shouldn't you go out with someone? If I met someone nice here, I'd go."

"Don't get upset again. Let's talk some more in the morning. We've got another early day, so let's try to sleep."

"Okay. Goodnight, Mary Ellen. I'm glad you had a good time."

"By the way, did I tell you about my nephew Lou? He's a year or so younger than you and goes to B.C. I can't help thinking you two would hit it off. I want to introduce you two when we get back."

"Great. Something to look forward to."

A knock at the door woke up Mary Ellen. Opening one eye, she saw that the girls were still sleeping. She pulled herself out of bed, cracked the door open. Larry was standing in the hallway, rumpled and bleary-eyed.

"Larry? What is it? What time is it?" Mary Ellen whispered.

"Quarter to six."

"And you're here . . . why?"

"Tai chi. Remember? Anna-Mei said she'd do it; I think you did, too."

Mary Ellen shook her head. "Did I really say that? Right now, I think I need sleep more than I need tai chi. I had a late night. Do you want me to wake up Anna-Mei?"

"Well, I don't want to go alone," he answered. "We did make a commitment to show up."

"And Erica doesn't want to?" she asked.

He shook his head. "I'm sorry to bother you. But could you just ask Anna-Mei for me?"

She held up a finger to indicate that he should wait a minute, then she shut the door. Anna-Mei was already awake.

"Who was that?" she asked groggily.

"It's your dad, honey. He wants to know if you want to go to tai chi with him. I'm not going to go after all."

Anna-Mei swung her legs over the side of the bed and blinked a few times. "I'd better go."

Mary Ellen opened the door again. Larry was leaning against the wall across from their room, rubbing his eyes.

"Anna-Mei is coming with you. She'll be ready in a few minutes."

Larry nodded. "Good."

"Is everything okay, Larry?" Lines she hadn't noticed before now ran from his nose to the corners of his mouth. His hair was sticking up in the back and his clothes were crumpled. It was the first time she'd seen him look anything but sharp.

"I . . . it's . . . ." His eyes filled.

Though she only had on a long t-shirt, Mary Ellen stepped outside into the corridor. She folded her arms across her breasts. "What is it, Larry?" What had she missed in the last twelve hours?

"There was some drama last night. Dakota told Erica and me to spend the evening alone and work things out. So, we did. Well, we spent the evening together, but working things out was not on my wife's agenda."

"I'm sorry, Larry. Were you able to resolve anything?"

He shook his head. "Erica is leaving me."

"Oh, I am sorry," she repeated gently. "Please tell me this doesn't have anything to do with me."

"No, no," he reassured her. "This is about her. Apparently, she just doesn't want to be with me."

The door to the room creaked open. Anna-Mei looked out into the hallway, uncertainty radiating from her sweet face.

Larry smiled, but it did not reach his eyes. "I'm glad you're coming with me, Anna-Mei. I promised our guide that we'd have some eager students. I guess it's just you and me."

"Mom's not coming?"

He shook his head. "Sorry to wake you, Mary Ellen. We'll see you at breakfast."

Mary Ellen climbed back in bed with a heavy heart. Poor Larry. And his daughters. Rooming with Dakota made Mary Ellen feel entangled in the mess. How could she not?

Right then, however, sleep beckoned.

The next thing Mary Ellen knew, the phone rang. Dakota answered it in a flash, indicating she'd been awake for a while.

Mary Ellen rolled over and looked at the time. Eight o'clock.

"Well, hello, sleepy head." Dakota was dressed in a t-shirt and short skirt, her hair wet from the shower. "That was Dad. He and Anna-Mei are in the restaurant. Weren't you supposed to join them for tai chi?"

Mary Ellen eased herself to a sitting position. "I couldn't deal with it at six a.m. When I agreed to it, I had no idea what a long day yesterday was going to be."

"Long, and exciting," Dakota said with a smile.

Mary Ellen remembered Larry's face and his sad news.

"What's wrong?" Dakota asked gently. "Second thoughts?"

"No, no. Look, I've got to get ready. Why don't you head downstairs and join your family without me?" She got out of bed. "Done in the bathroom?"

"Sure. Just let me grab the hairdryer." She trotted into the bathroom and quickly returned, hairdryer in hand. "Hey, how did my dad seem this morning?"

Mary Ellen paused.

"What?" Dakota was serious now.

"He looked tired. I think he could use a little moral support from you right now."

"Because my mother is such a fucking bitch?" She plugged the hairdryer in near the desk and turned it on.

Mary Ellen went over and put her hand on Dakota's shoulder.

Dakota flicked off the switch and burst into tears. "What is wrong with her? Why does she hate everybody?"

Mary Ellen rubbed her back. "Relationships can be complicated. For some reason, your mother is unhappy right now."

"My dad is great. Why can't she just be grateful for all she has? Why does she have to be so miserable?"

"I know it's hard to see, but your mom has her perspective, too. Don't be too hard on her."

A knock at the door caught them both off guard.

"Who is it?"

After a second of hesitation, Erica's voice sounded. "I'd like to speak with Dakota, please. Is she there?"

"No," Dakota hissed. "Tell her to go away."

"She's your mother, Dakota. How long do you think you can avoid talking to her?" Mary Ellen unlocked the deadbolt and opened the door.

Erica took a tentative step forward. "Dakota? Please, I need to speak with you. Alone."

Mary Ellen let Erica inside. Then she went into the bathroom, locked the door, and turned on the shower. As she closed her eyes and let the warm water cascade over her body, she said a silent prayer for them. She took deep, slow breaths, trying to assimilate the emotions of the past two days—from heady, wonderful, and hopeful, to feeling like she was treading on ground pocked with land mines. She pictured her mother sitting at their kitchen table, lips pursed, arms crossed. "*Honestly, Mary Ellen, the things you get yourself into,*" she would say. "*It serves you right for thinking that traveling to China, of all places, is something normal Americans do.*"

A surge of anger caused the sacrificial daughter to respond in a low voice. "It's called living your life, Ma. Not hiding out in your insulated little world, trying to keep everything from changing. Being open to people, places, and events, both good and bad." She wondered if she'd have the courage to say those words to Agnes in person. *No,* she thought. *Never.*

She turned off the shower, wrapped herself in a towel, and hated that now she felt out of sorts. She listened carefully but heard no voices. She poked her head out the door and looked around. The room was empty. A note sat on the bureau.

Mary Ellen,
 I'm going out for a walk with my mom. We'll be back in time to check out. Don't plan on us for sightseeing.
         – Dakota

Quickly dressing, Mary Ellen remembered she needed to pack up and bring her luggage down to the front desk. She noticed that Dakota's bag was packed and ready to go. Then there was another knock on the door. Mary Ellen yanked it open with more force than she'd intended.

Kate and Mariah stood there, obviously surprised at the rapid response.

"Oh, it's you guys," Mary Ellen said without smiling.

"Are we bothering you?" Kate asked. She looked baffled.

"No. Come on in." Mary Ellen sat down on one bed and gestured to the other. "Sit."

"What on earth is wrong?" Kate asked.

"Long story."

"Tell me."

"There's stuff going on with the Bishops."

"Yes, we witnessed some of it before we went out last night. It wasn't a happy evening."

Mary Ellen looked warily at Mariah, who was following the conversation with rapt attention. How much should she say in front of the girl?

"I haven't even packed yet," Mary Ellen said. She stood up and grabbed a plastic Ziploc bag from the bureau. "Mariah, would you please go in the bathroom and collect all the toiletries? I'll get my bag together while you do that. Thanks, sweetie," she said as Mariah headed to the bathroom.

The second she and Kate were alone, Mary Ellen wasted no time sharing the details of her conversation with Larry—and the scene with Dakota and Erica.

Kate shook her head. "What a mess. If you weren't rooming with Dakota, we could just take off by ourselves."

"I know. It's tempting, but I feel awful for the girls. I mean, it's not their fault. I hate to say it, but I think you and Danny and I are going to have to sit down with the unhappy couple and make some decisions."

Mariah came out of the bathroom with a full bag. "What kind of decisions?"

Kate and Mary Ellen exchanged a look.

"You don't miss anything, do you?" her mother asked. "The most important thing we have to do right now is to get the luggage down to the front desk and meet Qiu by nine o'clock. Which is in twenty minutes."

They arrived in the foyer with the luggage a little after the appointed hour. No one else from their party was there.

"If I'd known we'd be the only ones here, I would have had a cup of coffee," Mary Ellen lamented.

"Maybe they left without us," Mariah said.

Just then, Qiu walked in. "Good morning, everyone. Where is the rest of the group?"

"Good question," Kate answered.

Qiu was a model of patience. "Did you sleep well?"

Kate shrugged and Mary Ellen felt too tired to respond.

Danny strode in from the restaurant and waved across the lobby. When he reached them, he asked Qiu to go up to the Bishops' room and speak to Larry.

Qiu set off in that direction.

Danny turned to face the women. "Okay, here's the deal. The Bishops are having a family powwow. They won't be coming with us. They're going to try to make alternate arrangements, but I'm not exactly sure what that will entail."

"Anna-Mei isn't coming?" Mariah asked, the corners of her mouth turning down.

"For today, or for the rest of the trip?" Kate interrupted.

"I don't know. Larry was kind of vague. Not sure he knows."

Qiu suddenly appeared. "I am very sorry, but we will have to postpone our tour for about one hour. There is a wonderful park next to the hotel where you can walk and enjoy the sculptures. Also, food and beverages are there. I will meet you as soon as I can." He walked across the lobby, sat in a chair out of earshot from them, and pulled out his cellphone.

"What on earth is going on?" Kate wondered.

"Come on, let's go," Danny urged. "It may be that we'll no longer have traveling companions. Frankly, I'm thinking that's a good thing."

"Dakota won't be with us anymore, either?" Mariah looked stricken.

Kate put her arm around her daughter. "Mariah, sometimes things happen. This has nothing to do with us. We'll just have to wait and see."

Mary Ellen felt heavy-hearted thinking of the two sweet sisters, caught up in the mess of their parents' unhappiness.

When they got to the park, Mary Ellen tried to relax. She closed her eyes, allowing the trickle of water in the central fountain to soothe her, realizing that the stress of the past twenty-four hours was beginning to wear on her. She felt a twinge of resentment toward Erica Bishop, but she wished Larry and his daughters well in her heart. Then she opened her eyes to pay attention to her friends.

Nine

ERICA WAS GONE.

They'd spent an interesting, slightly unsettled morning at the Big Wild Goose Pagoda, which was surrounded by gardens, art museums, and shops.

The gardens were quiet and peaceful. Empty bird cages hung from some of the trees, and fat-bellied statues of Buddha appeared at every turn. Qiu said it was good luck to rub the laughing Buddha's belly, so Kate, Mariah, and Mary Ellen each put a hand on the smooth stone, while Danny took photographs.

Eventually they returned to the hotel and retrieved their luggage. Mary Ellen hadn't asked Qiu about the Bishops because he seemed reluctant to speak about anything other than the places they were visiting. She assumed they wouldn't be traveling with the others to Chengdu, and hoped they'd have a chance to say goodbye before boarding the bus to the airport.

Larry and his two daughters appeared, looking dazed and exhausted. Anna-Mei's eyes were red and puffy, no doubt from crying, and Larry looked pale and drawn. Only Dakota made eye contact with Mary Ellen briefly, shaking her head as if to say, "Wait 'til you hear this story."

The group boarded the bus to the airport, and Mary Ellen sat at the back with the O'Days. Before long, they pulled up to the front of the terminal. Qiu directed them to the proper check-in line and oversaw their passage through security to the gate.

Anna-Mei began to cry as they said goodbye to their guide. Mary Ellen wondered if the girl would always think of Xi'an as the city where her adoptive mother abandoned her.

Larry spoke to Qiu for a few minutes, pressing money into his hand while Mary Ellen put an arm around Anna-Mei and led her to a seat in the waiting area. She pulled some tissues out of her bag and handed them over. Anna-Mei blew her nose and softly thanked her.

Mariah approached cautiously. "Look," she said, handing her friend a bag of Skittles. "Chinese American candy." Anna-Mei examined the familiar-looking package that now had writing in Chinese characters.

"Thanks," she said, tossing her used tissue in the nearest trash bin. She gave Mariah a small smile. "Want to sit with me?"

Mary Ellen spotted Dakota in front of a shop across the way, examining a display of gorgeous silk scarves. She walked up behind her.

"Pretty, aren't they? Thinking of buying one?"

Dakota shook her head, leaning back against the window. "The only thing I'd like to buy is a ticket out of here." Tears came to her eyes. "We're so dysfunctional, Mary Ellen. I'm shocked that Bravo hasn't called with a deal for a reality show."

"Want to grab a quick bite to eat and talk?" Mary Ellen asked.

"Okay. I'll go see if Anna-Mei wants anything and catch up to you in a minute."

Mary Ellen pointed out a restaurant and walked slowly along the concourse toward it. Once there, she ordered tea and vegetable rolls.

Dakota arrived just as she found a place to sit and sat across from her.

"How are you feeling?"

"My mom's going home. She flies out tonight to someplace in the interior, then takes another flight to Shanghai. From there she goes direct to Chicago, I think, where she has a four-hour layover until she gets a flight to New York then to Boston." She looked tired from reciting it all.

"Did Qiu arrange her trip?"

"Yes. I sure hope it's worth all the hassle."

"Did she say why she's leaving?"

"Yes. She told me the whole sordid story on a bench near a rushing waterfall. Beautiful setting, horrible conversation. Surreal doesn't even begin to cover how it feels."

"Why did you say 'sordid'?"

"Apparently my mother has been having an affair with a man she works with. She claims she's in love with him. And that it's been going on for over a year."

"Oh, Dakota." Mary Ellen reached over and squeezed her hand.

"She thought going on this trip would make her forget him, would make her see how much she loves Dad and us. . . . You know, put everything back to normal."

"But it didn't work," Mary Ellen finished.

"No. Just the opposite. She told Dad last night. They decided to tell the travel agency she's sick and needs to get back to the States for medical treatment. That's what they told my sister, but I don't think she believes them."

"Why not?"

"Because Anna-Mei is smart. She's quiet and sensitive, so she usually has things figured out long before anybody explains. I think she knows there's nothing physically wrong with my mom. Maybe she doesn't know everything, but she knows Mom and Dad are splitting up."

"And your dad?"

"He's shell-shocked. Talk about having a bomb dropped on your marriage."

"I'm so sorry."

Suddenly, Larry was standing next to their table. "They just called our flight. We're getting ready to board."

The women got up and gathered their belongings, leaving the unfinished meal behind. Dakota took her father's arm, and they started to walk back to the gate. Mary Ellen wanted to say something to Larry, but the timing was off. And what could one really say? Silent until they reached the others, they forced smiles for the benefit of the younger girls. As they boarded the plane, Mary Ellen wished that the sadness could be left behind. She barely knew this family, and yet she couldn't pretend they weren't suffering. For Larry and the girls' sakes, she'd try to be compassionate and supportive. It wasn't what she'd signed up for, yet . . . Well, she'd told Dakota that relationships could be complicated. And now she decided that included even those among friends.

Ten

THE FLIGHT FROM XI'AN took only an hour. They were met promptly by a woman named Emily, who would be their guide in Chengdu. She was in her late thirties, plump, with shoulder-length hair and wire-rimmed glasses. She was also straightforward, to the point where Mary Ellen felt confident that she wouldn't need to make any decisions while Emily was in charge. Which was fine with her.

On their ride to the hotel, Mary Ellen listened passively to Emily's introduction to the city: Chengdu is home to twelve million people. There is almost always a cloud cover, and forty inches of rain falls in Chengdu every year, which is good for the pandas. Today they would go to the Panda Research Center (which was something they'd all been happily anticipating), after they checked into their hotel and had some time to unpack and freshen up.

Yes, Mary Ellen thought, Emily was in charge.

Mary Ellen's room was beautiful, and she had it all to herself. On the way over, Larry and Dakota had decided it would be better that way. Especially for Anna-Mei.

The phone rang as Mary Ellen headed to the bathroom to get changed. She dove across her bed to answer it. It was Danny, inviting her to come to their room to check emails.

She agreed; after all, she hadn't contacted her family since Beijing.

Mariah was using the computer when she entered.

Kate was in the bathroom, washing socks in the sink. "Get in here," she whispered. "We need to talk."

Mary Ellen sat on the closed lid of the toilet while Kate wrung out the socks and hung them on a line stretched over the tub. "First of all, how was your date with Michael?"

"Michael," Mary Ellen said. "Now *that* seems like a long time ago. We had a great time. He's a very nice guy. I think even my mother would like him."

"Huh. Do you think he has enough Irish in him?"

Mary Ellen chuckled. "His mother is half English, half Irish. Isn't that a hoot? He's handsome, don't you think?"

"Very." Kate slung a few more pieces of wet laundry over the line. "What do you know about the Bishops' situation?"

Mary Ellen hesitated. "How much do you know?"

"Not much. Larry said Erica is sick and going home for treatment. He didn't seem to want to give any details, so we didn't push it. What did Dakota say?"

"As I told you yesterday morning, Erica is leaving Larry."

"Why?" Kate demanded.

Mary Ellen hesitated again. "It's not my story to tell, and it's not a happy one. Larry and Dakota are still processing it. I'm pretty sure they'll tell you in due time, but Dakota spoke to me confidentially, and I don't want to betray her trust. I'm sorry."

"What about Anna-Mei? Does she know the story?"

Mary Ellen shook her head. "She was told the same thing you were, but Dakota thinks she's figured out what's really happening."

Mariah appeared in the doorway. "Hey, Mom. This looks like a Chinese laundry." She giggled. "Get it, Mary Ellen?"

"Yes, I get it. Very funny." She stood up. "Are you finished with the computer?"

"Uh-huh. It's all yours."

Mary Ellen logged into her email account and found no messages from her mother. For a second, it concerned her, until she remembered that Agnes had been at the Cape with Lou and the girls.

One email, however, was marked "urgent." It was from her sister:

> *I hope you are having a great time. Just wanted to let you know that Ma fell on the front steps on Saturday and badly sprained her right wrist. We're not sure what made her fall. She said she thinks she got light-headed, and her doctor thinks she might have had a mini stroke. That hasn't been confirmed yet, and she says she feels fine except for the wrist. Because it's the right arm she can't do much, so she's staying with us. I didn't want Lou to have to deal with food prep and helping her dress. She had to cancel the trip to the Cape, unfortunately, but the girls have been bringing over casseroles and cakes and cookies. It's like someone died. Anyway, I'm really missing you right now, and I look forward to your coming home. As a matter of fact, I'm counting the days. She's going to have her arm immobilized for at least two weeks, so prepare yourself. In the meantime, enjoy your freedom. Let me know you're okay when you can. Love from your frazzled, slightly insane sister.*

Mary Ellen clutched at her hair with both hands. "I don't believe it!"

"What's the matter?" Kate and Mariah asked, alarmed.

"My mother fell down the front steps and sprained her wrist!"

"Oh, no," Kate said. "Poor Agnes."

"Poor Agnes, my . . . " She looked at Mariah and stopped. "She couldn't just go to the Cape and have a good time with her friends. No, she had to injure herself so she had to move to Maureen's and be waited on. Her right arm, Kate. Not her left, so she could still function, but her right." She stood up and paced back and forth in the small space between the beds. "I'm so mad I could spit."

Mariah watched, wide-eyed.

Kate stepped into Mary Ellen's path and put her hands on her shoulders. "Calm down. Your mother, as crafty as she may be at times, certainly did not fall and hurt herself on purpose. Anyone can have a fall. Stop blaming her."

Mary Ellen sat down on the bed with a heavy sigh. "I guess it's just that I've been feeling so free here, you know? Now I have to go back to being the dutiful daughter. You know what Michael asked me the other night? He asked if I was the 'sacrificial daughter'—the one who sacrifices her independence in order to take care of her parents. And I am. I'm the sacrificial daughter, and I'm so damned sick of it."

She stood up and went back to the computer and quickly typed her reply:

> Sorry to hear about Ma. Please don't pamper her too much. Try to get her to do as much for herself as she can. I have a life, and I am not going to spend the rest of my summer being her personal nurse. See you in a couple of weeks. Love from your callous, selfish, seriously-pissed-off-freedom-loving sister.
>
> P.S. Don't read this to Ma.

She read it to Kate.

"Are you sure you want to send it?"

Mary Ellen looked boldly at her friend. "Yes, I do. I'm resigning my position in the family. The world can end when I get home. I'll let them get used to the idea while I'm thousands of miles away." She clicked the send button with a flourish. "Breakfast, anyone?"

Kate wanted to finish her washing, so Mary Ellen headed downstairs alone.

She found Larry at a table in the hotel restaurant, staring blankly at his coffee cup. "Mind if I join you?"

He jumped.

"I'm sorry. Would you rather be alone?"

"No, no. Sit down, please. Shall I get a waiter to get you some coffee?"

She shook her head and took a seat. "I'm sure one will be by soon." She spread the linen napkin on her lap and smoothed it out carefully. "I just feel so bad for you guys. Do you want to talk about it?"

He shook his head. "It's probably better not to. I need to keep it together for the girls. On the other hand, I'd love to be able to spill my guts to someone, but not here. Right now, I've got to be the strong one."

Mary Ellen wanted to get up and put her arms around him, but she crossed them instead, tearing up.

"Oh, Mary Ellen. Don't cry, please. I appreciate your compassion and the way you've looked out for the girls. I appreciate it more than you know. But I've got to get through the day."

Dakota and Anna-Mei made their way across the restaurant. Mary Ellen blinked back her tears, and she and Larry smiled at them.

"Ready to meet the pandas? This should be a fun day. Let's get some food first," Larry suggested.

"I'm not hungry," Dakota said.

"Neither am I," her sister agreed.

"You know, I'm not hungry either," Mary Ellen lied, "but we sure don't want to be touring all day with nothing in our stomachs. Let's go get something light, at least." She got up and headed for the buffet, relieved to find them following.

When they returned, they found the O'Days at the next table. Mariah was laughing at something her father said but sobered as soon as she saw them.

"Good morning," Larry greeted. "Did everyone sleep well?"

"We slept like logs," Danny replied. "Snoring logs, in Mariah's case."

"Dad. I do not snore."

"How do you know if you're asleep?" Larry teased. "Sometimes you've got to take your dad's word for it."

"Ha," Dakota said. "You shouldn't be pointing a finger at anybody."

Larry feigned outrage. "What are you implying?"

Anna-Mei was silent but watched the others intently. She gave Mary Ellen a slight nod as if to verify she understood the rules: they would not mention Erica's absence; jokes would be made, and she would make an effort to smile. Mary Ellen reached over and squeezed her wrist gently. Anna-Mei withdrew her hand and turned toward the window, refusing to accept sympathy.

As they were finishing their meals, Emily descended to round them up.

"Hey, are you going to see Michael again while we're in China?" Dakota asked suddenly.

"I don't know. He's visiting his grandmother in Chengdu for a few days. He knows where we're staying. I don't know if I'll hear from him or not."

"Do you want to?"

"Sure. Whatever." Their date seemed like it was weeks ago, not simply a couple of days. She'd been on such a high afterwards, but this mess with her traveling companions put her attention—and probably everyone else's—elsewhere.

They boarded the little white bus, and Mary Ellen watched the sprawling city, teeming with cars, bicycles, scooters, and hordes of pedestrians, go by. They sailed through a red light, narrowly missing a man who was carrying a big package and had stepped into the street.

Emily looked at them and shrugged. "Red lights are only a suggestion in China."

How comforting, Mary Ellen thought. Outside the window she saw workers wielding enormous mops, running them along the railings of a bridge. Emily was engaged in conversation with Larry, so Mary Ellen tapped Anna-Mei's knee and pointed. "I know everyone gets a job in a communist country, but dusting a bridge?"

Anna-Mei smiled.

They arrived at the Panda Research Center at nine-thirty. As they walked from the street into the park, Emily said, "Be careful on the footpaths. It is very wet here, and the pavement can be slippery. Now, who wants to hold a baby panda?"

"I do," Mariah said eagerly.

"The cost is 1000 yuan per person. You get to hold a baby panda while someone takes pictures. The money goes to formula costs for the babies for one month," Emily explained.

"Oh. We can't afford a thousand yuan, can we, Dad?"

"Mom and I already talked about it. One thousand yuan is one hundred fifty U.S. dollars. If you want to do it, we can afford it."

"Yes, yes!" She jumped up and down and hugged her father, then her mother.

Emily laughed. "Anyone else?"

Larry spoke to his daughters. "I want both of you to do it. This is an experience I don't want you to miss."

"Then I'll go make arrangements. Three, that's all? No adults?"

"Dakota is an adult."

"Of course," Emily said. "Two children and one adult. Same price, I think. If you go that way to the pandas, I'll find you," she said, as she pointed to a path that was lined with tall, slender bamboo trees.

They came upon an adult Giant Panda sitting in an enclosed area, munching on bamboo.

Anna-Mei turned to her father, smiling. "I can't believe he's so close. It's like something you'd see on TV, except it's not. He's real."

Larry smiled back and put an arm around her shoulders.

"Mom would love this," Anna-Mei added, a small catch in her voice. "She would just love it."

Dakota joined them by the fence. "Let's take lots of pictures, Anna-Mei. You can share them with Mom."

Her sister nodded. "Take my picture in front of him. Just me first."

Dakota and Larry each took photos, moving into various family combinations until Anna-Mei seemed satisfied.

The next enclosure held two young pandas, who were busy playing. Mary Ellen couldn't help but laugh as she watched. They were cute, like animated stuffed animals. A small group of Japanese tourists joined them, talking softly to each other, pointing out the pandas and chuckling as they snapped photos, too. Mary Ellen suddenly felt happy, aware of being exactly where she should be at that moment.

The next stop along the path was what Emily called a "kindergarten" of six two-year-old pandas. They climbed up on a fat tree limb. One lost its footing and fell to the ground a few feet below. A collective "aww" came from the crowd, which turned to laughter as the panda shook his little head and tried again. Even Anna-Mei seemed to forget her troubles as she watched.

Larry went to Mary Ellen. "This was certainly the right activity for today, wasn't it?" he said softly.

"Perfect," she replied, glancing over at his daughters. "They'll be okay, you know. It won't be easy, but you've got each other. In that regard, you're very lucky."

"Yes, I am. Thanks for reminding me."

The visit to the Panda Research Center continued throughout the morning. They saw a movie about breeding baby pandas (which Dakota later referred to as "Everything You Ever Wanted To Know About Panda Breeding and Much, Much More.") As instructed, the girls layered oversized bright blue hospital gowns over their clothes, donned yellow gloves, and had their turn at holding a nine-month-old panda. They took lots of photos of each other.

Their visit ended by a koi fishpond. The girls sat cross-legged at the edge of the water, feeding the fish, while the adults lounged at picnic tables, drinking bottled water and enjoying the view. Black swans floated on the tranquil water in the distance, as the fish, in shades of deep orange, light tangerine, and white with splotches of black, vied for crumbs of bread. Mary Ellen noted that everyone finally seemed content.

Just then, Mariah shot up and crossed her arms over her stomach. "Mom, I need to go to the bathroom. Quick!"

Emily jumped up and led Kate and Mariah to the back of a nearby building.

Danny followed a minute later.

Anna-Mei came over to her father. "I've been feeling kind of funny too, Dad, but I didn't want to say anything."

"Funny? How do you mean?"

"Sort of queasy. Ever since we left the baby panda house. I thought maybe I was just hot, but . . . ." Looking pale, she sank down next to him. A line of sweat broke out on her upper lip.

"Dakota," he called. "Can you bring Anna-Mei to the bathroom?"

The sisters disappeared behind the building where the others had gone.

"I hope she's not getting sick," Larry said to Mary Ellen. "Erica has always taken care of them when they're sick. I won't know what to do."

"Maybe this will pass. If not, there are plenty of us to help. Don't worry."

Emily returned, concern showing on her usually cheery face. "The two little girls are feeling sick. One has, you know . . . " she gestured to her intestinal area, "and the other one is vomiting. We will wait a few minutes, then take them back to the hotel. Anyone who is feeling good can come on the tour of the city."

They waited half an hour. Mary Ellen went to the restroom once and found Anna-Mei sitting on a bench with her head on her sister's shoulder. Dakota held a wet bandana to her forehead. Mariah was still in the toilet stall. Kate's feet were visible under the door. There was no sign of Danny anywhere. She went back to Larry to report on the girls and suggested that he look for Danny.

"He's sick, too," Larry replied. "Did they all eat something for breakfast that we didn't?"

"No idea." Mary Ellen hoped Kate hadn't eaten any of whatever had made the others ill. As much as she loved them, she didn't relish the idea of playing nurse to Kate's entire family.

Mary Ellen found a couple of plastic bags in the bottom of her tote bag and made sure all the sick people had one at their disposal. Only poor Anna-Mei vomited on the ride to the hotel. She cried pitifully into her hands as her father stroked her hair.

As soon as they arrived, the O'Days headed to their room. Dakota and Anna-Mei insisted that their father go on the city tour.

"That's ridiculous," he protested. "I need to be here. What if you need something?"

Anna-Mei took his hand in hers. "Daddy, go. There's nothing left in my stomach. All I'm going to do is sleep. Besides, Kate is here if we need anything."

"We'll be fine, Dad. Go with Mary Ellen. Enjoy yourself, and take lots of pictures," Dakota added.

Mary Ellen could tell that Larry wasn't happy about following his daughters' orders. She watched him as they drove through the wide city streets. "There really is no point for us to stay at the hotel, Larry. They're just going to sleep, and you'd be pacing the floor. Kate is there. And they have Emily's cellphone number if the girls need you."

He nodded.

Emily was uncharacteristically quiet for the first several minutes of their drive, but then began to point out the sights as they headed to "China Alley," a renovated hutong neighborhood. Back in Beijing, they'd already visited a similar neighborhood that was still inhabited by families who had lived there for generations; the courtyards were connected by alleyways, and they'd ridden bicycle powered rickshaws through the narrow streets. "This place is different," Emily explained. "This is old neighborhood made into shops and restaurants for tourists. Very nice. We go to a silk factory and then you have time to shop in the area."

"How long will we be away from the hotel?" Larry asked.

Emily assured him that her phone was fully charged and turned on, and that if his daughters needed him, they could go back right away.

Their first stop was the silk factory where a young woman showed them the various stages of silk making—from dried up silkworm cocoons, to the creation of lovely, expensive silk bedspreads and scarves. Mary Ellen bought an aqua scarf for Maureen and a deep blue one for herself.

"You're not going to buy anything?" she asked Larry.

"Better to let the girls do the shopping."

Their minibus dropped them off at China Alley and Emily gave them instructions to meet her at the entrance at three o'clock, leaving them on their own. Larry spotted a Starbucks and suggested that they stop for an American coffee. He insisted on buying while Mary Ellen found a table for two. She watched Larry from across the room. His face looked pale, and he had dark circles under his eyes. His light brown hair, graying at the temples, was starting to get long at the base of his neck, and the ends were curling from the humidity.

He returned with their coffees, Mary Ellen's a cold Frappuccino.

"How can you drink hot coffee in this heat?" she asked, twisting her hair up and clipping it with a barrette. "I feel like I've perspired buckets in the last ten days."

"I can drink hot coffee anytime. It's my one addiction. Better than booze, I suppose, although hitting a hotel bar sounds appealing right now."

"It probably wouldn't look so good if we're both sloshed when we meet Emily at three," she giggled. "Sorry. I know there's nothing funny about your situation." She squirmed inside, hoping she hadn't offended him.

"Someday I may laugh about this trip, but right now I'm still trying to figure out what the hell happened. I mean, is Erica losing her mind? Should I be with her, making sure she gets home safely? Or should I be relieved that I don't have to look at her resting bitch face every day, hearing her never-ending list of my failures and shortcomings?" He sipped his coffee and looked out the window.

"So, part of you is relieved, and part of you is worried about her."

"Can I be perfectly honest?" he finally asked.

Mary Ellen nodded.

"I feel so sorry for Anna-Mei. This trip was for her, you know? And now it's completely fucked up. And I feel for Dakota, though she's older. Erica was honest with her, but not with my sweet, sensitive Anna-Mei, the one person who deserves honesty. That part breaks my heart. But personally, I feel like someone just removed a hundred-and-twenty-pound tumor from my gut. To say that Erica and I needed a break from each other is a big understatement. But how did we get to this point? We loved each other once. We were happy. We raised two daughters. Why would she do this to me? I never cheated on her. I mean, I work a lot. Too much, I suppose. But was it my fault?"

Mary Ellen didn't know how to answer that.

"There's more to this. I don't know how much Dakota told you." He played with his napkin, avoiding Mary Ellen's gaze. "She told you, didn't she?"

Mary Ellen nodded.

"And what am I supposed to do with that? Wait until it runs its course and forgive her? Or do I file for divorce when I get home?" He shook his head. "I'm sorry. I'm sure you don't want to hear all this. 'How I Spent My Summer Vacation'—listening to some idiot's marital problems at a Starbucks in China." He laughed cheerlessly.

"Really, Larry. I don't mind. I'm happy to listen."

"You're a gem. It's beyond me how no one has swept you off your feet. We were complete strangers and you've taken in my daughters, listened to me vent, and put up with my wife. If there's anything I can do for you, don't hesitate, please. I owe you. I owe you a lot."

"It's not that big a deal."

"It is. You don't know." He ran the tips of his fingers along her hand. "Thank you."

She felt a tingle where his fingers touched her. She averted her gaze and saw a man outside who looked just like Michael Wong walking with a woman. She sat up straighter and craned her neck to get a better view.

"What is it?" Larry asked.

"Oh, nothing. I just thought I saw . . . ."

"What?" Larry asked, perplexed.

"Well, you remember Michael, the American man we met in Xi'an?"

"Yes. You went out with him."

"Well, I think he just walked by."

"That's right. He has family here."

Mary Ellen nodded.

"Would you like to go say hello?"

"Well, I don't . . . ."

Larry hesitated for only a second. "Come on. Follow me."

They left the coffee shop and headed down the pedestrian mall.

"Is that him?" Larry pointed to a man who was heads taller than anyone else.

"I think so."

Larry grabbed Mary Ellen's hand and powered through. Just before they reached the man, she pulled back. "Wait, Larry."

The man she thought was Michael moved closer to the woman. He pointed at something in a shop window, and she shook her head and giggled. He moved his face close to hers and spoke to her in Mandarin.

"Never mind. It's not him," Mary Ellen said, turning back the other way. She could feel her cheeks on fire. *Jilted again.* She felt Larry's eyes on her.

"Mary Ellen!"

They turned back around, and Michael was suddenly in front of them, reaching to shake their hands.

"Meet my cousin, Xia Ru. Mary Ellen and Larry. They're from the U.S."

Xia Ru greeted them in English as they shook hands.

"I called your hotel earlier," he said to Mary Ellen. "I was hoping to be able to meet you today. I spoke with Kate. She told me you were going on a tour of a silk factory and then to China Alley, so Xia Ru and I took our chances. I didn't think I'd run into you, but here you are."

"Yes. Here I am. I mean, here we are."

"Kate told me some of your party got sick. Unfortunately, that sometimes happens, because the food's so different than what we're used to. Even I have to be very careful what I eat here. It's a challenge with my grandmother because she assumes I'll eat everything she cooks. Hey, what time do you meet your guide?"

"Not till later."

He suggested that they find a shady spot and visit for a while. Larry hung back, but both Mary Ellen and Michael gestured for him to follow.

They found a quiet space that was furnished with stone benches and potted plants, and shaded by a canopy, which made it much cooler than on the sidewalk. Michael offered them bottled water from his large canvas bag, which they accepted.

They talked about the weather and the pandas. Mary Ellen asked Michael about how he'd been spending his time in Chengdu. He told them about his grandmother, the big meals she'd prepared for him, as well as the girls who kept dropping by her apartment, which he was pretty sure wasn't accidental.

Larry got up and asked Xia Ru if she would help him bargain to buy gifts for his daughters. Michael translated to make sure she'd understood, and they decided to meet later at a stall they'd passed that sold painted fans, silk purses and scarves, and little painted boxes.

As the two of them left, Mary Ellen suddenly felt shy.

"What do you think of Chengdu?" Michael asked.

"I haven't seen much of it yet, but it seems like a very vibrant city. So many people and vehicles. It makes Worcester look like a tiny village."

"The cities in China can be overwhelming. How much longer will you be here?"

"We fly to Hefei on Sunday. Mariah was adopted from an orphanage near there, and Danny and Kate want to take her to see it."

"Will you go as well?"

"I don't think so. I'd like to give them some private family time. Kate said there's a pool at the hotel, and a place to get a massage. I'm sold. What about you?"

"I'll be here three more days before flying to Hong Kong, and then home. May I call you once we're back in the States?"

"I'd like that. Do you still have my contact info?"

He assured her that he had both of her numbers in the States.

Mary Ellen reached her hand to his and shook it. "I'm so happy to have met you, Michael. Thank you for showing me Xi'an."

"It was my pleasure. I hope you enjoy the rest of your stay in China. I want to hear all about it." He squeezed her hand and released it.

On the ride back to the hotel, Mary Ellen quietly sorted out her feelings. It was so refreshing to receive attention from a nice, seemingly normal, well-adjusted man. And yet, she couldn't deny that she was drawn to the sad, complicated man beside her.

"Shall we meet for dinner?" Larry asked once they reached the hotel lobby.

"Let's play it by ear, shall we? We'll talk later." She let herself into her room and sprawled out on the bed, relieved to be alone in a cool, quiet space.

Eleven

SOMEONE WAS KNOCKING ON THE DOOR. The room was dark, except for a small stream of light that poured in from the city. Mary Ellen fumbled for the switch on the bedside lamp and groaned as she got out of bed. She felt groggy and her head hurt a little. She opened the door to find Dakota.

"What time is it?" she asked, squinting in the bright light of the hallway.

"Seven. Dad and I walked like ten miles to get Happy Meals for the girls. Someone at the desk gave terrible directions. My feet are killing me."

"They're eating McDonald's food after being sick? Yuck."

"Well, they're tired of Chinese food. And they both feel better now. I must admit that chicken nuggets and fries haven't tasted that good since I was a kid."

"Come in," Mary Ellen said. "You ate it, too? Was that dinner for everyone?"

"Just for the younger set. Dad's taking a shower right now, but he'd like to treat you and Danny and Kate to dinner downstairs. He told me to ask you guys."

"What did Danny and Kate say?"

"Well, I sweetened the pot by volunteering to stay with the girls. They're playing chess, so, it'll be a night out for the over-thirty crowd. If you're up for it."

"I'm exhausted, but I do need to eat something. The heat really sapped me today."

"Here . . . drink." Dakota produced a bottle of cold water, and Mary Ellen drank it down. "Now go take a shower and you'll be a new woman. I'll tell Dad it's a go. Come to our room when you're ready—5-1-6."

Mary Ellen found the O'Days and the Bishops together in Larry's room. Dakota was stretched out on the love seat reading an American newspaper. Danny was coaching Mariah's chess game until she turned to him with a look that said, "Get lost, Dad."

"Okay," Larry said. "I think it's time for dinner. I checked out the two hotel dining rooms; one is classy, the other is more casual. I'm opting for casual unless you folks object." He pulled a light sweater over his head. "Shall we?"

Mary Ellen couldn't help but feel as if this was a double date. Once they were out of the room and in the elevator, she sidled up next to Kate.

"Did you have a good day out on the town?" Kate asked.

"Yes. Emily took us to some interesting places. It must've been a hundred degrees out, though."

"Did Dakota tell you about our hike to the golden arches?" Larry asked.

"She did. Something about wrong directions and Happy Meals."

"Apparently, the woman at the desk doesn't know right from left. And we didn't run into any other English speakers to ask for clarification. We almost turned back when Dakota recognized the golden arches in the distance. Her eyesight is better than mine."

"I'll bet it was worth it to see Mariah's and Anna-Mei's reactions," Danny said. "It must have been like bringing them steak and caviar. Except they actually ate it."

"Are you feeling okay now, Danny?" Mary Ellen asked.

"Yeah, whatever it was, it was mercifully quick for all of us. I was really dehydrated, but I drank a ton of water, and now I'm going to celebrate my recovery with a beer."

"I don't think that's the wisest choice, do you?" his wife asked.

"You don't have to order one, Kate," he said, following the hostess to their table.

"I wasn't the one who was sick."

They glared from behind their menus, while Larry and Mary Ellen pretended not to notice. When the waiter came to take their drink orders, Danny asked for water, as did the rest. Kate looked somewhat smug.

"Don't look so satisfied," Danny said. "I may still order a beer."

"Well," Mary Ellen said, closing her menu. "Should we get several dishes to share?"

They ordered noodles, smoked duck, vegetables, and a beef dish. Larry ordered a chilled bottle of white wine. Danny poured an inch into his glass, but after a few sips, he nudged it aside.

"Okay, you were right," he said to Kate. "Go ahead and gloat."

Once they were relaxed and well-fed, Larry set down his glass and addressed the group. "I arranged this dinner without the girls because I wanted to tell all of you what's going on. Mary Ellen knows a bit more, but not all of it." He took a sip of wine. "First of all, I want to thank you for watching out for my daughters and for not asking a lot of questions."

Everyone remained quiet.

"Erica told me she's been having an affair. It's been going on for quite a while. I didn't suspect anything. We seemed to be growing apart, but I thought things would sort themselves out. Stupid me."

"That's a shame, Larry," Danny said. "Nothing's worse than being blindsided like that."

"Anyway, Erica is on her way home. There's nothing wrong with her health. I only said that to save face."

"Why did she agree to come in the first place?" Kate asked.

"She said she thought that being together as a family would help her appreciate what she had. She didn't anticipate the stresses of traveling in China—the heat, the lack of privacy, and, I suppose, how she would feel once she was separated from her . . . friend. It wasn't long before she started having migraines and being rude to everyone. I'm sorry about that."

"No need to apologize, Larry," Danny said. "You've been a real gentleman, and your daughters have done amazingly well despite the circumstances."

"I had a talk with them this afternoon. We were scheduled to go on to Hefei and take Anna-Mei to the orphanage, but she feels it will be too painful without Erica. She wants to go home. She wants her mother. She wants to understand what's happening. I wish I could give her some answers, but since I don't get it myself, I don't know what to say."

"It's all so sad. I feel terrible for all of you," Kate said.

"Thank you, Kate. With tomorrow our last day in Chengdu, I was wondering if I could impose on you once again. Could the girls go sightseeing with you while I work on adjusting our travel plans? I think it's best if we just head home."

"You'll lose all that money: the flight, the hotel, the trip to the orphanage. That's a big loss, Larry," Danny reminded him.

"Seems to be our theme—the trip of big losses." He stared into his empty wine glass.

There was nothing more to say. Mary Ellen told him they'd be happy to look out for the girls.

As Larry paid the bill, Danny offered an alternative. "Larry, we'll take your girls tomorrow, but would you mind if we leave Mariah with them a little longer? I'd love to take Kate out for a drink to have some time alone."

"Great idea. Take all the time you need."

Kate and Danny headed out, looking almost giddy, while Mary Ellen and Larry headed up on the elevator.

When they reached their floor, Larry said, "Look. If the girls are doing okay, can I come back to chat for a while?"

She took a deep breath. She'd given this guy her attention all day. Now she needed to take care of herself.

"Honestly, Larry, I need some time alone. It's been a long few days, and I haven't had time to process it all yet. Do you mind?"

"No, of course not. I'm sure you've listened to me more than enough today."

"It's not that. I just need some solitude."

He hesitated. "Look, I don't know how things will play out tomorrow. I don't know how much time we'll have before we leave. But I'd like to keep in touch. Can we exchange numbers before we forget?"

She agreed and they went into her room, where she found a notepad and two pens. They wrote down their information, and then she led him back to the door.

"Thank you for buying dinner. It was generous of you. And good luck tomorrow. I hope you can find a way home without breaking the bank."

"So do I. And thank you, Mary Ellen. You've helped me hang onto my sanity these past few days. I'm not sure how, exactly. But I imagine it's because you didn't let yourself get caught up in the drama."

She smiled. "It's a skill I've developed from living with my mother. The original Drama Queen."

"Well, then, thank your mother for me. I've benefited greatly."

There was an awkward pause before Larry drew her toward him. He wrapped his arms around her waist. She hugged him back, and as she pulled away, he kissed her. She started to pull away again, but it felt so good that she kissed him back. When they stepped apart, they both looked surprised.

He let out a deep breath. "Goodnight. I hope I'll see you again."

She closed the door behind him and sat on the edge of the bed, wrapping her arms around herself. *What was I thinking?* She'd forgotten how good it felt to be kissed. *But, Larry?* She closed her eyes and felt his kiss again. She decided not to analyze it; she didn't want to spoil the feeling, but rather, allow herself the pleasure of remembering.

July 1, 2010

We are in the air over Japan, experiencing turbulence. I feel like I'm on a bus with bad shock absorbers. I doubt I'll sleep, so I might as well write.

We had a great time in Shanghai. John Chung, a mechanical engineer who Danny met at a conference in the U.S., was our host. He treated us to dinner at a beautiful restaurant on the Bund that had a great view of the river. After, we sat on the rooftop deck and watched the people below. Colorfully lighted boats slowly cruised along the river, and the city on the other bank was lit up like a Christmas tree. Video streamed down along the sides of the buildings, and the lights twinkled and changed colors while my hair blew in the cooling breeze. As I stood on the terrace, I was filled with hope and excitement. I felt as if I was on the edge of something, and I was ready to finally take the leap into a new life.

I will admit that I felt the absence of Larry and his daughters. Dakota would have loved the excitement of Shanghai. I also admit to thinking about Michael. I never anticipated meeting a man on this trip, never mind two of them. I'm really looking forward to seeing Michael back home and getting to know him. And then there's Larry—and that kiss. I can still feel it, and I get a chill up my spine when I think of it. Funny, this trip was to be all about seeing the world and broadening my horizons to help me be a better teacher. Yet I learned more about myself in relationship to others than anything else. Which is good, I guess.

I heard from Ma yesterday. For some reason she couldn't type with her left hand, so her message came through Maureen. Suffice it to say, I am not looking forward to getting home. Her slightly veiled message in the email spelled out the rest of my summer: personal servant to the queen. However, since I've signed my own Emancipation Proclamation, this will NOT be the case.

Twelve

MARY ELLEN OPENED HER EYES and looked around the room. Home. Always a nice feeling, no matter where she'd traveled. The house was quiet. She stretched and rolled over to check the time: eight o'clock. Her room was a mess. Her suitcase and tote bag were lying on the floor, and the clothes she'd worn home were in a heap. She sat on the edge of her bed and took a deep breath. Her room felt safe and familiar, which she knew was dangerous. She hadn't come home to be comfortable, but to make waves. She threw on a pair of shorts and a t-shirt before wandering out to the kitchen. She was making a pot of coffee when voices came from the front hall.

"Do you think she's up?" Her mother's voice. "Oh, her bedroom door is open. Mary Ellen, are you here?"

"In the kitchen."

The door swung open, and Agnes entered. Her right arm was in a sling, but otherwise, she looked her usual, energetic self.

"Well, the world explorer has returned." She threw her good arm around her daughter and planted a loud kiss on her cheek. She stood back and studied her daughter. "You look peaked."

"Thanks, Ma."

"I think you look wonderful," her sister assured her, as she leaned against the doorway. "Are you happy to be home?"

"It was nice to sleep in my own bed."

"I didn't hear much from you. Only one postcard from Beijing," Agnes complained. "Was I the last thing on your mind?"

Mary Ellen quickly formed an answer. "It takes a long time for mail to get here from China, Ma. I sent a postcard from every city we went to. You'll probably get another one today. And I thought of you often. But we were on the go every day and a lot was happening. I knew you had people looking out for you."

"Well, a mother worries."

"Yeah, especially *our* mother," Maureen said, rolling her eyes.

"Roll your eyes all you want, kid, but when your child travels to Timbuktu you'll understand."

"Hmmm, I don't remember Timbuktu being on the itinerary," Mary Ellen teased. "Maybe next year. Coffee anyone?"

"Did you eat yet?" Agnes asked.

"Not since I got off the plane. I had a bagel while we waited for the limo service."

Agnes stepped into her "mother" role. "We have eggs, English muffins, cereal, fruit. I'd like to cook for you, but that's one thing I can't do." She lifted her right arm slightly.

"Where'd the food come from? Weren't you at Maureen's?"

"Yes," Maureen chimed in, "but yesterday she insisted we go shopping to stock the fridge. I put clean sheets on your bed, fresh towels in the bathroom . . . ."

"Fresh flowers in the foyer," Agnes added.

"That's so sweet. I was beyond exhausted when I got home, so I didn't notice. I did notice that the towels were soft and smelled nice when I got out of the tub. Then I passed out and slept until eight. My thanks to both of you for doing those things. Makes me feel loved."

"Well, we do love you. I'm so glad you're back." Maureen reached over and hugged her sister.

"Why don't you be really loving, Maureen, and make your sister some breakfast?"

"I can do it, Ma," Mary Ellen said, moving toward the refrigerator.

"No, I insist," Maureen said. "I live to serve, didn't you know? What would you like? What did you eat for breakfast in China?"

Mary Ellen sat at the table, where her mother joined her.

"I ate lots of strange things in the morning. Right now, I'm craving eggs over easy and an English muffin with butter and grape jelly."

Maureen winked. "Your wish is my command. But how was the food there?"

"We were taken to a couple of excellent restaurants in Beijing, but most of them catered to tourists. We sat at round tables with a Lazy Susan in the middle, and they brought out dish after dish. The food wasn't always identifiable. Truthfully, if I never go to another Chinese restaurant as long as I live, I'll be okay with that."

"Really? And you always loved Chinese food," Agnes observed.

"I'm not interested in going to a Chinese American restaurant, but I'll eat the food if someone who knows about Chinese cuisine cooks it."

"Where would you find someone like that?" Agnes asked.

"Well, I met a man in Xi'an who's from Massachusetts."

"What? That's a riot," Maureen said, flipping the eggs. "What was he doing in China?"

"He was visiting his grandmother and doing some sightseeing. His name is Michael Wong. Tall, handsome . . . ."

"Single?" Maureen asked.

"Uh-huh. Thirty-three years old, and he's a teacher. He took me out and we really hit it off."

"He's Chinese?" Agnes asked.

"Half. Get this, Ma. He's a quarter English and a quarter Irish."

"What's his Irish name?"

"I didn't ask."

"Does he look Chinese?"

"He looks like a mix of Chinese and European. Black hair and eyes, but quite tall, gorgeous teeth, beautiful smile. And very nice. You'll like him, Ma."

"Oh, I'm going to meet him?"

"I hope so. We exchanged numbers and talked about getting together when we got home."

"So, you met a man. No wonder you look so good," Agnes said.

"I thought you said that I looked peaked."

Maureen laughed as she handed over a plate.

The phone rang and Agnes got up to answer it.

Maureen sat across from her sister and imitated her mother's voice. "So, you met a man."

"Actually, I met two men, but one is married," she whispered.

"Mary Ellen! What are you saying?"

"Larry Bishop. Remember I told you we'd be traveling with another family?" She told her sister a one-minute version of the Bishops' story.

"Wow. That's some drama."

Mary Ellen nodded as she began to eat her meal.

"So, is this Larry attractive?"

"Very. We became good friends. We've got to get together to talk. Alone. I have so much to tell you."

"Sorry," Agnes said, returning to the table. "Betty wants me to go to a musical at Holy Name tonight. I don't know if I'm up for it. And I want to spend some time with you. I want to hear all about your trip. Did you take pictures?"

"Tons. But honestly, Ma, I don't know how long it's going to take me to get my days and nights right side up again. If you want to go out, don't worry about me. I've got to unpack, do laundry, and organize gifts. I also want to download my pictures onto my laptop. Are we going to do the usual Sunday dinner tomorrow?"

"Well, I can't cook." Agnes looked at Maureen.

"Oh, okay. I guess I could host." She looked less than thrilled.

"Why don't we do a potluck here?" Mary Ellen suggested. "I can manage some sort of main dish and you can bring dessert. I'll ask Rosie to bring a salad. What do you think?"

"We never do potluck on Sundays," Agnes protested.

"Do you have a problem with it?" Mary Ellen asked Maureen.

"No. I'd be happy to bring dessert."

"Good. That's settled then. I'll call Rosie." Mary Ellen got up and went to the phone.

"Well. I guess we're having a potluck Sunday dinner. Won't that be nice?" Agnes said to the air.

Mary Ellen returned and informed them that the first potluck Sunday dinner at the Kellehers' would take place tomorrow, and that she was going to make spaghetti with sauce from a jar. And garlic bread.

Agnes opened her mouth to speak, then apparently changed her mind and simply nodded.

By the time Mary Ellen finished unpacking, doing laundry, downloading photos, and napping, it was six o'clock. She headed to the kitchen and met Agnes just as she was on her way out.

"Did you have dinner?" she asked.

"Don't worry about me. Betty and I are going to Coney Island for a hot dog first," she said. The local eatery was a Worcester landmark, one of Agnes's favorite places to eat.

"I promise to be more helpful tomorrow." She kissed her mother's cheek and watched her leave.

Blissfully alone again, Mary Ellen checked the cupboards to see if everything was there that she'd need for dinner tomorrow. She'd have to go out in the morning to buy fresh bread, but otherwise, they were set. As a bonus, she found a bottle of red wine resting in the pantry. *Perfect. I'll serve that, too.*

Now that she had the house to herself, she grabbed the home phone and dialed Kate's number.

"Hello?"

"Hey there, how's everyone doing?"

"Mariah's been quiet. I think she's processing everything. She's eating junk food, and I'm letting her for the time being. We had Lucky Charms for breakfast, McDonald's for lunch, and pizza for dinner."

"Hopefully that will get old soon," Mary Ellen replied. Suddenly, she heard ringing in the distance. "Ugh. Somebody's calling on my cell."

"Do you want to get it?"

"No, I'll check it later."

"Maybe it's Michael. Have you heard from him yet?"

"I haven't even looked at my email. I'll do that tonight."

"So, you don't know what's happening with Larry and Erica?"

"To tell you the truth, Kate, I don't really want to know."

"It looked to me like you and Larry got pretty chummy there at the end."

Huh. You don't know the half of it. "Well, I'm not getting involved in their mess. I imagine we'll keep in touch, but he needs to straighten out his personal life."

"And then?"

"Let's not get ahead of ourselves. It could take a long time."

"Ever the romantic, Mary Ellen."

"My focus right now is to figure out another living arrangement. When I was standing on that terrace in Shanghai, it was clear that I am ready to move forward and make a change. But now that I'm home, it doesn't seem as clear. My mother has been reasonable. She made sure there were flowers and food and clean sheets for my homecoming. Plus, this is where I've lived my entire life. I'm comfortable here, you know? Do I really want to leave?"

"Beware of comfortable, Mary Ellen. Once she starts her emotional manipulation, you'll remember why you want a change."

"I suppose."

"Maybe you should let yourself settle in. Get over your jetlag. Don't expect to make life changes immediately. We've still got six weeks of summer vacation. There's time to think this through."

After making plans to have lunch on Thursday, she hung up and fetched her cell. Two missed calls. One from Michael; one from Larry. Michael had left a message, welcoming her back to the States and suggesting that he come to Worcester on Friday to take her to the art museum.

She called him back and left a message, saying she'd be happy to see him on Friday. She could show him around Worcester, and they could grab dinner after touring the museum. *And then maybe I can introduce him to Agnes.*

Mary Ellen and her mother spent a leisurely Sunday morning together, sipping coffee and reading the paper. Mary Ellen shared the highlights of her trip, and Agnes seemed genuinely interested. They went to ten o'clock Mass and then bought bread at the bakery on Water Street. Her mother was quiet, watching her daughter carefully, as if trying to discern whether this trip had changed her or not.

Agnes relayed the story of her falling down the front steps and how Betty, who luckily was waiting at the curb, drove her to the emergency room at St. Vincent's. She complimented Maureen for her support, then sighed deeply. "What if I was all alone in the world?"

"Well, you're not," Mary Ellen said briskly. "This episode showed that you have a tremendous support system. You didn't even need me."

Her mother was silent.

How will I ever be able to tell her I want to move out? It scared her to even think about it. She started to chatter about how much she was looking forward to cooking Sunday dinner. When they arrived home, she invited her mother to sit in the rocking chair in the kitchen, putting a hassock under her feet and handing her the latest issue of *People* magazine.

"Don't worry about a thing. Just relax. I'll get dinner ready."

Agnes read silently, or at least pretended, then quickly flicked her eyes off her daughter and back at the page whenever Mary Ellen glanced her way. Finally, she asked, "Are you nervous about cooking for everyone?"

"Nervous? Why would I be nervous? Ouch!" She ripped her hand from a steaming pot.

"Careful, there," Agnes warned. "You seem a little jittery."

"Just excited to see everyone, I guess. And maybe I drank too much coffee this morning."

The doorbell rang and Mary Ellen spun around, wondering if she could leave the stove to let her family in.

"I'll get the door," her mother offered. "You stay here."

"Are you sure you can manage?"

"I might not be able to cook, but I can certainly open a door."

Mary Ellen got the meal together and put it on a low burner to keep warm until serving time. She came out of the kitchen just as Rosie and Frank walked through the front door. Before she could finish giving hugs, the bell rang again. Frank ran down to open the door, and Maureen and her family clambered up the stairs.

"Dinner's ready, but I can keep it warm for a while. Let's sit in the living room. I brought presents from China for everyone," she said as she hugged Joe and the kids.

The children looked excited, so Mary Ellen gave them their gifts first. Teddy got a terracotta warrior statue from Xi'an; Joanna, a pretty silk box with a necklace inside.

"What do you say to your generous aunt?" their father prodded.

"Thanks, Aunt Mary Ellen." They each hugged her in turn.

"And now for the adults." Mary Ellen gave t-shirts to the guys, the silk scarf from Chengdu to her sister, and a stuffed panda and panda nightshirt to Rosie, who had requested panda paraphernalia.

She had already given Agnes a silk box and a scarf. Now, however, Mary Ellen took a hand-embroidered picture from the bag of goodies. "One more thing for you, Ma. This was handmade in Shanghai. Isn't it pretty?"

The picture was of a village. Mountains provided the backdrop with little houses nestled in the valley. Tiny people carrying baskets or pushing carts were rendered in stitches.

"Isn't that something," Agnes said. "Look at that needlework. It's so fine." She passed it around for the others to see. "Thank you, Mary Ellen."

"So, tell us all about your trip. What was your favorite place?" Rosie began.

"Do you mind if we eat while we talk? I don't want the food to dry up. It's already not going to be anywhere near as good as what Ma makes."

She got dinner on the table, aware that, once again, her mother was watching, lips pressed together as if to hold back the comments or criticisms lurking behind them. Once they all were seated, she asked Agnes to lead them in saying grace, but Agnes deferred to Frank, who obliged. Mary Ellen asked the children about their summer activities, and they told her about camps, swimming, and sleepovers. Then there was a brief lull.

"So, what's this I hear about you going on a date with some Chinese guy?" Frank probed.

Mary Ellen immediately felt irritated at the way he'd referred to Michael. "He's not 'some Chinese guy.' He's American. He lives in Chelmsford and he's a very nice man—a teacher."

Frank looked at his mother. "I thought you said he was Chinese."

"Did I say that? He's half Chinese. Sorry," she said, looking down at her plate.

"So how old is this guy?" Frank continued.

Mary Ellen deliberately took a big mouthful of food and chewed, ignoring him.

"Sheesh, Frank. What is this? The Inquisition?" Maureen said.

"What? I just want to know what kind of guy she was traipsing around China with."

Mary Ellen put down her fork and swallowed. "Frank, may I remind you that I am thirty-five and quite capable of choosing my friends without your approval? Not needed, and frankly, not wanted."

"Mary Ellen," her mother scolded. "Your brother is just looking out for you."

"If I were fifteen that might be appropriate, Ma. I don't interrogate him about his friends. I assume he can manage without my input. I'd appreciate the same respect. From you, too."

Her mother glared.

Mary Ellen glared back. "This is probably a good time to bring up something I've been thinking about for a while." She cleared her throat and took a sip of water. "I'd like to move out, get my own place."

Agnes gasped and clapped her good hand to her chest.

"Really, Mary Ellen?" Maureen sounded surprised.

"What the hell!" Frank said, pushing himself back from the table. "That's ridiculous. Who's going to take care of Ma?"

"She doesn't need to be taken care of. She's healthy, mobile—at least she will be once her wrist heals. She has good friends, children to check in on her. And I wouldn't move far away. I'd still be able to help, but I'd have my own life. I need that."

"Look at her, Mary Ellen," her brother continued. "You're breaking her heart." He nodded toward his mother, who still had her hand pressed against her chest. Her eyes were closed, and her lips were pressed together tightly.

"Change is always hard. It won't be easy, but I think it would be best for all of us. And Frank, if you're so concerned, we could sell this house, put an addition on yours, and Ma could live with you. You'd love to be closer to Frank, wouldn't you, Ma?" She noticed Rosie's eyes widen in alarm at that suggestion. "There are many scenarios that could work. We can all work together to find a solution that would be best for her. But I need to do something for myself right now. I'm ready for a change." Her hands were shaking. She clasped them together and put them in her lap.

Agnes stood up slowly and put her good hand on the back of her chair. "Frank, would you help me to my room, please? I need to lie down."

Frank leapt to his feet, glaring at his younger sister, giving his mother his arm. The room was silent as they shuffled through the door.

"Okay, raise your hand if you were at all surprised by that reaction." Mary Ellen laughed, then clapped a hand over her mouth.

"Are you losing your mind?" Maureen hissed. "This isn't funny."

"Sorry. I just can't believe I did it. I said it out loud. I asked for what I wanted. That feels great. I can't help it." She smiled apologetically, scanning the table for an ally.

"Way overdue as far as I'm concerned." Her brother-in-law Joe helped himself to another slice of bread. "She'll get over it. She always does."

"Joe! What are you talking about? This isn't just some . . . little thing," Maureen said.

"Frankly, Mary Ellen," Rosie said, "I don't know how you've done it this long. I support you one hundred percent, but please, please, don't mention the in-law apartment thing again." She smiled. "I'm sure there's some other solution."

"I can't believe you two. My sister drops this bomb, and you and my husband act like it's nothing. I need to get out of here. Kids, let's go," Maureen sputtered.

"But, Mom, we haven't had the chocolate cream pie you brought," Teddy pointed out.

"We'll take it with us. Come on kids. Now."

Mary Ellen stood and reached for her sister. "I'm sorry, Maureen. I should have told you. I've been thinking about this, but I didn't mean to blurt it out like that."

"I can't talk about it right now. I need to go." With that, she retrieved the pie and herded Teddy and Joanna out the front door.

A minute later, Joanna returned. "Dad, we need the keys." She held out her hand sheepishly.

Joe reached into his pocket and reluctantly handed them over. "Tell Mom to drive slow. And let me in when I get there, will you? I have a feeling she'll have locked me out, and I don't have an extra key."

"Okay, Daddy. How are you going to get home?"

"It's only five blocks. I can use the exercise."

"Thanks for the present from China, Aunt Mary Ellen," Joanna said as she walked to the door.

Mary Ellen got up and put her arms around her, kissing the top of her blonde head. "Tell everybody I love them, okay? It's going to be all right."

Joanna nodded soberly and left.

Thirteen

MARY ELLEN WOKE TO HER CELLPHONE RINGING. She grabbed it off the nightstand and flipped it open. "Hello?" she croaked.

"I'm looking for Mary Ellen Kelleher."

Mary Ellen pushed herself up to a seated position. "Larry, is that you?"

"Mary Ellen?"

"Sorry, I was napping."

"Oh. I'm sorry. Tough adjustment, isn't it? Took me a good week to feel halfway normal, and you've only been home a couple of days."

"We got back Friday night. I keep waking up at midnight and crashing in the afternoon."

"How does it feel to be back?"

"Yesterday I would have said it was all fine. Today? Well, I dropped the bomb at lunch, and now my mother and my siblings are no longer speaking to me."

"Bomb? What bomb?"

"I told them I wanted to move out and get my own place. My brother and sister are pissed. I assumed my brother would be, but Maureen? I never saw that coming."

"And your mother?"

"No surprises there. She buried her head under the covers as she does whenever she doesn't like what's going on. Now I see why it's taken me so long to assert myself. I've been avoiding the conflict."

"That's hard. I'm sorry it didn't go better. Was anyone on your side?"

"Both my brother-in-law and my sister-in-law supported me. So, they're in the doghouse with their spouses. Speaking of spouses, what's happening with Erica?"

"I've only talked to her on the phone. The girls have seen her a of couple times. Her friend, lover, whatever, apparently left his wife just before we left for China and got himself an apartment in Somerville. That's where she is. She moved out while we were gone."

Mary Ellen took a moment to take in Larry's news before she asked, "How's Anna-Mei?"

"She's putting up a brave front, but I think she's crying a lot. Poor baby. Abandoned as an infant, and now her adoptive mother walks out on her. She doesn't deserve this."

"No, but Erica hasn't abandoned her. She's abandoned you."

"It doesn't feel that way to Anna-Mei. Erica left, and she feels abandoned."

"Poor kid," she said, thinking of students she'd had who'd suffered through their parents' divorces.

"I still can't quite believe it, though I'm starting to see there were signs all along. I just refused to pay attention to them. The reason I called was to see if we could get together sometime soon. I need someone like you right now."

But I don't need someone like you, she thought. "This is a tough time, Larry. I've just created total chaos in my family. Maybe after I get things straightened out here."

"I see."

"I know you're hurting. We can talk on the phone, but that's all I can do right now. I'm sorry." She waited for a response.

"Okay. Well. Hey, I know I have no right to give you advice, but I'd suggest that you start with your sister. I remember you telling me that you two are close. Go talk to her. She'll see your side. Then you can deal with the others."

"Thanks. I think that's a good idea."

"I'll let you go. Good luck and stay strong. You can do it."

Mary Ellen got up and went to the kitchen. The mess mirrored her life. Dirty dishes littered the counters and a pan crusted with dried pasta sauce sat on the stove. *I don't have the energy for this.* She put the kettle on for tea and sat down in the rocking chair while she waited for the water to boil.

If she'd realized how difficult that first step would be, would she have chickened out? She rocked back, a slow creak escaping beneath her weight. The clock ticked on the wall, distracting her. Normally her mother would be here— watching TV, preparing food, or talking on the phone. Silence was rare. *If I move out, it will always be this quiet.*

The phone rang, startling her. She answered with some trepidation, half expecting Frank to start screaming. It was Maureen.

"Are you upset that Ma came back to our house?" Maureen asked.

"What? What are you talking about?"

"Ma called and said she wanted to come back to our house, so Joe picked her up. He said he left a note for you on the table. You were sleeping when they left."

Mary Ellen saw the note and crumbled it up. She wondered if this day could get any worse.

"Can I come over?"

"Of course! Come now," Mary Ellen almost shouted.

"Give me ten minutes."

Mary Ellen washed her face and brushed her teeth, and waited downstairs until Maureen arrived, carrying the leftover chocolate cream pie. As they hugged each other, Mary Ellen couldn't help crying with relief.

After they settled at the kitchen table with tea and dessert, Maureen began.

"First of all, I'm sorry about my reaction. I guess I felt a little betrayed. Why didn't you tell me you were planning to do this?"

"I decided when I was in Shanghai. I mean, it's been brewing for a long time, but I never thought I could do it. For some reason it all clicked into place when I was in China. Everything suddenly seemed possible. I really need to live my own life. I just can't do this dutiful daughter thing anymore. I love Ma, but you know, I don't always like her anymore, and I don't want to live with her. I hadn't had a chance to talk to you alone, and then Frank ticked me off, so I decided to go for it, to say what I've wanted to say for ages. I'm sorry I didn't talk it over with you first."

"I see. Now I guess we have to figure out a way to make this happen without allowing the family to fall apart. I'm pretty sure Rosie is working on Frank."

"Have you talked to her?"

Maureen shook her head. "I just know Rosie. She took your side immediately. And you know there's no love lost between her and Ma. Ma is like the mother-in-law from hell. Outwardly polite, but always ready to find fault. But I'll bet Rosie's working on our dear brother right now."

"He needs it."

"You can tell him to mind his own business. Remember when I started dating Joe? Mum and Dad were upset that he wasn't Irish, and Frank invited me out for a beer one night and tried to get me to see that Joe just wasn't the kind of guy someone in our family would marry. A Lithuanian? What was I thinking?"

Mary Ellen laughed at the absurdity. "What did you tell him?"

"Basically, I told him to shut up and mind his own business. Stop being his parents' henchman and leave me the hell alone. He didn't like it, but what was he going to do? I could've given him a hard time about marrying an Italian, but I love Rosie too much to use her like that. Eventually they all grew to love Joe, just as they'll grow to respect your decision."

"Gosh, I hope so. I have a feeling it's not going to be easy."

They drank their tea in silence.

"Maureen? What do you think I should do now?"

"How about starting with a note to Ma? Write it now, and I'll give it to her at breakfast tomorrow. Tell her you love her and care about her, then tell her what you told me. After she reads it, I'll suggest that we get together to talk it over. Just the three of us."

"Don't you think Frank will insist on coming?"

"We won't tell him about it."

"She'll tell him."

"Okay, so we set some ground rules. Like nobody speaks except you and Ma. Siblings can observe, listen, and support, but no talking."

"Frank will *love* that," Mary Ellen chuckled. "I'll be back."

She went to her room to compose the letter while Maureen washed the dishes. When she returned to the kitchen she said, "Okay, here goes."

> *Dear Ma,*
>
> *I'm sorry I upset you today at dinner. I didn't handle the timing on this very well and I hope you can forgive me. I want you to know that I love you very much and I always will, but I need to go and live my own life. I promise that I will always look out for you, just not from quite this close. Let's talk about this in person as soon as possible.*
>
> *Love,*
> *Mary Ellen*

"Perfect," Maureen said. "Short and sweet is always best."

Maureen changed the topic and told her how challenging it had been to have their mother move in after her accident, which was one of the reasons she could totally get why Mary Ellen felt the need to get her own place. Mary Ellen told her about meeting Michael and their wonderful evening alone together in Xi'an.

"You really like him," Maureen observed, noting the glow on her sister's face.

"I do. He's coming to Worcester on Friday."

"Okay, now tell me about Larry. What's the deal with him?"

Mary Ellen shook her head. "He's a very attractive, intelligent man with two wonderful daughters. But his wife's left him and he's in a vulnerable place. I talked to him today. He wants to see me, but I don't want to get entangled in that mess. There was no escaping it in China, but now that we're back, I'd like to keep my distance. I'm trying to get my own life in order. I told him we'd talk often on the phone, but that was all I can give him right now."

"Does he want more from you?"

She sighed. "I think so. He kissed me the night before he and the girls left. But let's face it—it's a rebound situation. His daughters are still reeling. I think they need to work through that before I show up as their dad's girlfriend, don't you think?"

"Agreed. What did that kiss feel like, if I may be nosey?"

"It made my toes curl."

"What does that mean?"

"Haven't you ever heard Ma's friend Betty's theory on how to choose Mr. Right? If your toes don't curl when he kisses you, forget about him. I never knew what she was talking about . . . until Larry kissed me."

"Hasn't Ma said that Betty was miserable all the years she was married?"

"Yeah, well, I didn't say her theory would hold water. Or maybe her toes didn't curl up when her husband kissed her, and she married him anyway. Maybe there's some old heartthrob out there who curled her toes, and she still pines for him to this day."

They laughed.

"Did Michael kiss you?" Maureen asked.

She shook her head. "Only handshakes thus far. He's rather formal."

"Well, your life has certainly gotten interesting. Now, are you absolutely sure you want to move out?"

"I think so."

"You think so? Frank is out filling a prescription for valium for Ma, and you *think so*?"

"Okay. I get your point. It'll be difficult, I know, but it's time. As for Ma, she plays the victim to manipulate us, but we all know she's strong."

"I have no doubt that Ma will be fine living on her own. I'm just not sure she'll be happy living *here* alone. Would you consider moving downstairs to the first-floor apartment? It'll be vacant soon. Although, she probably needs that rental income."

"Do you think that moving downstairs and living rent-free is an independent life? How could you think for one moment I'd consider that? I can afford to pay rent. I can afford a mortgage, for heaven's sake."

"Okay, sorry. What about living downstairs and paying rent?"

"Seriously? That's a terrible idea."

"I know. But I'm guessing that will be offered as a compromise."

"Yeah, well this isn't *Let's Make a Deal*. And Frank isn't Monty Hall."

"Maybe we're getting ahead of ourselves. Maybe the most important thing is to first smooth things over with Ma.

Who knows? Maybe she'd love to live somewhere else and has been staying here because of you."

"That would be too good to be true. I want her to figure out what would make her happy. And I need to do the same for myself. I think I'll call Nancy Shugrue tomorrow."

"Who?"

"A realtor. She's an old high school friend. I'm going to ask her to show me some houses."

"Gosh, Mary Ellen, I can't keep track of you. Three minutes ago, you said you weren't sure, and now you're planning to go house hunting."

"I'm processing, okay? I'm making it up as I go along. Bear with me, please."

"You realize you'll have to get approved for a mortgage and all that?"

She waved her hand at her sister. "Details, Maureen. First, I'll deal with Ma. Nothing will be right if she's not on my side. And house hunting will help me see if this is the right choice. Maybe I'll hate everything I see. Maybe I'll come running back here and decide to stay forever."

The sisters finally said goodnight at midnight. Mary Ellen watched the taillights of the minivan disappear around the corner. Then she headed to bed, placing her To Do list on her nightstand, telling herself that everything was going to be fine.

July 17, 2010

What's the karmic payback for deceiving one's mother? Will everything fall apart, leaving me to live with her in this triple-decker for the rest of her life? Her uncles were almost 100 when they died. What if Ma lives to be 90? I'll be 50 then, still single, childless, the old maid aunt. Perhaps I'll still be a beloved teacher, or I'll be bitter and disappointed. Okay, as Maureen would say, I'm getting way ahead of myself. As far as karma goes, I'm probably a lifetime or two ahead.

Maureen is taking Ma out to lunch today at The Purple Onion. I'm going to show up and discuss the situation with her. She won't be able to pull one of her dramatic stunts—I don't think she'd do that in public. I can't believe how nervous I am. I need to be calm, collected, and kind—with the tiniest hint of remorse for making my announcement without warning in front of the family. But firm. Inflexible. No, inflexible isn't right—unyielding, as I move toward my desired goal.

After lunch, I'll meet Nancy at her office. I already told her everything must be conducted in secrecy— Frank works with her brother, and I don't want him to know about this. Nancy assured me that confidentiality is her middle name.

I am so incredibly relieved to have my sister on my side again. When she reacted badly after my initial announcement, I felt as if the rug had been yanked out from under me. I couldn't do this without Maureen's support. But now, with her and Joe and Rosie on my side, I can picture this happening. Living in a small house that's mine and mine alone, not reporting my whereabouts or defending my choices to anyone. I can invite people over for dinner, I can have a lover—many, if I choose. And a cat. I can skip mass on Sundays and sleep in. I can become a vegan, or I can have pasta and meatballs and red wine every night. First, I've got to get ready for today. God give me strength. I was just kidding about the reincarnation stuff.

Fourteen

MARY ELLEN WALKED INTO THE PURPLE ONION, her eyes scanning the far corner, where Maureen told her they'd be sitting. She finally spotted them on the other side of the restaurant and made her way over.

"Hi, Ma."

Her mother looked up. She nodded to Mary Ellen. "Sit," she said.

Mary Ellen obliged.

"Maureen, you should sit next to me in case I need a little help eating. I'm still not great with my left hand."

Maureen got up and sat to the right of her mother.

Mary Ellen took a deep breath. "It's good to see you, Ma. I'm sorry about how things went on Sunday. I didn't mean for you to have to leave. It's your house."

"It's your house, too. You girls better decide what you want for lunch. That waitress will be back in a minute."

The women picked up their menus. Nothing looked good to Mary Ellen. She couldn't imagine swallowing anything until this conversation was over.

"What are you having, Ma?" she asked.

"A tuna fish sandwich."

"That's what you always get. Why don't you try something new?"

"I'm clinging to my routines right now. That's what people do when their lives are in an upheaval."

"I see. You really should come back home then, don't you think?"

Agnes shrugged. "I don't want to be a burden to you. I'll stay with Maureen for now. The children are a great comfort."

Maureen fidgeted in her seat. "I thought the kids were driving you crazy. The noise, the squabbling—you told me you missed the quiet of your own house."

"Maybe you should stay out of this, Maureen."

"*Excuse* me?"

"You got me here. Okay. But now your sister and I have a lot to work out. Why don't you go for a little walk and come back in a half hour or so? This is between the two of us, and I know whose side you're on now. I heard you come in after midnight the other night. Two against one isn't fair."

"I thought you needed help with your meal," she said coldly.

"I can handle it, I think. If not, Mary Ellen can help me."

"Fine. I'll go to McDonald's for lunch. Should I meet you in the parking lot?"

"Maureen, stop the drama. Just come back in a half hour. You can have dessert with us."

Maureen slid her purse over her shoulder and headed for the door.

"Was that really necessary?" Mary Ellen asked.

"I don't want an audience."

"You'd never guess that from what happened on Sunday. 'Frank, help me to my room.'" She imitated her mother's pathetic expression.

"Don't be fresh. I was hurt. It was a shock."

Right then a waitress appeared, ready to take their order. Agnes rattled off her habitual order; Mary Ellen requested the chicken Caesar salad. The waitress jotted down their requests, grabbed their menus, and disappeared.

Mary Ellen placed both forearms on the table and leaned forward. "Why didn't you answer my note? You got it, didn't you?"

Agnes reached into the pocket of her sweater and pulled out the note, which was now wrinkled at the edges. "I appreciate this, and I've been thinking it over. That's why I didn't answer. Now tell me, truly, what's going on with you?"

Immediately, Mary Ellen's eyes filled with tears. She squeezed them shut and pressed her lips together. *Don't cry, you idiot. Be strong.*

Her mother reached across the table. "Mary Ellen, you know how much I love you, don't you?"

Mary Ellen nodded her head as the tears dripped.

"So, you want a change. I understand. You want a taste of the life you glimpsed while you were in China. Am I right?"

Mary Ellen dug through her purse for a tissue and blew her nose. "Yes. I want what other people have. I want to try living independently. I want to be my own person, not just your daughter, or the little sister of the family. I love you very much, but I don't want to live with you anymore. Can you understand that?"

Now Agnes's voice broke. "I can understand it, but I don't want to be by myself. I like what we have together."

"Oh, Ma, I get it. Security is fine when you're seventy-five. But I've been living in this cocoon since I was born, and I've realized that when you step out of the cocoon, things happen. Good things, things you didn't even know were possible."

"Is it this Michael fellow? Are you in love with him?"

She shook her head. "No. It's too soon for that. But the possibility is there. The main thing is, I was with people outside my family for seventeen days. Nobody had any preconceived notions of me, and they saw things that I didn't see in myself. That I'm attractive. Likeable. Compassionate. I don't know how to explain it."

"Haven't I always told you how great you are? Why is this news to you?"

"I'm not sure. I just know that I don't want to go back to the way things used to be."

"Well, I have two ideas. Do you want to hear them?"

Mary Ellen nodded.

"The first suggestion is that you stay with me, but we live separate lives. I don't ask any questions; you go your way and I'll go mine."

Mary Ellen opened her mouth.

"Hear me out first, please," Agnes said, gesturing for her to stop. "The second idea is that you take the first-floor apartment when the Jackmans go. I haven't found anybody I'd consider renting to. You'd live on the first floor; I'd live on the third. We could look out for each other, but you'd have your own place."

"Could I have a cat?"

"No pets. You know the rules."

"I'd really like to have a cat. And a garden."

"You can resurrect the window boxes for the front porch," Agnes said. "They're in the basement somewhere. And you can dig up that part of the yard on the side of the driveway and put whatever you want in there."

"Would you let me have a cat if you never had to see it?"

"I'll think about it. Do you like the idea?" Agnes asked with hope.

"I don't know. I mean, I don't like the first one. It wouldn't work, and neither of us would be happy. I'll consider the second idea, but I want to explore some other options first."

"What's that buzzing sound?"

"Oh, it's just my phone."

"Well, see who it is. It might be Michael."

Mary Ellen smiled to herself as she fished her phone out. She looked at the screen and sighed.

"Is it him? Say hello."

"No, Ma. It's Frank, and I missed the call."

"Call him back. See what he wants."

"I'll get back to him later." She put her phone on the table, and it started to vibrate again.

Agnes reached across and flipped it open with her good hand.

"Hello, Frank, it's me. I'm having lunch with her. What do you need, sweetheart?" She moved the phone away from her face. "He said that Nancy Shugrue is a lousy realtor."

Mary Ellen sighed. "Let me speak to him." She took the phone. "What are you talking about, Frank?"

"I had lunch with Bobby Shugrue. He said his sister is showing you some properties. I wouldn't go with her if I were you. Nancy's kind of a flake. Are you and Ma making up? You haven't told her you're looking at houses, have you?"

"No, I haven't. And thanks for the info, but I need to get back to my lunch." She ended the call and threw the phone back in her bag.

"What's wrong?" Agnes demanded.

"Nothing. Where were we? Oh, yes. I'll think about the apartment. In the meantime, how 'bout I call Maureen and tell her to come back?"

"You mean we're finished talking about this?" Agnes asked.

"Not necessarily. Is there something else?"

"Did I ever tell you that I'd once planned to live with my mother for my whole life? I was also the baby of the family, you know. I had three older brothers, and I had to wait on them hand and foot while they were still at home. That was the old Irish way. My mother doted on her sons and insisted that I do, too. It drove me crazy. Finally, they moved out and got married, and I was thrilled to be alone with her. I wasn't interested in getting married or anything, so the arrangement worked. I didn't expect she'd die and leave me behind, but that's what happened when I was twenty-eight. That was old back then. To be single, I mean. Uncle John introduced your father and me. I wasn't the least bit interested, but for some reason he liked me, and he kept coming around. Eventually, he wore me down and I married him."

"Didn't you love him?"

"Not at first. I started to love him when I had my first baby. When I laid eyes on Frank, I knew I'd done the right thing. Then Maureen came along, and when I thought I was all done, you arrived. We were all crazy about you. The older kids were in school, so I had you all to myself. I loved having you with me. After I walked you to kindergarten on your first day, I cried all the way home. It broke my heart."

Mary Ellen squeezed her mother's hand. "I remember those days, too. You were my whole universe."

Agnes dug a wrinkled tissue out of her pocket and dabbed her eyes. "I never meant to do to you what my mother did to me. She loved me and she wanted me with her, but if she hadn't died, I would never have had you kids. I wouldn't have our house, or my grandchildren, or all the wonderful memories. I wouldn't deprive you of that for the world, Mary Ellen. I think I've just become too set in my ways. This will be good for both of us. It scares the heck out of me, but so did marrying your father, and look how that turned out."

"Thanks for telling me that, Ma, and for trying to see my perspective. I really appreciate it."

"Thank your brother and sister."

"Frank? Why?"

"He's the one who thought of the apartment. He figured out the finances for me and discovered that I can make ends meet without rental income."

"No. Absolutely not. I will pay rent if I decide to move there."

"I won't let you."

"But the point is to be independent, Ma. I can afford to support myself. I have a decent-paying job. I will not move into that apartment unless I pay you at least what the Jackmans are paying."

"How can I take money from you?"

"If you don't take it, I'll move somewhere else. And that's final. I won't consider living there without paying rent. If you think I would, then you don't get me at all."

The waitress arrived with their food just as Mary Ellen's cellphone rang. It was Maureen calling to say she'd gotten a call from the kids' day camp. Teddy was running a fever and felt like he was going to throw up. She had to pick him up and get him home. She asked if Mary Ellen could take Agnes home with her.

"Poor little guy," Agnes said once Mary Ellen had relayed the message. "Do you think I should I go over and help take care of him?"

"I think if he's running a fever, we should stay away from that house until the coast is clear. You don't need a stomach bug on top of a sprained wrist."

"I guess you're right. Maureen's good when the kids are sick. Must be that nursing degree she didn't do anything with."

"Ma, how can you say that? She worked at Saint V's for five years until Joanna was born. And she's looking for work now."

"She is? How can she work with two young kids? She's not going to farm them out to some crummy daycare, is she?"

"Maureen is a terrific mother. Her kids have come first since they were born. They're old enough to fend for themselves a little. Maureen feels she needs to get back to work before she forgets everything she learned about nursing. Don't criticize her for that."

Agnes looked up with an indignant expression. "Excuse me?"

"You've done a great job raising your children. But now we're all grown, and we have a right to choose what works for us without having to answer to you."

Agnes opened her mouth to speak but Mary Ellen continued.

"Why is it that only the females get criticized? Maureen, Rosie, me. Never Frank. Is it because he's so perfect? Maybe you should take a closer look at that habit of yours. You said you hated the way you had to cater to your brothers, but now look how you treat your son compared to us. Maureen and I are the ones who have been there for you through thick and thin, while Frank floats in once a week and pontificates on something, and you just glow like he's God's gift to humankind. I'm sick of it, and in case you haven't noticed, I'm not going to keep quiet about it anymore."

Agnes had stopped eating. "If I had a ride I would walk out of here right now."

"Well, I'm your ride and I'm eating my salad first." She jabbed the lettuce with her fork. "What's the point of escaping every time something comes up that you don't want to hear? If we deal with it, maybe we'll actually get to the other side of it."

"I was not criticizing Maureen. I'm simply concerned about my grandchildren's welfare."

"Okay," Mary Ellen said, laying down her fork. "Let me point out a few things if I may. First you said that Maureen had a nursing degree she never used, which is not true. But if it were, that's a criticism. You're implying you and Dad paid for her education, and that she wasted it. Then, when I tell you she wants to go back to work, you criticize her for wanting to use her education. Damned if she does, damned if she doesn't."

"May I have your phone, please?"

"What for?"

"Get Frank on the line."

"Can't you just work this out with me? Why do you have to call and ask him to leave work and take you home so you can crawl into bed? Do you know how frustrating that is?"

Agnes rose from her seat. "Never mind. I know his cellphone number by heart. I'll ask the hostess to call for me."

Mary Ellen sighed and threw her napkin onto her half-eaten salad.

"Fine. I will take you home. Wait here while I pay the bill." She returned a few minutes later with Styrofoam containers, dumping her salad into one and her mother's sandwich into the other. "Let's go."

Agnes walked slowly across the restaurant while Mary Ellen followed.

Why does this have to be so hard? She knew she should apologize, but that was the old Mary Ellen. The new Mary Ellen didn't have a clue what to do, so she simply helped her mother into the car, drove her home, and helped her to bed.

Fifteen

THE NEXT MORNING, Mary Ellen was driving to Kate's when her cellphone rang.

"What happened between you and Ma?" It was Frank.

"How surprising that she already reported to you. Skip the lecture, please. I spoke my mind, and she'll just have to look at some of these things head-on if she wants me in her life." She pulled into Kate's driveway. "I have to go now."

"Wait. Did you tell her I'm her favorite child?"

"No. I just pointed out that the females in the family get criticized frequently, but you never do. You can do no wrong in her eyes. It isn't your fault. But instead of talking about it, she wanted to go home. She hasn't spoken to me since. She refused food, but there were banana peels in the trash, and cracker crumbs in the peanut butter, so I know she's eaten something. I feel bad about this, but I refuse to tiptoe around her feelings for fear of causing one of her 'spells.' I've done it for years, and now I'm done."

"You realize that you're taking on Godzilla, don't you? Do you really want to do that?"

"You know, Frank, if *each* of her children tried to have a more honest relationship with her, it might help. We all love her. She's a wonderful woman, but she does have some flaws. I've lived in close quarters with those flaws, and I'm not going to do it silently anymore. Please don't undermine me in this."

"Hey, if you could get her to chill, more power to you. We'd all benefit. By the way, she needs to be taken to the doctor's tomorrow for a checkup on her arm."

"I know. I'm planning to take her."

"Well, just so you know, she's calling the Elder Bus, so she won't have to listen to your lecture in the car."

Mary Ellen threw her head back and looked up at the sky through the sunroof. She sighed.

"Listen," Frank continued, "I'll call her later and tell her to let you take her, that you promised me you wouldn't lecture her. Just be nice. She'll be happier when she gets an all-clear from the doc, and I know you two will work things out."

Mary Ellen hung up and got out of the car. She made her way up to the house, rang the doorbell, and waited patiently.

"I'm out back," Kate yelled.

Mary Ellen walked around the house to the small deck that was adorned with pots of petunias. Window boxes were filled with fragrant geraniums. The glass-topped table was set for two with quilted placemats, pink linens, and clear glass plates. Kate slid the screen door open and stepped out, bearing a bottle of chilled white wine.

"Wow, you've been busy. The deck looks great. Where did this Martha Stewart-ish energy come from?"

"I have no idea. Mariah left with Danny's parents for five days in Maine, and I woke up with this urge to beautify. I was at the greenhouse when they opened and had all the plants in by ten. Then I made quiche and salad and something yummy for dessert, and now I'm ready to sit. Wine?"

Mary Ellen nodded. "I take it your jet lag is a thing of the past."

"Oh, I didn't say that. I'll probably fall asleep in my blueberry cobbler after a glass or two of this," she said, raising her glass and taking a sip. "You look exhausted. Is everything okay at home?"

"Funny you should ask."

She filled Kate in on the events of the last twenty-four hours, including her brother's latest call.

Kate shook her head. "Your mother is something else. Maybe at her age the thought of change is too hard. Or more likely, her patterns are so deeply ingrained that even when it seems like she's coming around, she can't sustain her new outlook. Do you think if you consistently refuse to give in, she'll give it up?"

"I wish I knew. It seemed promising for a while yesterday. Maybe I'm asking too much. I just got back and announced that I wanted to move out, and then I called her out on her behavior. I mean, it needed to be said. But maybe the timing was off. Do you think I should apologize?"

"I don't see how you can get things back on track without an apology. On the other hand, I'd hate to see you back off your intention to be more outspoken. Let me think about it and report back. In the meantime, come and help me bring out the food."

Mary Ellen followed her into the kitchen and carried the salad out. Kate served slices of tomato and garlic quiche, and they piled on the greens.

"Ah, summer," Mary Ellen crooned, inhaling the wonderful garlicky aroma of the quiche.

"And garden tomatoes. Not my garden, but still, local and fresh."

"My mother said I could have a garden plot next to the driveway if I take the first-floor apartment. Maybe we'll eat tomatoes from my garden next year."

Kate ate silently.

"Do you think moving downstairs is a bad idea?" Mary Ellen asked.

"Well, I'd love to see you get away completely, but maybe you don't think that's realistic. If you're in the same house with Agnes, she'll still feel secure, but you'll have to be firm on setting boundaries. It might be a good compromise for now. If it doesn't work, you always can rethink it."

Mary Ellen took a forkful of the quiche and thought about Kate's advice.

Around three o'clock, Mary Ellen unlocked the front door and let herself in. Agnes was talking on the phone in the kitchen. Mary Ellen walked softly to the door, hoping to ascertain her mother's mood.

"Oh, Betty. Mary Ellen and I have lived happily together since she was born. I don't understand what's happening to her." She paused to listen. "No, no. She's never been selfish or spoiled. I don't know what I'll do. I don't want to be here alone, and I don't want to give up my house. You know how that goes. We've seen it with the girls who are ten years older than us. Elderly apartment, assisted living, nursing home, death. It's just a question of how long it will take, but that's the road, isn't it?"

Mary Ellen walked quietly to her room to put her things away. When she entered the kitchen, Agnes was still sitting at the table, her phone call finished.

Mary Ellen took the seat across. "Ma, I'd like to apologize for upsetting you yesterday. I'll take the downstairs apartment. I'll pay what the Jackmans were paying. And I still want to take you to your appointment tomorrow."

Agnes said nothing.

"Oh, Ma." Mary Ellen went over and put her arms around her mother. "Please don't be upset. I love you more than anyone in the whole world, don't you know that?"

Agnes's eyes filled with tears as she stroked her daughter's hair. "I'm just so afraid," she whispered.

"I promise I won't abandon you. I'll be nearby and we'll look out for each other, just like we always have. Please don't be afraid." She rubbed her mother's back.

The phone rang. Agnes pulled a tissue out of her pocket and blew her nose before answering.

"Oh, I'm glad he's feeling better," she said into the phone. "Is his fever down?" She turned to Mary Ellen and whispered, "Teddy's better, running around the house." She switched back to Maureen. "By the way, I'm sorry I threw you out of the restaurant yesterday. I wasn't at my best, but I'm better now. Mary Ellen's moving downstairs as soon as the Jackmans move out. Isn't that great?"

Mary Ellen could hear her cell ringing in her bedroom. She and Agnes smiled at each other as she left the room.

She picked up just before it went to voicemail.

"Hi, Mary Ellen. Are you recovering from the trip?" The sound of Michael's voice made her happy.

"Still recovering, absolutely. But I feel fine. Are you still coming to Worcester tomorrow?"

"Yes, but I need your address."

"Aren't we going to meet at the museum?"

"If I pick you up at your place, we can travel together instead of having two cars to try and find parking spaces for."

"Makes sense." *So. There would be no way around Ma.* "Oh, I just remembered. I need to take my mother in for a checkup at ten. Can we do two o'clock?"

Michael agreed. Once they ended the call, she lay down on her bed. She thought about how life seemed to be jerking her this way and that since the China trip. Her life wasn't boring anymore, but a part of her longed for everything to be safe and predictable again.

Sixteen

"*People, people who need people . . .*"

After arriving home the next day from seeing her doctor, Agnes was in the kitchen, singing along with Barbra Streisand, while attempting to use her right hand as she put the dishes away. The doctor had said she was doing very well. He prescribed physical therapy to help strengthen her weak muscles, so she scheduled a string of appointments. As Frank had predicted, Ma was in a good mood. "*Lovers are very special people,*" she crooned.

"Ma, what are you doing?" Mary Ellen looked slightly frantic, her hair wild, brush in hand.

"I'm singing. What's wrong?"

"Please don't be singing about lovers when Michael gets here," she moaned.

Agnes laughed. "I'll turn it off before he arrives. Why are you in such a tizzy? Sit down and let me brush your hair."

Mary Ellen hesitated.

"Come on. Sit. Take some nice, deep breaths. I'll try to brush with my right hand. It will be good therapy for both of us." After a few swipes the brush dropped out of her hand. "Damn. This is going to be a long process." She picked it up with her left hand and awkwardly drew it through her daughter's hair. "Is that what you're wearing on your date?"

"It's not a date. And what's wrong with what I'm wearing?"

"Nothing. I was just wondering. You look nice. There's also nothing wrong with calling it a date. You like this man. He likes you. It's a date."

"Please stop calling it that. Let me finish getting ready. Thanks for trying to help." Mary Ellen got up abruptly and headed for the bathroom. Agnes followed.

"Why don't you want this to be a date?" she asked, as Mary Ellen pulled the sides of her hair back into a barrette. "That looks pretty."

"Thanks. Because I hate dating, that's why. I feel like I never know the right thing to say. I wish I could just skip all this. I wish I knew right now whether we were right for each other or not."

"I used to feel that way, too. You just have to figure it out as you go along. You'll be fine."

The doorbell rang just as Mary Ellen finished putting on lip gloss.

"Okay, here we go. Please be nice, okay? Please don't stare at him or interrogate him about his family, or . . . ."

"Sheesh, Mary Ellen. Give me a little credit, will you? Answer the door. I promise to be a shining example of supportive motherhood."

Whatever that means. Mary Ellen forced herself to slow down and take her time on the stairs. Through the window on the door she thought he looked taller than she remembered, and maybe a little nervous. That thought calmed her down until he looked through the window and smiled. Was devastatingly handsome too strong a description? She wiped her palms on her slacks and opened the door.

There was an awkward moment when she wondered if she should shake his hand, but he reached out and hugged her.

"Gosh, it's so nice to see you," she said, stepping back. "Come on up and meet my mother." She turned and led the way upstairs, her stomach flip flopping with each step.

Agnes was sitting on the sofa in the living room, casually turning the pages of a magazine.

"Michael, this is my mother, Agnes Kelleher."

Agnes started to rise, but Michael insisted that she sit as he shook her hand and greeted her warmly. "Is this the recently freed arm?"

"Yes, it is. And it was freed just this morning. Please, sit down. Mary Ellen, get Michael a cold drink."

She hesitated to leave her mother alone with him, but she didn't know how to refuse. So she poured iced tea into tall glasses and mentally crossed her fingers. When she returned to the living room, Agnes and Michael were chatting amiably. They thanked her as she handed the tea glasses around.

"You didn't tell me that Michael was a Harvard graduate."

Mary Ellen sat across from the sofa. "I didn't know that. Harvard. Wonderful."

"And you teach at the Groton School," Agnes added. "That's a very prestigious place, isn't it?"

"I suppose," he answered. "Lots of wealthy families send their children there, and so it does have a certain reputation."

"Tell me about your family," Agnes said smoothly.

Mary Ellen gave her mother a look of warning, which she ignored.

"My parents live in Brockton. My mother is English and my father Chinese American, as you probably know. They met at MIT back in the sixties. I'm their only child. My father is now retired, but my mother is a physician with a very busy practice in Boston. I see them frequently, but I live in Chelmsford to be closer to my job."

"That's how it is nowadays, isn't it?" Agnes asked. "In my day you lived with your parents until you got married. Times have changed. Mary Ellen is moving out; did she tell you? She's taking the first-floor apartment right here. It'll be a big adjustment for me. She's been in this apartment since she was born."

Shut up, Ma, Mary Ellen willed. She stood up. "We should probably get going to the museum, Michael. The galleries close at five, and I'd hate for us to be rushed."

"Oh, that's a shame," Agnes said. "We were having such a lovely visit. Well, another time, I hope." She reached her left hand out to his and gave it a squeeze. "Maybe next time you can come for a meal. We have a big family gathering every Sunday for lunch."

"That would be lovely, Mrs. Kelleher."

"Please, call me Agnes." She fluttered her lashes.

"Mary Ellen, may I use the restroom before we go?" Michael asked.

Mary Ellen showed him the way and then returned to the living room.

"How did I do?" Agnes asked in a loud whisper.

Mary Ellen opened her mouth to speak but decided to kiss her mother on the head instead.

"He is very handsome," Agnes added. "And polite and well-educated. Seems like quite a catch. And to think you had to travel to the other side of the world to meet him."

"Okay, Ma. That's enough. I'll see you tonight. Don't wait up."

She joined Michael in the hall, and her mother waved from the sofa. "Have a lovely time, you two."

As they walked downstairs, Mary Ellen imagined Agnes sprinting to the phone to let her bevy of Irish beauties know that Michael was a real catch.

"She's very nice," Michael said as he unlocked the car door and held it open. "I have to admit I was a little nervous about meeting her. I thought she might object to you dating someone Chinese. Did you tell her that I'm a quarter Irish?"

So, this is a date, Mary Ellen thought as she settled into the passenger seat and put on her seat belt. "Yes, I did. I think she was a little nervous about meeting you, too, but you seem to have won her over."

He laughed. "Which way to the museum?"

Mary Ellen directed him, pointing out Worcester landmarks from the top of Vernon Hill as they went. He lingered at the stop sign, taking in the number of triple-decker houses stacked up and down the hilly streets. She pointed out the site of the old St. Vincent's hospital, where she was born, the street where Danny and Kate lived, and the hill in the distance where her school was proudly perched, the windows catching the light of the afternoon sun.

They merged onto the highway.

"You don't have far to travel to school or to your friend's house. And now you'll be traveling as far as the first floor of the house where you grew up. I wouldn't have taken you for a homebody when I met you in Xi'an."

"The apartment is a compromise. It'll be vacant soon and my mother needs to rent it. I was planning to buy a house of my own, but what can I say? My life is closely entwined with my mother's. She's afraid of growing old and being alone. She doesn't want things to change, and I have to be understanding of that. This way I'll see what it's like to be on my own, but I'll be close enough to look out for her. I hope it's the best decision."

"Why do you want to live alone?"

"I guess I'm looking for *me.* I want to hear my own thoughts, feel my own feelings. I want to buy my bread from the bakery instead of the supermarket. Have a glass of wine when I feel like it without having my mother worry that I'm becoming an alcoholic. Do my own laundry, pay my own bills, decorate my very own Christmas tree. I want a cat. And a garden. I want to be able to sit in my living room at night and watch a James Bond movie without having to hide in my bedroom."

"James Bond? I would have taken you for a romantic comedy sort."

"Action movies are my guilty pleasure. My mother hates them."

Suddenly she felt silly, like a spoiled child who needed her own way. "I'm sorry. I know this must all sound ridiculous coming from a woman my age."

Michael pulled into a parking space outside the museum and turned off the motor. "Not at all. Most people want to structure their lives according to what they love. I couldn't wait to leave for college for that very reason. Did you live in a dorm?"

"No, my parents bought a used car for me, and I commuted fifteen minutes for classes. No one suggested that I live in the dorm. My father was still alive then, and he presented it as a done deal: I would accept the car, they would pay my tuition, I would sleep in the same room I'd slept in my whole life. I wasn't given a choice, and it didn't even occur to me to ask for one."

"So, you're making the break you never made. How about your brother and sister? What did they do?"

"Frank lived away at Boston College, but Maureen lived at home while she went to nursing school. Of course, she made the break when she got married. I'm not following the expected plan." Then her eyes grew wide as she realized something else. "Maybe moving to the first floor is just playing into my mother's hands. It's not making a break, it's just more of the same. Why didn't I see that?"

"That's one way to look at it. But the other side is as you first presented it. Your mother is afraid of being alone, and she wants you nearby. You need and want space, and living on the first floor will allow you to offer your mother a feeling of security. That's important. Your mother won't live forever, you know. Life goes on and things change, whether we want them to or not."

"So, you don't think this is some kind of trap?"

"Anything can be a trap if you allow it to be. It's up to you to make this into a happy move that's right for you."

Mary Ellen thought about his words as she waited for him to pay their admission fee.

"Thank you for helping me see that, Michael," she said as they approached the stairway to the galleries. "It is up to me to make this a positive move. Now, let's get lost in the museum. I need to focus on something besides myself."

It was easier to do than she'd expected. Michael seemed enchanted by the small museum, admiring the mosaic floors, the tiny ancient stone chapel, the ornate staircase. He knew more about art than Mary Ellen did, and he shared his knowledge freely in a way that made her feel like an intelligent companion rather than a student. Eventually they made their way to the modern art gallery, stopping to rest in front of Jackson Pollock's *Equine Series II*.

"It looks like a child's drawing, doesn't it?" she observed.

"In a way it does," he agreed. "Can you see the horse? You may have to step back to change your perspective."

Mary Ellen got up and walked a few feet behind the bench. "Yes. The horse does sort of come into focus. But the closer I get to the painting, the more details I see." She sat next to him and pointed. "See the ghostly figures? And that right there looks like a clothesline. Those are flying houses, blown by a tornado. What do you see?"

He smiled. "I see a huge ball of energy—the energy of life. And there," he said as he gestured, "is a black demon-like creature creeping onto the canvas." He stood and moved closer. "Look at the variety of brush strokes and the thickness of the paint. It's whimsical, yet intentional."

Then a guard approached them. "Excuse me," he said, "but the museum is closing in fifteen minutes."

Mary Ellen was amazed that it was almost five o'clock. "Oh, I wish we had more time. Sometimes I feel totally saturated after an hour in a museum, but I feel like we're just getting started."

"Well then, we'll have to come back again. Or explore other museums. There are so many great ones in this state."

Mary Ellen led the way to Institute Park on the corner of Salisbury Street and Park Avenue. On a hot afternoon there was usually an empty bench near the pond in the shade, and, indeed, they found one. Mary Ellen slipped off her sandals and wiggled her toes.

"I'm having such a nice time, Michael. I haven't had this much fun since that evening in Xi'an."

"Same here. You're a perfect sightseeing companion. Maybe we should consider traveling together. Where would you like to go? Someplace you've never been, of course."

"I'd like to go to Iceland, to Antarctica, back to Italy, to Paris, England, Greece, Bali, Ireland, Prague, Germany . . . let's see . . . are those enough places?"

Michael laughed. "If you have Antarctica on your list, it sounds like you're game to go anywhere."

"If the opportunity presented itself, I'd consider traveling anywhere, unless it was a war zone or something. Unfortunately, a trip to the South Pole isn't going to happen on a teacher's salary. How about you? Where haven't you been before?"

"Oh, so many places. I'd like to see more of this country. I'd like to see the national parks out West, and I'd love to go to Seattle and north to Vancouver. I'd also love to visit Greece and Turkey. I've seen most of the British Isles. The cities of Florence and Paris do sort of call to me, though I've been to both. The museums there are incomparable. You can get lost in them for days. Hey, let's think about April vacation in Paris. If our vacation weeks match up, that is."

Mary Ellen laughed as an electric surge of happiness traveled down to her bare toes. "April in Paris. Isn't that a song?"

"Yes, but I'm not much of a singer. I do play violin, but I don't have one handy."

As they grinned at each other, Mary Ellen's phone chirped. She tried to will it to silence, but it chirped again. She apologized, saying she needed to make sure nothing had happened with her mother. It was a voicemail.

"Sorry. I'll just check this quickly. It's probably nothing."

"Mary Ellen, it's Dakota. Oh my God, I miss you so much. Can we meet for lunch or something? I have so much to tell you. And I want to meet your nephew. You promised. Okay, so call me back at this number. I can't wait to talk to you."

"Is everything okay?" Michael asked.

"Fine." She put her phone back in her purse. "It was a message from Dakota Bishop. The girl I roomed with for much of the China trip. You met her parents, Larry and Erica."

"Oh, yes. I never did hear how the rest of the trip went. Just about everybody in your party was sick when I saw you and Larry in Chengdu. I trust everyone recovered."

"They were all feeling better by the time we got back to the hotel. The girls ate Happy Meals from McDonald's for dinner. The next day we went to the Temple Market area and ate in a hot pot restaurant. Now, that was an experience. Have you eaten in one of those restaurants?"

"Many times. Chengdu is famous for them. Did you like the food?"

"I did. However, one of the waiters put a chicken foot in Dakota's bowl—complete with a claw."

Michael threw back his head and laughed. "Oh, no. What did she do?"

"She covered it with a bowl so that she couldn't see it, then proceeded to eat only white rice. I was thankful she was using the restroom when I put my chopsticks into the hot pot and pulled out a whole chicken head with a beady little eye staring at me."

"Then you had the full hot pot experience," he laughed. "No trip to China is complete without it. Where did you go after Chengdu?"

Mary Ellen was silent, remembering Larry's kiss.

She realized that Michael was watching her closely. She felt herself blush. "I'm sorry. We said goodbye to the Bishops after the hot pot episode. We were headed to Hefei so Danny and Kate could take Mariah to the orphanage where she lived for her first year. The Bishops headed home. It was quite sad, saying goodbye. They'd been through so much."

"How so?"

Mary Ellen realized that he didn't know about Erica having left her family and gone home. She related an abbreviated version.

"I'm sorry to hear that," Michael said. "They seemed like a very nice couple. I never would've guessed they were unhappy."

"Well, it was clear to the rest of us, believe me. And poor Dakota often vented to me, which made me uncomfortable. I tried to be supportive, but I hardly knew them. And I never imagined that I'd get drawn into their family drama."

"And now you're in the middle of your own."

She smiled. "Yes, but it's of my own making. My drama pales in comparison to theirs; I don't have so much at stake." She stood up. "Now, let me show you how to get to Shrewsbury Street. There are wonderful restaurants there. Mexican, Italian, seafood, Chinese, whatever strikes your fancy. Personally, I'm still on hiatus from Chinese food."

They decided on Mac's Diner, which served some of the best Italian food in the city. Since it was a BYOB place, they picked up a bottle of Montepulciano on the way; once they were seated at the back of the restaurant, Michael lifted his glass in a toast.

"To new beginnings. A new apartment for you, excellent school years for both of us, and the hope of April in Paris."

They clinked glasses, and Mary Ellen said a silent prayer that those three wishes would come true.

Seventeen

THE JACKMANS MOVED OUT the following weekend. Early Sunday morning, Agnes handed Mary Ellen the keys. "Here you go. For your very own castle."

Mary Ellen wasted no time heading down to the first floor. She wandered the rooms alone, trying to sort out her feelings. While she was excited about the prospect of making it her own, another part of her felt, well, she couldn't quite put her finger on what was bothering her. As she walked around the apartment, she realized that the layout was exactly the same as it was upstairs. Nothing felt new. Now that it was empty of furniture, she could see that the woodwork was scuffed in several places, the linoleum was cracking in a spot near the refrigerator, and the kitchen cabinets needed to be painted. And the whole place needed a thorough cleaning. It was disappointing.

She was wiping dust onto her jeans, just as Agnes knocked and let herself in.

"So, what do you think? What kind of shape did they leave it in?" She didn't wait for an answer, but prowled through the rooms, taking everything in. "Heavens. She wasn't much of a *hausfrau*, was she? That bathtub ring will need to be sandblasted."

Mary Ellen managed a weak smile. "I've got my work cut out for me. Want to help?"

"I don't know how much I can do until I can really use my right hand. But don't worry. We'll get some help. Show me what you want done."

Mary Ellen led the way around the apartment, pointing out the peeling cabinets, the cracked linoleum, the window trim that needed painting.

"I'll call Bruce O'Malley. He'll do the painting and any other handyman jobs. Just make a list."

Relieved, Mary Ellen ran upstairs to get a pen and legal pad. As she reached her bedroom, her phone rang.

"Dakota, I'm so sorry I didn't call you back. Things are a little crazy here."

"My dad said you were thinking of moving."

Mary Ellen explained that she had gone beyond the thinking stage and was, in fact, checking out her new apartment right now. She took her phone with her and headed back downstairs, pad and pen in hand.

"I want to see you so badly," Dakota pleaded. "Can you meet me for lunch tomorrow? There's an adorable little place in Chestnut Hill, not far from B.C. Maybe your nephew can meet us there?"

Mary Ellen hesitated. She was overwhelmed with how much she needed to do, yet Dakota's enthusiasm made her realize she missed her.

"I can't get there until two at the earliest. I've got a lot to deal with here. Would that be okay? And Lou is working every day, but I'll give him a call. I did tell him about you, and he's looking forward to meeting you."

Dakota gave Mary Ellen the address.

After hanging up, Mary Ellen wandered from room to room, her list growing long. She tried to picture the place with clean windows, new curtains, buffed hardwoods, the thought of which provided a glimmer of pleasure.

When she returned to the upstairs kitchen, she found her mother hanging up the phone.

"Lucky for us, Bruce is on an outside job right now. It's going to rain, so he won't be able to work there for a few days. Instead, he'll be here tomorrow morning at eight. Where's your list?"

Mary Ellen handed it over.

"Holy Moley, Mary Ellen. You want a new kitchen floor?"

"Ma, how old is that floor? It looks like vintage 1980s."

"That sounds about right."

"Okay, so that's thirty years. I think it's time, don't you? I'll pay for it."

Agnes read the list silently, shaking her head. "You're going to be more trouble than Mrs. Delaney. Remember her? She thought she was living at the Plaza Hotel, and I was the concierge. Always something."

Mary Ellen crossed her arms over her chest. "I'll pay for the upgrades, Ma. I don't think there's anything unreasonable there. Besides, I won't be living here forever, and this way you'll have a nice apartment to rent. You can ask for more money if it's in good shape."

"You're thinking of moving out already?"

Mary Ellen squatted in front of the cabinet under the sink and pulled out a bucket, rubber gloves, sponges, and cleaning products.

"Do we have any bleach?"

"On the floor of the bathroom closet. You're going to start scrubbing now? It's after seven."

"I'm going to start while I still have energy. I promise to be quiet when I come back up."

"How long are you going to work?"

"Why? Is there a problem?"

Agnes's hands were on her hips, transmitting her disapproval. Suddenly, she dropped them to her sides.

"I'm sorry. I'd like to help you, but I get tired at this time of night. And my wrist still isn't strong enough."

"I know that," she said gently. "I don't mind working alone. You take it easy. Can I do anything for you first?"

"Maybe just fill the kettle. Don't put much water in, so I can lift it. Let me find the bleach for you."

Mary Ellen made a couple of trips between apartments to bring supplies. She tucked her phone into her pocket and poured her mother's tea. When Agnes was settled in her rocking chair, she kissed her on the forehead and went downstairs.

Before tackling the dirty bathroom, she called Lou and invited him to meet her and Dakota at the restaurant. He said he wouldn't be able to get there until two forty-five. Mary Ellen told him she and Dakota had lots to catch up on, so that shouldn't be a problem.

When she tiptoed into the upstairs apartment at ten-thirty, the place was quiet. She got ready for bed, climbed in and closed her eyes, expecting to be asleep in minutes. Instead, her mind whirled, reviewing all she'd accomplished that evening, adding to her mental list of jobs to tackle in the morning. How would she be able to go to Paris in April if she spent all her savings on the apartment? Maybe this wasn't the right decision. Her mother wasn't *that* hard to live with. In fact, she'd gotten noticeably better. Why was she trying to change everything? It would be so much easier to maintain the status quo.

When sleep finally came, she dreamed that she was already living in the apartment. She was setting the table in the kitchen while a pot of soup simmered on the stove. From somewhere in the apartment, a man was singing. *Michael.* She smiled contentedly as she walked to the bathroom to tell him dinner was ready. But when she opened the door, Larry, not Michael, was standing naked in the tub, his body dripping from his shower. The sleeping Mary Ellen was as shocked as the one who woke up to a knock at the door.

"Mary Ellen," Agnes said, "it's after seven. Bruce will be here soon. You probably should get up now."

"Thanks," she managed to croak. Shaking her head at the weird remnants of her dream, she rolled out of bed. She dressed in shorts and an old t-shirt, ran a brush through her hair, then plopped on a baseball cap.

Her mother was at the stove cooking scrambled eggs, and the coffee was already brewed and waiting.

"Can you butter the toast, Mary Ellen? I can wield a spatula pretty well, but I can't butter toast."

Mary Ellen wasn't hungry, but she knew she should eat. She would miss her mother's cooking but didn't dare say so.

"Look, here comes the rain," Agnes observed. "Just as Bruce predicted."

As if on cue, the doorbell rang. Mary Ellen thanked her mother for the breakfast and, list in hand, she headed downstairs to greet the handyman.

"So, I hear ya' gonna move down to the first floor. Cheaper than getting your own place, that's for sure. This is a nice house. I wouldn't mind takin' an apartment in here myself. Agnes is a good egg. Always liked her." Bruce kept talking as Mary Ellen unlocked the apartment door. "Oh, yah, I remember this place. Did some painting and plumbing in here a few years ago. Okay, so whaddaya' got?"

Mary Ellen went through her list.

"New floor, huh? This all okay with your mother?"

"Yes."

"Ya' pick out the new one yet? Whaddaya gonna do? Tile? Linoleum? I don't do linoleum, ya' know. But I can do a beautiful tile job."

Mary Ellen asked about the difference in price.

"Tile's prob'ly a little more, but it'll last longer. Good investment. I'm sure I can talk Agnes into it if you want."

"What are you going to talk me into, Bruce?" Agnes appeared in the doorway.

"Tiling the kitchen. Lasts longer, looks beautiful."

"How much?"

"Ma, I'm going to take care of it, remember? Bruce, could you measure the space so I can get an idea of how much tile you'll need? Then I can go online and get prices."

"Sure, I'll measure, but I wouldn't be able to start the job for a while. Once it stops raining I need to finish my outside job, and I got another one lined up after that. Might not be able to get to your floor until the middle of September."

Mary Ellen was disappointed, but then she realized that would give her plenty of time to choose the tile carefully and plan her kitchen décor. "That's okay. There's plenty for me to work on in the meantime."

Bruce measured the kitchen, and then started to tackle several small jobs while she went upstairs to grab her laptop. She found the names of a few local kitchen design places and tile stores and decided to check them out in person. By noon she'd ordered tile and bought paint for the cabinets. She found a used kitchen set at a consignment shop that could be delivered the next day. She checked in at her apartment to find that Bruce had removed the old, mildewed grout from behind the bathroom sink and replaced it with a fresh white line. The kitchen window had a new lock, and the faucet had stopped dripping. He was under the kitchen sink, cleaning out the drain. She showed him the tile sample she'd brought home and gave him the soft green paint for the cabinets.

"Yah, that'll look beautiful. Ya' mother will be happy."

She found his constant reference to Agnes a little annoying.

Convinced that she'd done everything she could for the time being, she headed upstairs to shower and change for her lunch date.

Agnes was in the kitchen with Maureen, Teddy, and Joanna.

"Hey, how's it going?" her sister asked. "Can we see the place?"

"Can you wait a day or two? I've got to get to Chestnut Hill to meet Dakota by two. Besides, Bruce is down there working. It'll look much better once he's had some time there."

"Where have you been? I saw your car leave ages ago," Agnes asked.

Mary Ellen smiled broadly. "You won't believe this, but I found some perfect tile for the kitchen, a new paint color for the cabinets, and an adorable kitchen set at Bargains Galore."

"Bargains Galore?" her mother repeated. "Isn't that the place that sells other people's junk?"

"Well, at the risk of sounding trite, one man's trash is another man's treasure."

Agnes's mouth was puckered up in distaste. She shook her head.

Before she could speak again, Mary Ellen headed for the shower. "I'm sorry I can't show you the place today, guys. I really have to get going. I'll call you tomorrow, Maureen."

Mary Ellen managed to find a parking space in Chestnut Hill, a busy neighborhood near Boston College. She walked along the block in search of the restaurant. In the distance she noticed a tall, slender young woman coming toward her, walking arm in arm with an older man. Suddenly, the young woman shrieked and ran toward her, leaving her companion behind.

"Mary Ellen!" Dakota exclaimed, pulling her into a long embrace.

As she pulled away, Dakota's companion reached them. Larry.

"Hello, Mary Ellen." He wore a blue shirt that showed off his eyes. His hair had been cut short, and he had two days of stubble on his face.

"I didn't expect to see you today, Larry."

"He insisted on coming," Dakota said. "I thought it would be nice to have some girl time, but I couldn't shake him." She laughed, but Mary Ellen could tell that she'd meant it.

"I hope it's okay," Larry said.

"It's fine. It's nice to see you both."

"Mary Ellen, you look so beautiful. I love your hair all curly like that," Dakota said.

Mary Ellen laughed. "It's what you'd call *au naturel*. Too busy to do anything with it."

Dakota linked her arm in Mary Ellen's and led them to the restaurant. Eight tables were squeezed into a small room. The walls were painted an intense mustard color and abstract paintings in various shades of purple seemed to pop off the walls. Mary Ellen thought she might have to put her sunglasses back on. Fortunately, the air conditioner was cranking, and the cold felt good to her. She took the seat across from father and daughter. They ordered cold drinks immediately and scanned the menu. When the waitress came back with the drinks, she ordered a bowl of gazpacho and a garden salad, asking for the soup to be brought first.

"I've been doing things for the apartment since early this morning, and I'm famished."

"Dakota tells me you're moving," Larry said.

"Yes. To the first floor of the house I've lived in since I was born."

"It's your mother's house?"

"Yes, she'll stay on the third floor. It's sort of a compromise. Thinking that I'd move out completely was very upsetting to her, so she offered me the first-floor apartment when it became available. I was going to buy a house of my own, but my relationship with her is too important. Hopefully, this will be good. We can still look out for each other, but I'll have more autonomy."

"Is the second floor rented out?" Larry asked.

"Yes, Mr. Stevens has lived in that apartment for twenty years at least."

"He'll be the buffer between you," Larry joked. "Well, congratulations. I know it's a big step for you."

"Thanks. It's a huge step. I still can't quite believe I'm doing it."

"Is there anything I can do to help?"

"It's nice of you to offer. I'll let you know." She turned to Dakota. "So, how does it feel to be home?"

"Great on one hand, and totally weird on the other."

"Weird in what way?"

"Well, my mom is gone. She's living with her—sorry, Dad—lover, and she wants Anna-Mei and me to go over there for dinner to meet him. She really doesn't get it. Like we're going to just go and be like, 'Oh, it's nice to meet you. Thanks for breaking up our family, asshole.'"

"How does Anna-Mei feel?" she asked.

"Horrible," Dakota responded.

At the same time Larry said, "She's doing as well as can be expected."

"Really, Dad? She cries herself to sleep every night. She eats hardly anything, have you noticed?" She turned back to Mary Ellen. "If you ask me, she's a mess. She's really hurting."

"I'm so sorry to hear that. Where is she now?"

"She's with Erica." Larry looked sick with worry. "I have to pick her up later. I didn't realize she wasn't eating. I mean, I noticed, but I . . . I'll have a talk with her today. Maybe we should get her some counseling."

"What about you, Dakota? You seem angry," Mary Ellen pointed out.

"Don't I have every right to be?"

"Of course. But what are you doing with that anger?"

"Well, I'm venting, believe me. I go out for runs, and when nobody is around, I scream as loud as I want. I suppose what I really need to do is to flip out at my mother, but right now I'm afraid I'd do her bodily harm."

"How often do you speak to her?"

"She calls or texts every day. Sometimes I answer. I've only seen her once since we got back. I drove Anna-Mei over, and I told her I wasn't interested in meeting Gregory. That's his name. Sounds like a twit, doesn't he? Not Greg, mind you. Gregory. Pretentious, presumptuous, home-wrecking Gregory. I hate him, sight unseen."

Dakota's phone vibrated. "Oh, it's Julie—my roommate at school." She excused herself to take the call, stepping outside into the heat.

"Well," Mary Ellen said to Larry. "Not much ambiguity on her part."

Larry shook his head, staring vacantly across the room.

"What about you?"

He made eye contact and folded his hands. "Me? I'm okay. Well, nights are tough. Once the house is quiet, I seem to sink down into a place where I've spent very little time in my life. I don't remember ever being depressed. Erica went through her dark days at various times in our marriage. I pointed out that she had a beautiful life, and she answered by saying I didn't understand. Now I do."

"But this depression is situational, Larry. It's in response to your marriage falling apart. You're still adjusting to everything that Erica's leaving means. If you're a naturally optimistic person, you'll come through this. Even wiser and stronger."

Larry reached across the table and took her hand in his. "You know, I wasn't kidding when I said that I needed a friend like you right now. Since I've known you, I've been impressed with your clarity and your willingness to support others. Please say you'll let me come and spend a day with you in Worcester. I'll help you with the apartment. I'll run errands; I'll peel wallpaper—anything. I'm pretty handy around the house."

"Peel wallpaper, huh? You may have just talked yourself into a deal."

"Please tell me I'm not just a pair of hands to you, though. I'd like to think there's more between us."

She felt her color rise as she returned his gaze.

Suddenly Dakota was pulling out her chair and sitting down. "Sorry about that."

They released hands quickly.

"Did I interrupt something?"

Larry cleared his throat. "I was just thanking Mary Ellen for her help and support when we were in China. She made a difference to all of us, don't you think?"

Dakota nodded. "Meeting you was the best thing that happened on that trip."

"Thank you, Dakota. I don't feel as if I did anything out of the ordinary, but I'm glad we're friends." Now it was Mary Ellen's turn to be interrupted by her phone. "Oh, it's Lou. He's here."

As she stood to look for him, he burst through the door. She hugged her tall, grown-up nephew, remembering how when he was six, with scabby knees and grungy sneakers, he had proudly presented her with a garter snake. She introduced him, and he took a seat across from Dakota.

"It's nice to meet you guys. Mary Ellen told me a lot about you."

"We heard a lot about you, too," Dakota said. "Your aunt is crazy about you, have you noticed?"

Lou grinned shyly. "Yeah, Aunt Mary Ellen and I have always been buddies. She used to take me everywhere— Disney on Ice, the circus, high school musicals, the library. When I got older, we went to concerts and museums and stuff. I think she kept me from becoming a complete moron."

"With or without me, you were never in danger of becoming a moron."

"Little do you know," he said. "And you were much more fun than my parents. They were all about achievement and doing the right thing."

"May I remind you that I was fifteen when you were born? That may have had something to do with the difference." She turned to Dakota. "Lou is being modest. He plays lacrosse for B.C. and is an accomplished pianist. He's a young Renaissance man."

"Okay, stop," Lou said with a laugh. "What did you folks think of China?"

Loaded question, Mary Ellen thought as her soup arrived. "Sorry we didn't wait to order, Lou. I was starving."

"That's okay. I ate a couple of hours ago. You guys eat, and I'll talk, which shouldn't be a problem. I'm half Italian. We're really good at talking. And eating. And drinking."

Mary Ellen hadn't seen her nephew in a social situation outside of their family for years. His dark eyes flashed and his Irish dimples framed his smile as he regaled them with stories about working for his mother's cousin, packing frames in boxes in an old warehouse. By the time they finished dessert, Dakota seemed to be enjoying his company immensely.

Larry glanced at his watch. "Oh, no. I've got to pick up Anna-Mei. Let me get the check."

He signaled the waitress, pulled out his credit card, and handed it over before Mary Ellen could even open her purse. "Dakota, I'll be back to pick you up. You'll be okay here for a while?"

She assured him that she'd be fine.

"Mary Ellen, would you walk out with me?

"I'll be back," she said casually.

They went outside and walked in silence for a few minutes until Larry asked, "Could I persuade you to come with me to pick up Anna-Mei?"

The image of Erica's face flashed in her mind. She'd love to see his daughter, but she certainly didn't want to run into his wife. "No. I mean, I'd love to see her. Why don't we make plans for you to bring her to Worcester? You could come and see the apartment, and then I can arrange for her to spend some time with Mariah. Oh, I forgot. She's away with her grandparents. How about next week? Can you get away on a weekday, say, next Tuesday or Wednesday?"

Larry stopped walking.

"Why are you stopping?"

"Here's my car." He laughed.

"What's funny?"

"I was just remembering that night in Beijing when you got the giggles and then hiccupped all the way back to your room."

"I suppose I made a total fool of myself."

"Not at all. I thought you were delightful. I still do." He reached over and pulled her in a close embrace. "May I come see you on Sunday? Without Anna-Mei?"

All Mary Ellen could focus on was his body pressed up against hers as she breathed in his scent. She could feel his heart beating. She wasn't sure if hers had stopped. She stepped away and looked into his eyes. The longing in them caused her to take another step back. She was aware of everything—the fact that he was married, that he was hurting and vulnerable, that she'd already set her boundaries with him. Yet she was also aware of the attraction between them. *Would it hurt to spend some time with him alone?*

"Yes," she said quickly. "Come on Sunday after three so we can avoid the weekly family dinner."

Larry nodded. "I'll get there at four. I think I've got the address. First floor, did you say?"

"Yes. See you Sunday."

She walked down the sidewalk toward the restaurant. When she turned back to look, he was still watching. They each raised a hand before she went back inside. Dakota and Lou leaned toward each other, conversing. Mary Ellen went over to say goodbye.

"I love you, Mary Ellen," Dakota said as she hugged her. "Thanks for coming. And for introducing me to Lou."

She smiled and he jumped up to hug her.

"You're the best," he whispered in her ear. "Thanks."

Heading back to Worcester, she felt totally relaxed, unbothered by the rush-hour traffic. She'd done another previously unthinkable thing. She'd recognized her attraction to Larry Bishop and had opened that door an inch or two. She knew the path might be challenging, but she wanted to see where it would lead. Being cautious and well behaved had gotten her nowhere. It was time for a new approach to life.

Eighteen

WHEN MARY ELLEN GOT HOME, she found Agnes watching TV in the living room.

"Guess who's coming to dinner on Sunday."

"Let's see . . . Sidney Poitier?"

"Guess again," her mother said in a teasing voice.

"Ma, could you just tell me, please?"

"Michael!" Agnes exclaimed.

"Michael who?"

"Your new friend, Michael. The handsome, charming, half-Chinese man."

Mary Ellen sat down on the other end of the couch and turned off the TV. "What are you talking about?"

"He called here looking for you. Said he couldn't reach you on your cellphone. We had a nice chat. He's very smart, I can tell. He speaks English so well."

"Ma, he's American."

"I just mean he's very articulate and well-spoken."

"What exactly did you chat about?"

"Oh, this and that. I told him what a wonderful teacher you are and how much you love children. How much you enjoyed meeting him in China and how God works in amazing ways."

Mary Ellen tilted her head back and closed her eyes. *This is not happening.* "And you invited him to dinner?"

"And he very graciously accepted. He'll be here on Sunday at one o'clock."

"I don't believe this." She crossed her arms tightly.

"What? Don't tell me I did something wrong. I thought you liked Michael."

"I do like him, but I've made plans for Sunday. Besides which, I'd like to be able to decide when and where I'll see my friends. I don't need a matchmaker."

"Well, excuse me." Agnes crossed her arms, mirroring her daughter. "I was just trying to be helpful."

They were silent for a few minutes while Mary Ellen thought things through.

"I suppose you could call him and cancel."

"No." She stood up. "It's fine. I'll tell him I have plans at four o'clock and that he'll have to be gone by then. Right now, I'm going to go downstairs and see what Bruce accomplished. And then I'm going to go to bed early."

Agnes gave a hopeful smile. "You're not mad at me?"

"No, but in the future, please check with me before you invite my friends to dinner, okay?"

She didn't wait for an answer but headed out the door and down to her apartment. The streetlights outside cast enough light for her to see as she wandered through the shadowy rooms. She couldn't wait to have this place to herself. She wished her bed had been moved down already, and that she could lie down on it and be alone.

Flicking on the kitchen light, she saw a note Bruce had left. It detailed what he'd done and what he planned to tackle the next day. The cabinets had been scraped, primer applied to the bare spots. He'd painted one section of a cabinet with the green paint, which she liked. It was going to look great with the floor tiles. She leaned against the counter and surveyed the room until she could picture it with sheer white curtains, green and white dishes stacked up on the open shelves, a bright yellow tea kettle on the stove. Flipping over the note, she jotted down a list of items she'd need to purchase and then headed back upstairs.

Her mother had moved into the kitchen and was talking softly on the phone.

Mary Ellen waved and blew her a kiss.

"Hold on, Nora," she said into the phone. "Want a bedtime snack, Mary Ellen?"

She shook her head. "Just sleep. It's been a long day. Good night."

"Sleep well."

She undressed, pulled a soft t-shirt over her head, and climbed into bed with her cellphone and a novel. She gave Michael a call and was relieved to hear it go to his voicemail. She left a message, then realized she'd forgotten to brush her teeth.

Just as she got to the bathroom, her phone rang.

She sprinted back and nabbed it off the flowered bed sheets. "Hello."

"Hello, Mary Ellen. I just got your message. Would you prefer that I don't come on Sunday? I hesitated to agree before checking with you, but your mother insisted."

"Oh, no, it's fine. If you'd like to come, that is."

"I would. I understand I'll be meeting the whole family."

"Yes. Not everyone gets invited to the family Sunday dinner, so my mother must really like you."

"I'm honored. What can I bring?"

"Do you like to cook? My mother's right hand is still somewhat limited so maybe you could come at noon and help us in the kitchen. I bet she'd enjoy that."

"So would I. Noon it is."

After she'd settled in bed and turned out the light, she couldn't help but laugh. Two months ago, she'd had no prospects in the love department, and here she was, going to entertain one guy and try to slip him out the door before the second one arrived. *If only Ma knew.*

Mary Ellen kept busy with the apartment, willing herself not to think too much about Michael or Larry. She'd taken Agnes grocery shopping on Saturday. Her mother was hell-bent on getting everything just right for Sunday dinner. She'd wanted to make chicken *chow mein*, complete with crunchy noodles from a can, but Mary Ellen convinced her to make a nice stir-fry with beef and peapods. She suggested they have it over rice, but Agnes went online and found a recipe for *lo mein* noodles. She worried that it would seem strange that her Irish American mother would insist on cooking a Chinese meal, but she decided that Michael was easy-going enough to take it in stride and could teach them something about cooking in the meantime.

On Sunday morning, Mary Ellen stayed mostly silent as she watched her mother fuss and fret about the table linens, the flowers, and the shine on the crystal water glasses, until she couldn't stand it anymore.

"Ma, why are you making such a fuss over this dinner?"

"You don't need to have a doctorate from Harvard to see that Michael is a great catch. He's cultured, smart, good looking, polite. . . . Really, I could go on and on. I want him to see our family in the best possible light, that's all. Now help me fold these napkins so they look interesting. Can you make them into swans?"

Mary Ellen bit back a laugh as she attempted to shape the gold cloth into a bird. She thought they didn't look half bad, actually. She was just finishing the last one when her mother reentered the dining room, wearing lipstick and a clean apron.

"All we really need is the guy," Agnes sang out in a Broadway belt, her left arm outstretched in a pose. She stopped and looked her daughter over from head to toe. "I

think you should change. Put on a nicer blouse and maybe some jewelry. Are you wearing makeup?"

"He saw me in China, Ma. Sweaty, wrinkled, frizzy-haired. He didn't seem to mind at all."

"Go change, Mary Ellen. Sweaty and wrinkled is okay when you're traveling or when you've been married for ten years, but not at this stage of the game."

"Okay, I suppose you're right." She went into her bedroom and rifled through her closet looking for something cool to wear. A peach-colored cotton dress with a flounce on the bottom caught her eye. She hadn't worn it in ages; she pulled it over her head, looked in her full-length mirror, and turned sideways. She'd lost a few pounds in China and the reflection of the tall, lean woman with a hint of a tan pleased her. She brushed her hair and twisted it up off her neck, securing it with a cloisonné barrette, and then put on mascara and lipstick. She found some sandals under her bed, slipped into them, and went back to the kitchen for her mother's approval.

"Better?" she asked.

"Much. In fact, you look adorable."

The doorbell rang.

"I guess the guy we need is here," Mary Ellen pronounced as she headed to the door.

Michael held a stunning bouquet of summer flowers.

"Where did you get them? They're gorgeous."

"From my parents' garden. Now that my dad's retired, he's discovered that he loves to grow flowers and vegetables. He's got quite the green thumb."

"I'll say."

When they reached the third floor, Agnes was nowhere in sight.

"Ma?"

"In here."

They followed the voice to the kitchen where they found her sitting at the table, nonchalantly browsing through her Asian-inspired recipes. She looked up and smiled.

"Hello, Mrs. Kelleher," Michael said. "These are for you— from my parents' garden."

Mary Ellen was slightly taken aback that the flowers weren't for her. She watched her mother accept them with a rush of compliments at their size and beauty. "Would you get a vase for these, Mary Ellen?"

As Mary Ellen rummaged in the pantry, she heard Agnes invite Michael to sit next to her so he could answer her questions about the recipes. As Mary Ellen had expected, Michael was very gracious to Agnes.

"These dishes are simple to make once you've assembled the ingredients," he said. "Do you have a wok?"

"That's one pan I didn't have, but Mary Ellen thought of that yesterday, so we bought one."

"Wonderful. Shall we prepare the ingredients together? I'd be happy to do the actual cooking when it's time. If you don't mind, of course. I grew up watching my father do this, and as soon as I was old enough, I became the stir-fry cook in our house."

Mary Ellen pulled out fresh garlic, ginger, and pea pods, and laid them on the table. She produced a couple of sharp knives and cutting boards, and she and Michael peeled and chopped while Agnes washed the pea pods and stirred the bowl of marinating beef strips. They put the vegetables into small bowls and lined everything up on the counter. Mary Ellen put a pot of water on to boil for the noodles as her mother poured them each a glass of Riesling.

They moved into the living room just as the doorbell rang. Mary Ellen ran down and found her siblings, their spouses, and their children dressed in their casual best, looking a bit nervous.

"Why are you all looking like that?" Mary Ellen asked with a frown. "Is something wrong?"

"No, no. Everything's fine," Maureen assured her brightly.

Mary Ellen regarded them suspiciously before leading the way up the stairs.

Michael sat next to Agnes on the couch. He stood up when her family entered and shook hands all around.

"Mary Ellen, get drinks for everyone, would you?" Agnes ordered.

"I'll help," Maureen insisted.

The sisters went through the dining room into the kitchen; Maureen shut the door behind them. "Wow. You set a beautiful table. You must really want to impress this guy."

"That is our dear mother's doing. She wants to show our family in the best possible light since Michael is such a good catch. 'It doesn't take a doctorate from Harvard to figure that out, you know.'"

"She said that?"

"Verbatim."

"Hmm. He is good looking, I'll say that. And so tall. I thought the Chinese were short."

"He's half Chinese. He told me his mother is quite tall. But the Chinese come in all sizes, just like everyone. What would the kids like to drink?"

"I guess they can have soda today. Is there more wine?"

Mary Ellen poured two glasses of wine and put them on a tray with cold beers for Joe and Frank. Maureen filled glasses with ice and poured orange sodas.

"It smells good in here. Who's going to cook?"

"Michael came early and helped us. He'll be our chef. I'm guessing Ma will want us all to socialize for a bit before we eat."

They returned to the living room and served the drinks. Their family members, even the children, were sitting quietly, listening to Agnes tell everything she knew about Michael—his education, family background, his grandmother in China, how he met Mary Ellen at the terracotta warrior pits. Michael smiled pleasantly, clearly well practiced at humoring old ladies.

"Ma, maybe Michael would be more comfortable talking about something else."

Agnes glared at her for a moment, then softened. "I'm sorry," she said, reaching over to touch Michael's hand. "I hope I didn't embarrass you."

"No, no. After all, I'm the new kid around here. I'd like to get to know everyone, though. I've heard so much about each of you."

"Uh-oh. I'll bet my sister didn't have anything good to say about me."

"I didn't know you realized that, Frank," Maureen joked.

"Did your grandfather look anything like this?" Teddy asked, holding up the little terracotta warrior statue that his aunt had brought him from China.

Michael reached out for the statue and looked it over carefully. "I never knew my grandfather. He died before I was able to meet him. But he was born a thousand years after this guy was. I've seen a couple of pictures. No mustache, for one thing. And he was tall and skinny."

"I always thought Chinese people were short."

"Teddy. Go in the kitchen and get some chips." Agnes looked nervous.

Teddy frowned. "Oh, okay."

Michael turned to Mary Ellen. "How's your apartment shaping up?"

"I sure hope we can see it today," Rosie chimed in. "I heard you bought a secondhand kitchen set."

It was Rosie's turn to receive Agnes's glare.

"I'm sorry. Was it a . . . surprise or something?"

"Not at all. In fact, I can't wait to show it to you. It arrived yesterday. Needs a little touch up here and there, but it's a perfect fit for the room, and the price was right. I could give a tour before dinner if you'd like."

"We just served the drinks, Mary Ellen." Agnes's lips were pursed.

"After the drinks, then." She raised her wine glass and took a long sip.

Mary Ellen decided to sit back and watch the scene. She didn't feel invested in whether or not her family liked Michael, or if they passed some kind of test for him. She refused to turn this into a mating ritual. Joanna sat on the hassock in front of her; Mary Ellen reached out, took her silky blonde hair into her hands, and fashioned it into a French braid. Michael and Frank raised several topics of conversation as if trying to find some common ground, only to discover they didn't have any. Michael wasn't a numbers guy. He preferred world literature, the arts, and travel. He suspected that Frank was a sports fan. It would fit his type— Boston College graduate and all. Michael had no interest in sports; neither did Mary Ellen.

"What do you teach?" Joe—always her supportive brother-in-law—asked Michael.

"World history to sophomores, world literature to seventh and eighth graders. I also tutor high school students in a variety of things—Latin, French, writing skills. Oh, and I run the Mandarin Language Club. Unfortunately, the subject isn't offered, but I have nine high school kids who are interested in learning it, so we have fun a couple of afternoons a week. It gives me a chance to practice the language. I learned it in college, but I don't really have anyone to speak it with, except when I go to China."

"What about your father? Isn't he originally from China?" Joe asked, downing the last of his beer.

"No, he was born here but raised by immigrants. He only speaks English. He doesn't understand why I wanted to learn Mandarin. He's only been to China once when he helped his mother move back after my grandfather died."

"Was your mother in the picture then?" Mary Ellen asked.

"Yes, they were newly married. She didn't go with him, and when he showed his grandmother her picture, she nearly collapsed. She couldn't understand why he would marry an ugly white woman." He laughed. "It's funny because my mother is beautiful."

"Ethnic pride runs deep in certain generations," Joe observed. "Agnes here almost keeled over when Maureen brought home a Lithuanian. Only the Irish were good enough for you, right Agnes?"

Agnes stiffened. "Really, Joe. I have opened my heart to the people my children love, don't you think?"

"Aw, yeah, eventually. But you'll have to admit it felt like an interracial marriage to you in the beginning."

Mary Ellen stood up. "How about we go on that tour of my apartment?"

"Why don't your mother and I start cooking now?" Michael asked. "I can see the apartment later. We'll need about a half hour to get the food on the table."

"Perfect. Come on, the rest of you," she said, herding the other nine out the door.

"Jeez, Joe. You have an amazing capacity for political incorrectness," his wife said as they got to the first-floor landing.

"Okay." Mary Ellen raised her voice. "Enough. You are now about to enter my sanctuary. Granted, it still needs work, but I'd prefer no negative energy." She led the way into the dining room. "As you can see, it's exactly the same layout as Ma's apartment. Not in the same shape, unfortunately, but I'm working on it."

The kids wandered off on their own, amazed that it was just like their grandmother's place, only without the lace curtains and familiar furniture. Frank whistled softly as he surveyed. Joe knocked on a few walls, opened cabinets, and peered at door hinges. Maureen and Rosie followed Mary Ellen as she presented her plans for the place—wall colors, floor tiles, a couple of wool rugs on the floors. They offered their services to help with window washing and floor buffing, which Mary Ellen gratefully accepted.

Agnes joined them as they were touring the kitchen. "You won't believe how good it smells up there," she said. "It's like watching a cooking show. He's amazing. If you marry him, Mary Ellen, you'll never go hungry."

"You're gonna get married, Aunt Mary Ellen?" Teddy looked delighted at the prospect.

"Ma, really," Mary Ellen scolded. "Don't say things like that." She turned to her nephew. "Michael and I are just friends. Grandma has an overactive imagination. No one is to say the word marriage for the rest of the afternoon, understand?" She turned back to her mother. "You left him alone up there?"

"He asked me to tell you that dinner is almost ready."

They headed upstairs to find Michael putting huge platters of food on the table. He wore one of Agnes's aprons. Teddy giggled at the sight.

"Like it?" Michael asked him.

They took their seats and found chopsticks next to their plates. Michael gave a lesson on how to use them, and everyone applied serious effort, motivated by the wonderful aromas. The children proved to be quite adept; the adults—except Mary Ellen, who'd had lots of recent practice—were not quite as talented. Finally, Frank set down his chopsticks in frustration. "Screw this," he muttered. "I'm using a fork."

Agnes opened her mouth to scold him just as Michael laughed. "It's amazing how we adapt to whatever we know best, isn't it? It's a little like trying to drive a stick shift when you've had an automatic for years. Yet the kids do it easily."

"I guess my brain isn't flexible anymore, either," Joe said. "I'm going for the fork, too."

Rosie continued to try using chopsticks, laughing at herself each time she dropped another pea pod. "Is this why you lost weight on your trip, Mary Ellen?"

Mary Anne Kalonas Slack

"Partly. But the food we had in China wasn't anywhere near as delicious as this."

"I'm going to admit something to you, Michael," Agnes said coyly.

"Oh?"

Mary Ellen held her breath. *What now?*

Agnes giggled. "I don't even like Chinese food. I never go to Chinese restaurants. I like the taste of fortune cookies, but that's it. But this is one of the tastiest meals I've ever eaten."

"Thank you, Mrs. Kelleher," Michael said, reaching over to put another helping of *lo mein* on her plate.

"Remember? It's Agnes."

"Agnes, then. I find good Chinese restaurants are few and far between. There's one in Cambridge I like, and a couple in Chinatown. Other than that, I'd much rather cook it myself or eat my father's meals, which are very good."

The meal slowed them all down.

Lou looked at his watch. "Oh, Dad. My softball game starts in forty-five minutes. Can you give me a ride?"

"You can't stay for dessert?" Agnes said sweetly.

The sisters exchanged a glance. Was this really their mother? Either she was tipsy, or falling in love with Michael herself. The thought made Mary Ellen laugh.

Michael looked at her and smiled. "And you have a commitment later yourself, correct?"

"Yes. At four." She felt her face get hot. "What time is it now?"

"Two-twenty," Lou said. "Sorry we have to leave, Grandma. If I had my own car I could just take off."

Rosie brought their plates out to the kitchen, while Frank and Lou said goodbye. Lou hugged Mary Ellen and whispered in her ear. "I have a date on Wednesday with Dakota. I think she actually likes me."

"And why wouldn't she?"

"'Cause she's hot and I'm not?"

"I think you're gorgeous, Lou. Dakota is lucky to have a chance with you."

Maureen served the ice cream in cones, and Joe took the children outside to eat them in the yard since there was a cool breeze. Mary Ellen left Michael to chat with Agnes while she and Maureen washed the dishes.

"I think Ma is falling in love with Michael," Mary Ellen observed.

"She's smitten. Isn't that the funniest thing? What do you think the attraction is?"

"Probably the Harvard degree. And the parents who went to MIT. She's always been impressed with that stuff. Who knew she couldn't resist a man who cooks?"

"And what about you?"

Mary Ellen shrugged. "He's very charming, but his charm sort of keeps him at arm's length. An armor of charm. I haven't gotten past it yet."

"It's not just because he's on his best behavior with your family?"

"No, I just realized that it's always like this with him. I don't know him all that well, though. Maybe it takes time."

"What are you doing at four o'clock, by the way?"

Mary Ellen lowered her voice. "Seeing Larry."

Maureen looked at her sister for a moment, before turning back to the dishes.

Mary Ellen felt an urge to defend herself. "What?"

"I didn't say anything."

"Okay, what were you thinking?"

"What's his status with his wife?"

"They're getting a divorce. She's living with her boyfriend. The girls are with him."

"Isn't that a messy situation to get into?"

"I'm fully aware, Maureen. Love can be messy."

"You love him?"

"I'm very attracted to him. I don't know how it's going to play out, but I'm not going to run away just because it might be difficult. I've played it safe long enough. Being with him seems like I'm flirting with danger and yet . . . ."

"You realize if Ma finds out she'll have a fit."

"I'm not planning to tell her until he's divorced, and I'm sure of things. If that day comes, I mean."

"How are you going to hide a relationship from her when you'll still be living in the same house?"

"I don't know. I'll figure it out as I go along."

Michael came through the swinging door. "Mary Ellen, your mother suggested that you show me your apartment, and then we walk around the neighborhood before I leave. What do you think?"

"Great idea."

"I'll finish up here," Maureen said. She wiped her soapy palm on a dish towel and reached out to shake his hand. "So nice to meet you, Michael. The meal was great. It gave me a new appreciation for Chinese food."

Once they were downstairs, Mary Ellen showed Michael the apartment, then they went outside and said goodbye to Joe and the kids. As they wandered around the neighborhood, Michael admired the architecture of the houses; he admitted he'd read up on the famous triple-deckers of Worcester, and he pointed out architectural details that she'd never noticed before.

"I can't remember if I told you I'm going away again," he said, after they'd walked a few blocks.

"This summer?"

"Yes. My mother wants me to go to London with her to visit her sisters. I haven't been since 2000, and I'd love to see my cousins. Mom's footing the bill, so how can I say no?"

She felt somewhat relieved. "What a great opportunity. How long will you be there?"

"Two weeks. We leave Friday morning. I feel as though you and I were just beginning to get to know each other, and here I am taking off on another trip. I'm sorry about that."

"Don't be silly. It's only two weeks. We can see each other when you get back."

Mary Ellen noticed a silver Audi pull up across the street. She took a discreet look at her watch. Ten minutes to four. Michael and Larry would overlap. She stopped at the end of the driveway, about six feet behind Michael's Ford Escort.

"Thank you for coming today. And thanks for cooking. The meal was great. I hope my mother wasn't too . . . ."

"Attentive?" he said with a laugh.

"You could put it that way. She can come on pretty strong when she has a mind to. I hope she didn't make you uncomfortable."

"Not at all. She's rather cute."

They both laughed, and then Michael reached out and hugged her. "I'll call when I return?"

"That would be nice. Do you know how to get to the highway?"

She heard the sound of Larry's car starting up.

Michael looked in the direction of the sound.

She saw a look of recognition on his face when he spotted Larry in the driver's seat. She opened her mouth to speak but didn't know what to say.

Michael looked uncomfortable. "Well, good to see you, Mary Ellen. Tell your mother I said thank you again." He got into his car.

Mary Ellen waved as he drove away. Then she crossed the street and rounded Larry's car, opening the passenger door and sliding inside.

"Did I interrupt something?" he asked, looking straight ahead.

"No. He was just leaving. My mother invited him to Sunday dinner."

"Your mother?"

"Uh-huh. I told him I had plans at four, and so he left. You're a little early."

"Sorry."

"Look. If I didn't want to see you, I would've called you to cancel. Let's go somewhere and have a drink. I've had to behave all day, and now I want to relax."

He turned to look at her. "You look pretty. I like your dress."

"Thank you."

"May I kiss you?"

"Are you serious?"

His face fell.

"I'm sorry. I just mean, not here. My mother could be looking out the window, and I haven't figured out how to explain you to her."

"I see."

"So, let's go. Let's get out of Worcester, in fact. Take a left at the corner."

He pulled out and followed her directions. "I noticed that Michael didn't kiss you."

"That's because we're just friends." Which was probably true now, even if she hadn't been sure of it earlier.

"And what are we?"

"That remains to be seen."

He nodded once and pulled onto the highway.

Nineteen

THEY ENDED UP AT AN IRISH PUB just outside the city, settling into a green leather booth and ordering tall draft beers. The bar wasn't crowded, and the noise level was low. Larry ordered a platter of nachos after discovering that it was one of Mary Ellen's favorite foods. She didn't have the heart to tell him she was still full from the amazing Chinese dinner.

"So, tell me what's happening in your life," she began.

He took a long draught of his beer and set it down. "I had a long talk with Anna-Mei last night. She agreed to talk to a counselor. She told me that she's having a hard time with the notion that Erica would travel all the way to China to adopt her as a baby, but then would leave the family. After all those tears she shed in China, she seems to be getting angry."

"I suppose that's part of the process, though I hope she moves through it quickly. I can't even picture an angry Anna-Mei. She's such a sweet girl."

"She's always been even-tempered, even as a baby. Dakota was only six when we adopted her, and she had some jealous feelings at first. But Anna-Mei was so lovable, Dakota started hauling her around, calling her 'my baby' within a week of us coming home."

"Erica is keeping in touch, isn't she?"

"She's already broached the subject of Anna-Mei coming to live with her and Gregory. I certainly don't want that to happen. I never imagined I'd have to be in a custody dispute with her."

"Anna-Mei is fourteen. I would think that a judge would speak to her and take her wishes into consideration. But then she'd have to choose between the two of you, and that's a terrible thing for a kid of any age to have to do."

"The thought of that enrages me. It's probably better to change the subject. Have you gotten much done in the new apartment?"

Mary Ellen brought him up to date on her renovations thus far, and on her plans for the remaining weeks of her summer vacation. "I hope to be living there by the first of August at the latest. The kitchen floor won't be installed yet, but that will only take a day or two in September. I hope it'll be okay. I mean, my mother invited Michael to Sunday dinner without asking me first. It's going to be a struggle to get her to let go and focus on her own life, rather than mine."

The waitress brought over a platter heaped with nachos. Larry ordered two more beers.

"Am I allowed to ask about Michael?"

"What about him?"

"Are you seeing him?"

"Only a couple of times. He's very nice. I'm not sure I'll see him again."

"Because?"

"I don't know. Can we talk about something else?"

"Of course."

After killing off the nachos and beer, Mary Ellen suggested they head over to her apartment.

As they pulled up in front of the house, she said, "Listen, please don't take this the wrong way, but my mother is old-school Catholic. No one in our family has ever divorced. My cousin Eddie once filed for divorce, and she ranted for days about how the family name was being dragged through the mud. But he and his wife got back together. No one in my family is married to a divorced person. My mother knows nothing about you except that you were on the China trip. I haven't told her about Erica." She looked up toward the third-floor windows. "I know this seems ridiculous, but let's be very quiet going in, okay? I'd prefer for her not to see or hear us."

"Mum's the word. Let me know when I can speak."

"If she does come down, let me do the talking, okay?"

He agreed. They shut the car doors as softly as possible and went up the driveway to the back entrance. Once inside, Mary Ellen shut and locked the door behind her. She slipped off her sandals and whispered, "Would you mind taking off your shoes?"

Larry obliged. "Isn't she two floors up? Is her hearing that acute?"

"I'm not taking any chances." She turned and gestured around the area. "So, this is it," she said, her voice still soft. "Living room, dining room, kitchen, one bathroom, two bedrooms, and a small room off the kitchen that will be my study. I realize it requires a little imagination."

"Not at all. It's a great space. Look at the beautiful moldings," he said, running a hand over the window frame. "It would cost a lot to replicate this nowadays."

"I've never lived anywhere else. I hear people at work complain about shoddy workmanship when they've built houses, but I've never been able to identify with their problems. This place is so solid."

"Well, you've got a great foundation on which to build. It takes time to make a place really yours. Do you have furniture and things to hang on the walls?"

"I'm assuming I can take my bed with me, but I haven't actually discussed it with my mother. She may want it for when my niece and nephew stay over. Maybe it's time for a new one, anyway." She blushed, aware of Larry's proximity.

"Come on, I'll show you the bathroom. It's got a great claw-foot tub." As she stepped into the room and turned on the light, she remembered her dream of Larry standing in her shower, his bare chest glistening. Her blush deepened.

"Wow, what a space. It's huge compared to most bathrooms."

"The one upstairs is like this, too. We have a stackable washer and dryer in ours, but I think I'd rather find an old vanity table or chest to put in here. I'm picturing lace curtains, maybe blue or teal accent colors. I'd like it to feel like an oasis."

"You seem to be seeking peace by moving in here." He inched closer. "I'm afraid that getting involved with me will get in the way, because my life is anything but peaceful right now." He put his arms around her waist.

She raised her face to his and they kissed, gently at first, then more urgently. Her mind resisted, yet her body felt the sexual energy emanating from him. She could not pull away. His hands caressed her bottom, and she realized she wanted to make love to him badly. Her knees buckled, and Larry responded by holding her tightly, bending his knees so that they dropped to the floor. He reached for the buttons on her dress. Her hand was shaking as she helped him. Oh, why hadn't she brought her bed downstairs yet?

Then there was a knock at the door. "Mary Ellen, are you in there?"

They froze. "No, no, no," she whispered. "Can you hide in here until I get rid of her?"

"Are you sure you want to do that? Why not be honest from the start?"

Mary Ellen stood, smoothing down her dress. "Please. Do I look like I've been . . . "

"Mary Ellen? Is that you in there or should I call the cops?" Agnes hammered on the door.

Larry smoothed out her hair with both his hands. "Take a deep breath. You're a grown woman. You're not doing anything wrong."

"Tell that to her. Just don't come out at first, okay?"

He nodded and partially closed the bathroom door.

She unlocked the front door. Her mother stood there, her brow furrowed with anxiety.

"Where on earth have you been? I've been worried about you. I called your cellphone and heard it ringing in your room. And you just disappeared."

"Ma, didn't we discuss our intention to live our own lives?"

"Well, sure we did. But that doesn't mean I can't look out for you. Couldn't you have told me you were going?"

"I told you I had plans at four o'clock."

A floorboard creaked behind the bathroom door.

"Is somebody with you?" Agnes asked, craning her neck to look into the apartment.

Larry stepped out of the bathroom and came to the door. "Hello, Mrs. Kelleher. I'm Larry Bishop." He offered his hand.

Agnes looked shocked but shook it. "I—oh, you're the fellow that Mary Ellen traveled with in China. You and your family, right?" She looked around the apartment. "Is your wife here, too?"

"No, she isn't."

Agnes looked him up and down and then looked her daughter over, taking in her red face and her mussed hair. Her look held a world of suspicion and assumptions. She turned to Larry.

"Well, it's nice to meet you. It's been a busy day for Mary Ellen, what with spending time with Michael and everything." She studied Larry's reaction, but he continued to smile. "Did you meet Michael in China?"

"Briefly, a couple of times."

"Isn't he great? I think he's just the nicest guy. I'm hoping he and Mary Ellen will get together."

"Well, Ma, I'd like to show Larry the rest of the apartment. I'll be up soon."

Agnes just stood there.

Larry stuck out his hand again. "It's been a pleasure, Mrs. Kelleher. How is the wrist healing by the way?"

She gave him just the tips of her fingers this time. "It's improving slowly. Thank you for asking. Well, good night." She looked pointedly at her daughter. "Come see me before you go to bed."

Mary Ellen nodded and watched her mother climb the stairs slowly before shutting the door. She leaned against it.

"That wasn't too bad, was it?"

"You have no idea. I'll get the third-degree when I get up there. 'Why were you alone with a married man?' 'What kind of a wife lets her husband go visit a single woman?' Yada, yada, yada."

"What will you say?"

She thought for a moment. "I think I'll defer the conversation until tomorrow morning. I need to think this through, and I'll need a rested mind, not to mention a fresh cup of coffee, to take her on. Even better, a Bloody Mary."

She finished showing him around, and they talked about him coming back to help her move in. They kissed again at the door, and she watched him drive away before reluctantly heading for the stairs. As badly as she wanted to savor the memory of Larry's kiss and his desire for her, she knew she needed to face the music. She felt like a guilty fifteen-year-old. But she was an adult, she told herself. She would not apologize or explain.

Agnes was sitting in the living room. Her rosaries were in her left hand; her eyes were closed.

Mary Ellen went inside, shutting and locking the door behind her.

Agnes blessed herself and kissed the crucifix before dropping the beads onto her lap. "So, do you want to tell me what's going on?"

"Going on? What do you mean?"

"You know exactly what I mean."

"Are you accusing me of something?"

"Mary Ellen." Agnes leaned forward. "Married men don't generally leave their wives behind to spend time with an attractive, single woman unless something is going on."

"We're not having an affair, if that's what you're insinuating." That was strictly true, though probably not for long.

"Good God. That thought never crossed my mind. An affair? My daughter? I know you better than that."

"Thank you."

"But still. What's this guy looking for?"

"We're friends, Ma. We all got to be close on our trip. Men and women can have platonic relationships, you know."

"Yes, but you're the single one. What if you fall in love with him? It happens, you know. Then he goes home to his wife and kids, and you're left alone with a broken heart. I think you're playing with fire."

"I appreciate your concern. But I'm not a kid. I know what I'm doing. Now, I'm going to go to bed. Is there anything I can do? Can I help you get ready for bed?"

Agnes shook her head.

Mary Ellen kissed her mother's cheek. "Good night. Sleep well."

"Good night," Agnes said softly, and her daughter could hear the disappointment in her voice.

Mary Ellen crawled into bed and lay awake for a long time, unable to stop her racing thoughts.

Allowing herself to sleep in a little the next morning, Mary Ellen eventually woke to the smell of freshly brewed coffee. She crawled out of bed, tossed on her old bathrobe, and followed her nose to the kitchen, where she was surprised to see that it was nine o'clock. She was even more surprised to see her brother and sister sitting at the table with their mother.

Play it cool, she told herself as she headed for the coffee. "Good morning, all. To what do we owe this early visit?"

"We stopped by to see how Ma is doing," Maureen said.

"Do you always sleep this late, Mary Ellen?" Frank asked. "Even Lou gets up earlier than this."

"I had a busy weekend. I decided not to set the alarm. This is my summer vacation, after all."

"Sounds like your weekend was busier than most of us realized," he continued, holding out his coffee cup. "Give me a little more, would you?"

Mary Ellen stared him down and returned the pot to the counter. "Get it yourself."

"Mary Ellen." Her mother's voice was sharp. "Don't be rude. Get your brother a cup of coffee."

Mary Ellen sat at the table and looked over at Maureen, whose sympathetic expression gave her a little courage. She took a sip of coffee.

"I honestly don't know what's gotten into you, Mary Ellen. You lie to me, you're disrespectful to . . ."

"What do you mean I lie to you?"

"You and that man are not just friends. There's something going on. I'm not stupid, you know."

"I see. You think Larry and I are more than friends, and so you invited these two over to . . . what? Talk some sense into me? Shame me into thinking I'm doing something wrong? Take me to confession at St. Brendan's?"

"Well, I don't know what to do. I can't sit idly by while you ruin your life."

"Isn't that a bit arrogant? How could you possibly know if I'm ruining my life? Maybe I'm choosing happiness. Maybe Larry Bishop is the best thing that's ever happened to me.

You are making a judgment before you've even gotten to know him."

"He's a married man. You're committing a mortal sin."

"Oh, please. Divorce, annulments, remarriage—they're all quite common these days. Even Catholics divorce and remarry."

"No one on either side of our family has ever done that. You're not going to be the first."

"And you're not going to be the one to make that decision. I may very well decide that Larry isn't the man for me, but it will be my decision, not yours." She turned. "Frank, did you really come all the way over here before work so you could tell your adult sister how to live her life?"

He rubbed his face. "I'm here because Ma asked me to come. Truthfully, I think you're old enough to decide who to get involved with."

"Gee, thanks."

"But you know very well that dating a married man is stupid, right?"

"I'm not dating him. And his marriage is breaking up. They are planning to file for divorce very soon."

"Okay. So, you'll be dating a divorced man sometime in the near future?"

"Possibly."

Agnes blessed herself. "Holy mother of God, help me."

"Ma, really. This sort of thing is not uncommon today," Maureen said. "And choosing to have a relationship with a man that you care about is not a bad thing."

"There are plenty of men around. There's Michael. He's not married. Why do you have to pick somebody who's wrong? This is so unlike you, Mary Ellen. You've always made such good choices in your life. Now suddenly, wham! I knew you shouldn't have gone on that damn trip."

Mary Ellen set her cup on the table and noticed her hand was shaking slightly. "I'm going to take a shower. You three can continue to have a nice discussion about what an idiot

I am." She stood up and left the room, stopping outside the door to listen.

"I've got to get going. I've got a meeting at ten o'clock." Frank downed his coffee and rinsed his cup out in the sink. "I know this is tough for you, Ma, but this is the twenty-first century. Fifty years ago, this would be a scandal. But now? There are six guys in my office. Two are on their second marriages, one is married to a woman who was married twice before she met him. Two others live with their girlfriends. Aside from me, only Steve has been married to one woman for a long time. We're in the minority."

Thank you, Frank.

"You take marriage vows, you keep them. No matter what."

"No matter what doesn't fly anymore, Ma," Maureen said quietly. "People have had miserable marriages for centuries. They stayed together for the children. But it's not like that now. You don't even know the whole story about Larry and his wife."

"And you do?"

"She told me that his wife left the family in China to be with her boyfriend in the States."

"Why didn't she tell me that?"

"Maybe because you didn't seem to be in a listening mood. And Mary Ellen's point is she's a grown woman, perfectly capable of recognizing her own feelings and acting on them. She's always done the right thing, hasn't she?"

"Up until now."

"Give her a little credit, will you? I'm sure this isn't easy for her. If you get off her case and support her, she'll even confide in you, I'll bet."

"I hear what you two are saying, but still. Your father will roll over in his grave if she marries that man."

Frank took his car keys out of his pocket and walked toward the back door. "Dad loved Mary Ellen. He'd want her to be happy. I haven't met this Larry guy yet, but if he makes her happy, then I'm all for it. I've got to go. Don't worry. I'll call you tonight, okay?"

As soon as Mary Ellen heard his footsteps leave the kitchen, Agnes started to cry.

"Oh, Ma. Please don't." Maureen said.

"Hand me the box of tissues," Agnes sniffed.

A second later, she blew her nose. "I'm so tired, Maureen. There's been too much drama this summer between her going to the other side of the planet for three weeks, this stupid wrist of mine, then her moving out of the place she's lived since she was born. Now this. It's just too much for me."

"It is an awful lot to deal with at once. But on the other hand, I see some wonderful changes in her. She's reaching out to life and saying yes to what makes her happy. She got tired of being the good little girl of the family. No one can blame her for that. She wants love and romance. She wants to try living alone. It has nothing to do with you or with any of us. It has to do with her. She's following her heart."

Mary Ellen couldn't listen to any more. Though she appreciated her siblings' support, she was seething at her mother's lack of trust. She walked quietly to her room and started throwing shoes, clothes, pillows, and books into a big box.

"Mary Ellen, what are you doing?" Maureen suddenly said from the doorway.

"I'm packing. What does it look like?"

"Stop for a minute. I want to talk to you."

Mary Ellen ignored her, unplugging a table lamp and raising her hand to launch it toward the box.

Maureen grabbed her arm. "Stop. You need to calm down."

Mary Ellen let her take the lamp. Then she sat on her bed and burst into tears. After a few minutes, Maureen put a box of tissues on her lap.

"Don't I deserve to be happy?" she asked her sister. "If I'm not truly happy living here, teaching school, and coming home to Mommy, don't I have the right to change that?" She paused to catch her breath. "If I don't do it now, Maureen, I'll still be living alone in this house fifty years from now, dusting Ma's knickknacks and bouncing *your* grandchildren on my knee. I'm thirty-five. I have a chance at love. Why isn't anybody happy about that?"

"Ma is just overwhelmed by all the changes. You couldn't have honestly thought that she'd welcome Larry with open arms. But she wants you to be happy. She made such an effort with Michael yesterday."

"I don't think I want Michael," she said softly. "Wouldn't it be simple if I did? He's too nice, too perfect. With Larry, there's chemistry. There's a spark. I mean, it may not go anywhere. He's been with Erica since he was in college. He's furious and hurt now, but that could change. He could forgive her."

"And that would be a heartache for you."

Mary Ellen shrugged. "At least I would've taken the risk. I don't think they'll get back together. I think they're done and have been for a while. Whatever happens with Larry and me will have to happen slowly. I know that. Maybe that'll give Ma time to adjust to the idea."

"I think you're probably right. She's come around on everything else. She needs a little understanding and compassion right now. You're rocking her boat like it hasn't been rocked ever before."

A small smile emerged. "A little part of me is pretty proud of that. I needed to rock the boat. I was way overdue." She surveyed the mess she'd made of her room. "I guess this isn't really the way to pack, is it?"

"Not if you want things unbroken, not to mention being able to find what you need later."

Mary Ellen started pulling items out of the box, placing them on her bed. "How is Ma now?"

"She's lying down."

"Ha. Figures."

"Mary Ellen, I appreciate the fact that you're trying to take care of yourself and your desires, but you can't just leave Ma out of the equation. She's not young anymore, and she's experienced a whole lot of stress in the last month or so. She's exhausted from it. She really didn't look good when I helped her to bed. Please be kind to her and try to see her side."

"That's hard for me right now. I don't want her meddling in my life. I'm not giving her the right to do that anymore."

"Okay, fine," Maureen said, heading for the door. "I'm going home. I suggest you don't ignore her. I doubt that, in your quest for true love, you want your relationship with your mother to be a casualty. Nobody loves you more than she does. Don't forget that."

Mary Ellen took in her sister's words. She heard Maureen go to her mother's room, no doubt to check on her. She listened to her sister's footsteps move through the house as she left. When the sound of the van drifted up from outside, Mary Ellen lay back on her bed and closed her eyes. Sorrow filled her chest; her tears flowed again. She thought of the quote from Julian of Norwich that she'd learned in religion class in high school: *All shall be well, and all shall be well, and all manner of things shall be well.* She said it again and again as a mantra, and, eventually, she fell asleep, feeling as exhausted as her mother, who by then was most likely sleeping fitfully in the room across the way.

Twenty

A SHORT WHILE LATER, Mary Ellen woke up. She made coffee and prepared a bowl of Cheerios, trying to be quiet so as to not bother her mother. But as she sat down to eat, she heard a soft moaning sound coming from her mother's room. She dismissed it as the usual theatrics, but then it started again. She stopped chewing to listen more carefully. Fear rose in her chest. She jumped up and ran to open the bedroom door. The shades were drawn against the light, but she could see her mother lying still on the bed.

"Ma, are you okay?"

Agnes moaned again.

Mary Ellen turned on the bedside lamp. Fear and confusion painted her mother's eyes.

"What's wrong? What hurts? Tell me. Should I call someone?"

Then she noticed Agnes's mouth was sagging on the left side.

"Oh, God. Ma, try to smile. Can you lift your arms? She reached over and raised her mother's left arm, which fell like a heavy weight back onto the bed. She tried to recall the acronym for diagnosing a stroke, but all she remembered was the part about smiling. Whatever it was, it didn't look good. "I'll be right back. I'm going to call for help."

She called 9-1-1 and asked for an ambulance, then she rang Frank. His secretary said he was in a meeting.

"This is urgent. Tell him to call Mary Ellen immediately. I need him."

Then she tried Maureen, but her sister didn't answer her cellphone. Leaving a frantic message to come as soon as she could, Mary Ellen went back to her mother. Agnes still looked frightened, unable to speak or move.

Mary Ellen started to cry. "Oh, Ma, I'm so sorry. Oh, God. Help is coming right now. You'll be all right." *Please, please,* she prayed, *let her be all right.*

Time passed in a blur of uniformed EMTs crowding the kitchen and bedroom, their radios crackling. Mary Ellen sat in the living room, her heart in her throat. She found her mother's rosary beads still on the sofa; she picked them up and fingered them. She whispered a "Hail Mary" over and over, trying to calm herself until Maureen burst through the door.

"What happened? Why is an ambulance here?"

"Oh, God, Maureen. I think she had a stroke. I heard a noise and went in to check on her, and she couldn't talk or move, and her mouth was drooping. I called 9-1-1. They came right away. I think if you get help right away, then there's a drug they can give you so that there's no damage. That's right, isn't it?" She reached for Maureen's arm.

Maureen stepped back from her sister. "I need to see her." She headed for the kitchen, leaving Mary Ellen.

"I thought it was best to get out of the way and let them do their work," Mary Ellen called after her.

She thinks I've killed her. They're all going to think I've killed her. This is all my fault. She sat back down on the sofa and put her face in her hands.

She heard furniture being moved in the dining room and got up to help, pulling the heavy chairs to the wall. She sat on one and watched as the EMTs rolled the stretcher swiftly out of the kitchen and across the dining room. Maureen walked in front of them and opened the front door, telling them she'd drive behind them.

"Come on, Mary Ellen, let's go." The phone in the kitchen started to ring. Mary Ellen sat, frozen to the chair. "Did you call Frank?"

Mary Ellen nodded and pointed toward the kitchen, unable to speak. Maureen ran over and grabbed the phone, then told Frank the details, UMass Medical Center.

"It's okay, Mary Ellen," she said, returning to her sister. "You acted fast and she's getting help. You must've caught it right away. I only left a little over an hour ago, and she was okay then. Get your purse and keys and anything else you need. I'm sure we'll be there for a while. I'll call Joe so he'll know to pick up the kids at camp today."

Mary Ellen managed to pull herself up from the chair and walk to her bedroom. She saw the indentation on the bed where she'd been only minutes ago, crying for her own problems while her mother was having a stroke. She started to cry again.

She managed to find her purse and her cellphone. The battery was nearly dead. She looked for the charger but couldn't find it in the mess that she'd created. She found some sneakers and a sweatshirt, threw a book into her bag, and finally ran across the phone charger, tangled up on her dresser.

"Maybe you want to put on some clothes."

She looked down at the nightgown she still wore.

Maureen pulled open her closet and tossed some things to her. "Get dressed."

Mary Ellen wiped her eyes on her sleeve and nodded.

Maureen rubbed her back for a moment. "Hang in there. We'll get through this together."

When they pulled into the hospital parking lot, Maureen pulled a box of tissues from the back seat and set them in her sister's lap. "Please try to pull yourself together. I know this is hard, but it's not going to help any of us if you're falling apart."

"You didn't give Ma a stroke. I did."

"Don't be ridiculous. You can't give someone a stroke. She's almost seventy-six. This isn't uncommon. Besides, you sprang into action. And you were right: there's a drug that, if administered in the first few hours after symptoms appear, will help reduce the damage. I'm certain we're within that window of time. I'm going in now. Do you want to sit here for a few minutes?"

Mary Ellen nodded, blowing her nose.

She tossed her the car keys. "Don't forget to lock up."

Mary Ellen took several shaky, deep breaths as she tried to calm herself. *How am I going to get through this? What's going to happen to my life now? Listen to yourself. You are so selfish. Ma is suffering because of you, and you're worrying about yourself.*

Her cellphone rang, breaking her stint of self-loathing.

"Hello?" she croaked.

"Mary Ellen?"

"She had a stroke, Larry. I'm outside the emergency room right now."

"What are you talking about?"

"My mother. I found her a little while ago."

"You're kidding."

She took a deep breath. "Oh, if only. I woke up to find she'd called in the troops to tell me the error of my ways after I saw you yesterday. I wouldn't listen. I told her to mind her own business and let me live my own life. Later on,

I heard a funny noise from her room, and I went to check and . . . " She paused to hold back a sob. "And when I went in, she could not move or speak. Her mouth was drooping on one side and . . . " This time she sobbed out loud. "And she looked so frightened, Larry. Her eyes looked desperate and scared. It was terrible."

"I'm so sorry."

"I feel so guilty. I've been so caught up in the excitement of my own life that I didn't really see what was happening to her. It's all my fault."

"Don't blame yourself, Mary Ellen. Your mother is elderly."

"That's what Maureen says, but I've caused her a huge amount of stress since I got back from the trip. This was the last straw. Now the camel's back is broken, and everyone's going to think that her spoiled, selfish, rotten daughter is the cause."

"I think you're wrong. But who cares what anyone thinks? Put this stuff out of your head. You can't support your mother if you're beating yourself up. Focus on her. She needs you now, and if you're there for her, hopefully, all these feelings will recede."

"I don't know about that."

"Would it help if I came?"

"No, absolutely not. I can't see you anymore, Larry."

"Please don't do this. Things will work out. It looks bleak right now, but everything will work out."

Mary Ellen's phone beeped. She looked at it and saw the low battery signal flashing. "I have to go. My phone's about to die." And with those words, the call was cut off.

Mary Ellen sat with her brother and sister in the waiting room. The medical staff had asked them to wait there while they stabilized Agnes and got her ready to be moved to a bed upstairs. Maureen texted Rosie and Joe, while Frank paced across the room.

"Frank, could you please sit down?"

He ignored Mary Ellen.

"Frank? You're driving me out of my mind."

He stopped in his tracks. "Maureen, you're a nurse. What causes a stroke, anyway?"

Maureen looked up from her texting. "It can be caused by a blood clot—something that keeps the blood from circulating to the brain."

"Yes, but what causes that to happen?" he asked. "I mean, can stress cause a stroke?"

Mary Ellen's voice quivered. "You're asking if it's my fault. Is that it? Well, don't waste your time. I've already taken full responsibility for this. If she dies, I may as well have murdered her."

"Stop it," her sister hissed. "Believe it or not, you're not that powerful. Ma has high blood pressure. I'm pretty sure her mother died of a stroke. She had some risk factors." She looked at her brother. "So, the answer is no, Frank. It's not stress-related."

"You're sure?"

"Why don't you Google it? Or ask her doctor."

Mary Ellen started to cry again.

"Frank, please step outside. I want to talk to you."

"No, Maureen," Mary Ellen said. "Whatever you want to say to him, do it in front of me."

"All I know," Frank continued, "is that Ma was fine this morning. I just want to know what went on after we left."

"She was tired and asked me to help her to bed," Maureen said. "She seemed unsteady and really exhausted. Nothing else happened. A little while later, Mary Ellen heard her moaning. She called 9-1-1. She responded quickly, Frank. She feels bad enough without you adding to it. She needs support, not judgment. This isn't her fault. Promise me you'll stop these ridiculous questions."

"I want to know, that's all."

"And what the hell difference would that make? Will it turn back time? Restore Ma to perfect health? No. Let it go. Be kind. Please."

They heard the click of high heels on the linoleum floor and turned to see Rosie coming down the hall, dressed for work in a navy suit and fuchsia blouse.

Rosie kissed her husband and sisters-in-law. "I came as soon as I could. How's Agnes?"

Noticing Mary Ellen's red eyes and nose, she sat and put her arms around her. "How are you doing, sweetie?"

"I feel terrible. I just wanted to live my own life. I didn't think it would kill her. She's so tough, you know?"

Rosie had no idea what she was talking about. "Of course, she's tough. She's a strong, feisty woman. I'm sure she'll be fine, you'll see."

One of the doctors who had been working on Agnes came into the waiting room. "Hello. I'm Doctor Mitchell. Are all of you relatives of Mrs. Kelleher?"

Frank shook his hand and introduced his wife and sisters. "How is she?"

"She's holding her own right now. We've decided to move her to the Critical Care Unit so we can keep a close eye on her. The next forty-eight hours are the most crucial. We administered a clot-busting drug that can mitigate the stroke's damage, but we don't know yet how effective it was. She needs to rest."

"If the drug works, will she wake up and be fine?" Frank asked.

"Unfortunately, a stroke is quite debilitating. There will be damage. She may not be able to speak or walk or move on one side of her body at first. She'll need therapies and a long recovery time, but she could regain all her abilities. There's no way to know right now. I know this is difficult for you, but it's a waiting game. The best thing for you to do is to go home and get some rest. She'll be sleeping for a long time, so you can plan to come back tomorrow. Only two visitors at a time are allowed in the CCU. We keep the place quiet and calm so our patients can heal."

"Will you be her doctor?" Mary Ellen asked in a small voice.

He gave her a tired smile. "No, I work in the ER. But there's a fantastic staff up there on the third floor. They'll take excellent care of her and keep you folks informed of her progress."

Mary Ellen zoomed in on the word progress. She stood up. "How long does it take to recover from a stroke?"

"Anywhere from a few months to a lifetime, I'm afraid. It depends on the extent of the damage, the general health of the patient, and the person's desire to get better. How was your mother's health?"

"She was healthy. And strong," Mary Ellen replied softly.

"Not to mention strong-willed," Rosie added.

He smiled. "Then she may do very well." He shook hands all around and wished them luck.

Rosie put her arm around Mary Ellen. "Why don't you come home with Frank and me? You look like you could use some chicken noodle soup and Italian cookies. You can sleep in the guest room as long as you like."

As Mary Ellen gave her a hug, she noticed that Frank was trying to catch his wife's eye. "Thanks, Rosie. That's sweet of you, but I think I'll go home."

"Don't you need a break from there? Just for today?"

"Thanks, but I've got a lot to think about. I'm going to have to refigure everything in light of all this."

"What do you mean?" Maureen asked.

"If she can't walk, she can't go back to the third floor. I'll need to speed up the renovations downstairs and get the place ready for her."

Her sister placed a hand on her shoulder. "Whoa. Let's wait and see how she is in forty-eight hours. If things go well, she'll be in the hospital a while, and then she'll have to go to a skilled nursing facility for rehab. Once we see how she's doing, there will be time to make decisions. I think it's a great idea to go home with Rosie, or with me. Get out of your head for a while. You're going to exhaust yourself."

"I am exhausted," she said, sinking into the nearest chair. "What time is it, anyway?"

"It's after three," Frank said. "I've got to go into the office for a couple of hours. I'll talk to you tonight, Maureen. Come on Rosie, let's walk out together." He took his wife's hand.

Rosie allowed herself to be pulled along by her husband. Then she called over her shoulder, "You take care of yourself, Mary Ellen. Call if you need anything—a meal, a glass of wine, a chat."

"Thanks, Rosie. I will." She watched them walk away, Rosie practically running to keep up with her husband. She turned to Maureen. "I want to go home. I'm going to sleep, then I'll come over in the morning. We can come back here together. They'll call if . . . you know . . . she takes a turn for the worse, won't they? I don't want her to die alone. I need to tell her how sorry I am."

"Oh, Mary Ellen." Maureen put her arms around her sister.

They held each other silently, dry-eyed for now, and left the hospital hand in hand.

August 5, 2010

Nearly three weeks have passed. I'm sitting here in Ma's room at Bright Star Rehabilitation Center. We managed to get a private room for her, and I've been sitting beside her bed, feeding her at mealtimes, wiping the drool from her chin, and staying nearby while the physical therapist works her paralyzed left arm. She still can't speak. I've been told it takes time and that progress will be slow. It's very depressing. I know I have to stay optimistic, but it's hard. Even though the staff is great and Ma is well cared for, I still hate that she's here. I hate that I'm here, too, and I feel like I'm doing penance for my sins.

To add insult to injury, Michael called last night. He told me all about his trip to England, how he'd toured all the London historic sites with his cousins and took day trips to Windsor Castle and Oxford and some other places I'm not remembering. He sounded so alive, whereas I felt half dead. Eventually, he came around to asking about my mother and me, and I told him the news. He got very serious and said all the right things, but he must have felt like he was talking to a zombie. He'll probably never call again. If he knew what I'd done to cause this nightmare, he'd disappear for sure.

Maureen is supposed to come and sit with Ma soon so I can go home. I've been here for almost four hours. The thing is, I don't know what to do at home. There are so many unanswered questions: Should I go back to school, or take a leave of absence until Ma is better? What about my apartment? Should I get it ready for Ma and me to move into? That would mean packing fifty years' worth of her stuff from upstairs. I don't have the energy for that. Truthfully, I'd like to climb into bed and be taken care of for a week. Rosie offered, but there's Frank, who frowns whenever he sees me, making me feel guilty. God knows I don't need any help in that department.

One sliver of hope is that Ma seems happy to see me when I come in. She becomes less anxious, and there's nothing in her eyes that hints that she blames me for this. Of course, she probably doesn't remember what happened right before her stroke. Hopefully she never will.

Twenty-One

AGNES WAS MOANING IN HER SLEEP. Mary Ellen bent over her and adjusted the edge of the blanket up by her chin. She stroked her mother's right arm for a few minutes, and when it looked as if she was settled, Mary Ellen sat back down. She read over the page of her journal and imagined being enfolded in Michael's arms, feeling warm and safe. She tried to imagine how she'd feel in Larry's arms but could only remember with embarrassment what they'd been doing when her mother found them together. If only she hadn't been so hell-bent on getting what she wanted without regard for her mother's feelings, she might be living in her new apartment now, her mother adjusting to the new arrangement, the two of them sharing a few meals a week.

Larry didn't seem to feel the least bit guilty. Although Mary Ellen hadn't seen him since the night before her mother's stroke, he'd called every day without fail. At first she didn't answer, but when his messages continued, she relented. All he really wanted to do was to support her. How could she deny him that, especially when he could be preoccupied with the dissolution of his marriage? He told her repeatedly that she wasn't at fault, that she was living her life, which was how it should be, but she couldn't help but feel guilty.

Bless me Father, for I have sinned. Yes, she thought. Sitting here was definitely her penance.

"Hi." Maureen came in with a bag of sandwiches from Subway. Teddy was trailing behind her. She kissed her sister and turned to her mother. "Sleeping peacefully, I see. Did she have therapy yet?"

"No. They'll get her up for lunch and take her to PT after that. She's been asleep most of the time I've been here." She reached for her nephew. "Hey buddy, come give me a hug." Teddy scrambled onto her lap and allowed her to put her arms around him and rub her nose in his sweet-smelling hair. "Somebody's had a shampoo."

"Yeah, Mummy made me get cleaned up. I'm going to smell like nursing home when I leave anyway, so I don't know why I bothered."

"Shh, Teddy. That's not nice." Maureen brought another chair closer to the bed. "We brought you lunch. Teddy picked out your sub. I hope barbecued chicken's okay."

It wasn't Mary Ellen's favorite, but she smiled as she reached for it. "Good choice, Teddy."

Maureen looked her over carefully. "You've been losing weight. Have you been eating?"

"My appetite's lousy these days. I have a bowl of cereal around nine o'clock when I realize I haven't had dinner."

"Why don't you just plan to eat with us every night?"

"Like you need another person to feed." She took a small bite of her sandwich, chewing and swallowing carefully, gauging whether or not her stomach could handle it.

"You're eating like an anorexic."

"Stop, Maureen. I'm in no danger of starving to death. You don't have to take over Ma's job."

"Sorry. I'm just a little concerned."

"Be concerned about her, okay?"

"Did you talk to the social worker today?"

"Briefly. I asked about taking her home. She said at this point she needs full-time care, and that she has to improve quite a bit before we can attempt that. I'm trying to make some plans, but there are no answers. I just have to wait."

"Plans? What are you thinking?"

"Well, I could take a leave of absence from school in the fall to take care of her. Of course, at some point I'd have to go back . . . I won't get paid for that time off, and I can't afford to be without a job."

"Mary Ellen, please don't take all of this on yourself. This should be a family decision. You are not solely responsible for her care, you know. The three of us can figure out what's best for her and make a reasonable decision." She lowered her voice to a point where Mary Ellen could barely hear her. "She might not be able to come home at all. You realize that, don't you?"

Mary Ellen nodded sadly.

"I wish you would go and do something good for yourself. Go spend some time with Kate. Or maybe with . . . ."

"Don't say it, Maureen."

"Please stop punishing yourself. I know you've had martyrdom modeled for you all your life, but I never thought you'd take it on yourself."

"You think I'm being a martyr?"

"To some degree, yes. And we both know how effective that is. Live your life. Do what makes you happy."

Mary Ellen stood up, wrapping the remnants of her sandwich in paper and stuffing it into her bag. "What would make me happy right now is to get out of here."

"Don't be mad. I'm sorry. I just . . . ."

Just then her mother's eyes opened. Mary Ellen forced a smile and kissed her on the forehead. "I'm going now, Ma. You've had a good sleep. Maureen and Teddy are here, and they'll help you with your lunch. Then you'll have some physical therapy and another rest, and Frank or Rosie will be here to help you with supper. I'll be back either tonight, or in the morning. I love you."

Agnes made a grimace that Mary Ellen told herself was an attempt at a smile. She brushed Agnes's cheek with her hand and turned from the bed. "Bye, Teddy. Take good care of Grandma."

He nodded somberly and climbed up on the bed. Mary Ellen could see Agnes's eyes light up at the sight of his face.

Maureen followed her sister out to the corridor and reached for her arm, squeezing it gently. "Call me later. Or come over and eat with us."

"I'll see. I don't know what I'm going to do right now." She extricated her arm and walked down the hall, her sneakers squeaking on the linoleum.

Once outside, she thought about tossing the sandwich in the trash, but then thought better of it and sat on a bench in the sun to finish it.

She replayed Maureen's words and realized there was some truth there. She'd felt guilty, so now she was going above and beyond the call of duty to make sure others could see how dedicated and blameless she was. It probably would be good to step away for a bit to get some perspective. Larry's invitation to his home was an open one.

Come to Westwood one night this week, he'd told her when they'd spoken last night. *I'll make you a wonderful dinner. I'm an excellent cook, and I'd love to show off. Just give me a little notice, and I'll make sure the girls are here. They'll smother you with love and attention, and we'll send you back to Worcester well fed and revived.* She'd said no, that she couldn't possibly be away from her mother that long.

But maybe she could. Not to be alone with him, but to spend time with all of them. She set down her sandwich and reached for her cellphone to shoot off a text: *Decided to accept your offer for dinner. What night would work for you three?*

Would he answer, or had she blown it? She finished eating, threw her trash away, and heard her phone chirp.

Thrilling news! You've made my day! How about six o'clock this evening?

Tonight? She quickly thought of several reasons why tonight was too soon. Then she understood his reasoning. If she waited, she'd change her mind. She texted her acceptance and headed for the parking lot, feeling lighter than she'd felt in weeks.

On her way home, she passed the hair salon she often used. On impulse, she pulled over, noting with satisfaction that the sign *Walk-ins Welcome* was still in the window.

Jennifer, her regular stylist, was sitting at the front desk. "Mary Ellen! You don't have an appointment, do you?"

"No, I don't. My mother had a stroke three weeks ago and I haven't been doing much besides sitting by her bed. But I was driving by and wondered if you were free to wash and trim my hair. Maybe a manicure, too, if someone's available."

"It's your lucky day, hon. My twelve-thirty just cancelled. And I can do your hair and your nails. Follow me." She led her to a sink and tucked a cape around her neck. "Now, settle back, girl. I'm going to give you a nice scalp massage. How about a deep conditioning treatment?"

Mary Ellen told her to do whatever she wanted and allowed herself to savor the feelings of warm water, of the capable hands threading through her hair, and the somewhat mindless chatter of the other stylists who were at work on their customers. Two hours later, she walked out with her hair nicely cut just above her shoulders, her curls straightened and styled. Her neglected hands were reborn, too; the skin was smooth and French tips enhanced her fingernails.

At home, she donned rubber gloves and cleaned the bathroom and kitchen, vacuumed the apartment, and put out the trash. She stripped her bed and started a load of wash. Then her phone rang; she answered it in a cheerful voice.

"Hey, Mary Ellen," Frank said. "You going to see Ma tonight?"

Her mood immediately crashed. "I thought you or Rosie were on for tonight."

"Something came up."

Tears sprang to her eyes. "Oh, Frank. I really wanted to take the night off. I was there this morning, and Maureen is there this afternoon. It's your turn."

"I've got a night meeting I can't get out of. Do you think it's okay if nobody goes? Rosie has plans, too."

"No, Frank. It's not okay. I don't trust the staff to make sure she's fed and not in pain. That's what her family is for." She checked her watch. "They'll be serving her dinner around five-thirty. What time is your meeting? Can't you stop by on your way?"

He sighed. "It's a bit of a pain, that's all."

"Really? You do realize it hasn't been exactly fun and games for me to sit by her bed for hours every single day since her stroke."

"Yeah, but you're off for the summer."

"Look, just tell me. Can you stop by to check on her, or do I have to cancel my plans and do it myself?"

"Well, my meeting's at six thirty. I can go and stay until six. It's not convenient, but . . ."

"Spare me, Frank. Thank you for keeping your commitment to Ma. Tell her I'll see her in the morning." She hung up. Feeling annoyed and agitated, she called Maureen, anxious to make sure Agnes was okay before she headed out to the Bishops.

"We stayed until after her therapy. She's still weak, but Janice said she could see a little progress. She was up in her chair when we left. I told her that Frank would be along soon."

"Yeah, well, he called and tried to get out of it. I told him I needed a night off, and finally he agreed to stop by on his way to his meeting. I don't know why I get so pissed at him, but the favored son should be a little more attentive to his mother, don't you think?"

"He's not comfortable with illness, Mary Ellen. Remember when Dad was dying? He could barely stand to be in that hospital room."

"And I seem to remember Ma making excuses for him. Maybe she's doing the same thing now."

"Well, don't worry about it. I'll call the nursing home around seven and make sure everything's okay. What are you going to do?"

"I'm driving to Westwood to have dinner with Larry and his daughters. I'm leaving now. Do you think I should stop by the nursing home on my way?"

"No. Absolutely not. As a matter of fact, turn your phone off and put Ma out of your mind. I'll check on her later. Go and have a wonderful time. That's an order."

For once, she was in the mood to obey. She grabbed Larry's address and was quickly en route to Westwood, her phone on the seat beside her just in case.

Twenty-Two

S HE PULLED INTO THE DRIVEWAY a little after six. Through a front window of the two-story home, she could see Larry's daughters. They waved, making their way outside and down the front steps.

The girls greeted her warmly while Larry watched from the doorway. He wore a yellow and black striped apron with the logo: *Man in the Kitchen—Beware!*

"Nice apron," Mary Ellen commented, passing him by without a hug as she entered the living room.

"This old thing?" His smile crinkled the corners of his blue eyes.

Dakota stepped between them. "Mary Ellen, I've concocted some amazing frozen drinks. Coconut rum and lemonade. Come have one with me on the back porch."

"I drank those in Florida once. Delicious, but lethal. I hope you went easy on the booze. I haven't had a drink in weeks."

She followed Dakota through the kitchen where the smell of fresh basil and garlic stopped her in her tracks. She inhaled deeply.

"What are you making, Larry?"

"Bruschetta with tomatoes and basil from the farmer's market. Go have your cocktail and chat with the girls. I won't be long."

She stepped onto the screened porch.

"Sit here," Dakota ordered, gesturing to a wicker love seat, the cushions upholstered in a tropical design. She poured a tall, frosted martini glass full of yellow liquid and handed it to Mary Ellen. "Did I tell you I'm taking a bartending course? I signed up on my twenty-first birthday. It's so much fun. I learned this one the other night." She handed another glass to her younger sister.

"Um, didn't they teach you it's illegal to serve a fourteen-year-old?"

"No alcohol, Mary Ellen. Don't worry," Anna-Mei laughed. "Just lemonade."

Mary Ellen took a sip of her drink and, almost immediately, the liquor rushed to her head. She set it down on the table in front of her. "Wow. Potent."

Larry entered from behind, carrying a tray of toasted slices of baguette topped with tomatoes and basil. "When was the last time you ate, Mary Ellen?" He looked at her with what she thought was a rather stern look.

"Around the time I sent you the text, I think."

"You look awfully thin. Maybe you've been forgetting to take care of yourself? Please eat before you drink any more of Dakota's potion."

"Gee, Dad. You make me sound like a witch."

Anna-Mei giggled.

"And it's safe to assume that there's no alcohol in your sister's drink, yes?"

"Sheesh, Dad. What do you take me for?"

Larry sighed and sat next to Mary Ellen on the loveseat. "I'm sorry, Dakota. Now, may I have one of your refreshing-looking beverages, please?"

Dakota got up slowly and poured her father a drink. "Hopefully you'll find this acceptable."

Mary Ellen ate a slice of the bruschetta slowly, gauging the dynamics of this newly diminished family as she tried to keep from dropping tomatoes onto her lap. Something seemed off with them. She felt slightly disappointed. She'd so hoped to be able to take a night off from stress. She took another sip of her drink and felt relaxation begin, starting with her arms and working its way down into her belly. *Maybe I'll get delightfully, embarrassingly drunk*, she thought with a quiet smile.

"I'm so glad you decided to come tonight," Larry said. "We've been driving each other a little crazy lately, and we decided you'd be a good influence. It's great to see you."

"I'm not in any shape to be a good influence on anybody these days, I'm afraid. I've just been muddling along since my mother got sick."

"I'm sorry it's taken me so long to ask about your mother. How is she?" Larry asked.

"She's holding her own. We see tiny improvements day to day, but recovery will be a long process. Thanks for asking. Now, let's talk about you folks. How are you, Anna-Mei? I haven't seen you since we got back. You look like you've lost some weight, too." She suddenly remembered the conversation between Dakota and Larry about Anna-Mei's not eating, and wished she could take back that last remark.

Anna-Mei looked into her drink for a moment. When she looked up, her eyes glistened with tears. "It's been a hard time for me, too. Sometimes I forget to eat, or I don't feel like it when I'm sad. But I'm kind of getting used to things. It still hurts, but I know my mom didn't do this to hurt us. And it's not our fault. She told me that. I guess I have to believe it."

They were silent.

Larry spoke first. "This is tough for all of us. I have to keep reminding myself that I can't change anyone else. I can only control how I react. And, I guess, try not to make things worse in the process."

"Is that what I've been doing, Dad?" Dakota asked. "Am I making things worse by being so enraged at Mom? Maybe I need to talk to a counselor."

"I didn't mean that, Dakota. You're entitled to your feelings. God knows I've been angry at her, too."

"And you're not now?" Dakota looked directly at Larry, her face now open and vulnerable.

"It comes and goes. Thank God it's not a constant thing. It flares up when I talk to her on the phone, or when I see one of you girls hurting. Then I could . . . ." He shook his head. "Never mind. It's hard, that's all."

Mary Ellen felt her tears start once again and tried to hide them behind a cocktail napkin.

"Oh, Mary Ellen. I'm sorry." Dakota turned to her dad. "We didn't invite her here to make her cry. Let's change the subject."

"It doesn't take much to make me cry these days, Dakota. I've always been a crier, but it's been worse lately. Just ignore me. It will pass. I really admire you three for being able to discuss your feelings and struggles so openly."

"Yes, but talking about our personal pain while drinking these things could be dangerous." Larry raised his glass and peered at the yellow liquid. "How much rum did you put in this, Dakota?"

"They are a little strong, aren't they? I could have sworn I followed the recipe exactly, but maybe I was a little heavy-handed on the rum. Good thing I got to practice on you guys. Take a couple of gulps, and then I'll dilute them with lemonade."

"And here I was thinking I'd become a lightweight," Mary Ellen said as she reached for the bruschetta. "I've had about four sips, and I feel like I've had a bottle of wine. I think you're right, Larry. I need something in my stomach."

"Indulge yourself. I'm going to light the grill."

"May I ask what you're cooking?"

"We're having surf and turf. Grilled lobster tails, steak tips, corn on the cob, and a green salad."

"Wow. I think I'd better lay off the bruschetta if I'm going to eat a meal like that."

"You'll have plenty of time to metabolize the appetizers, believe me," Dakota assured her. "Dad's a fantastic cook, but it's not exactly fast food."

"And he makes the biggest mess of the kitchen," Anna-Mei added. "And guess who has to clean it up?"

"Only fair, girls. I cook, you eat, and then you clean up. Anytime you want to switch roles, let me know."

Dakota rolled her eyes as her sister smiled from across the room. This was the family banter that Mary Ellen had witnessed on their trip before the drama. She felt reassured. She sat back and took another sip of her drink.

"Okay, I'm ready to have this drink diluted before I do something embarrassing like fall off my chair."

"Anna-Mei, why don't you give Mary Ellen a tour of the house?" Larry called from the yard.

"Would you like that?" she asked.

Erica's house, Mary Ellen thought. *With her decorative touches, and the bedroom she'd shared with Larry . . .*

"It's okay if you don't want to," Anna-Mei said.

"No, no, I'd like to see it. Especially your room. And your sister's. I want to see where you guys hang out."

The girls led the way through the kitchen into a cozy dining room, then crossed the foyer into the spacious living room. A fireplace was flanked by bookcases with shelves so full that books spilled over onto the floor.

"Now this is my kind of room," Mary Ellen commented. She liked the messy, lived-in look of it. "It must be so nice in the winter to curl up in front of the fire and read."

"That's Dad's idea of a good time, too," Dakota observed.

They made their way up the staircase. Family photos hung on the wall. School portraits, vacation photos, the girls as babies and toothless six-year-olds. At the top, there was an empty space where a picture had once hung. The wedding portrait?

"This is my room." Anna-Mei opened the door to a tidy bedroom. The twin bed was made up with a peach bedspread, a flowered pillow arranged at the head. A bureau, a nightstand, and a wooden chair stood against the walls, with not a speck of dust visible. Under the window, a small bookcase held a dozen books, a Teddy bear, a Chinese fan, and a photo of the Bishop family at Disney World.

"What a nice space," Mary Ellen observed. "Do you always keep it so neat and clean?"

"Yes, aggravatingly so," Dakota growled. "Wait until you see my room."

Dakota's room was next door. Mary Ellen took in the orange walls, the electric blue bedspread, a rug with big, geometric shapes. A desk was piled with textbooks, boxes, and shopping bags.

"I know it's a mess," Dakota said. "I'm getting ready to go back to school."

"Your décor is stunning. Did you decorate it yourself?"

"Yes, back in junior year of high school. You like it?"

"I love it. You have such a flair. I don't know if I could fall asleep in here, though—the colors are so vibrant."

"Hmm. Actually, I find it restful."

"Oh, look at these," Mary Ellen interrupted as she caught sight of a wall that was entirely covered with collages of photos. Proms, graduations, parties, beach trips with friends. Dakota looking stunning in every one. "Has a bad picture ever been taken of you?"

"No, aggravatingly not," Anna-Mei answered for her sister, and they all laughed.

"Mary Ellen?" Larry stood in the doorway. "You have a phone call."

She looked at him, puzzled. "I thought I turned my phone off."

"Your sister called on our home phone. Why don't you take it downstairs in the study?"

Mary Ellen stood still, looking at his grave expression. "Is it about my mother?"

"I don't know. She didn't say. She'd like to speak with you. Follow me." He turned and walked toward the stairs.

Her heart beat rapidly as her stomach churned. She suddenly wished she hadn't taken even a sip of that drink. She wanted to run but forced herself to take her time on the stairs, trying to breathe. *Ma's okay,* she told herself. *She's fine. Everything's all right.*

Larry opened the door to a room the girls hadn't shown her. "The phone is on the desk. I'll hang up the extension after you pick up."

She nodded and picked up the receiver. As soon as she heard her sister's voice, she knew her mother was dead. As she struggled to listen to Maureen explain what had happened, her knees grew weak; she sank to the floor.

"Are you there, Mary Ellen? Are you okay?" Maureen asked.

She tried to speak; tears tore at her throat and ran down her face. She sobbed from her gut and dropped the phone, then ran out into the hall, where Larry was waiting a discreet distance away.

"Bathroom," she whispered, and ran in the direction he pointed, barely making it to the toilet. Yellow liquid rushed out, searing her throat. When she finally stopped heaving, she sat back on her heels and sobbed for several minutes. Finally, Larry cracked open the door.

"How can I help?"

She closed her eyes and shook her head. He stepped into the tiny bathroom and handed her a wad of tissues. He wet a washcloth with cool water and pressed it into her other hand.

"Come with me," he said gently.

She wiped her mouth with the cloth and followed him out through the kitchen into the living room where the girls were waiting. She sank down onto the sofa and closed her eyes so as not to see their stricken faces. Anna-Mei got her a glass of water.

"Thank you," she whispered, taking a sip. She looked at Larry. "I dropped the phone. Can you please tell my sister I'll call her right back?"

He left the room.

"Is it your mother?" Dakota whispered.

Mary Ellen nodded and pressed her hands against her face to hold back the torrent of tears that were breaching the surface.

Larry returned and sat next to her. "I told her you needed a few minutes. She said she was going to go home to talk to her kids and would call your cellphone later."

Teddy's angelic face sprang into her mind. He loved his gnarly grandmother so much. This would break his little heart. She stood up and walked back to the bathroom. She ran the water in the sink to cover the sound of her sobbing. *Oh, God. How can this be happening?*

After about ten minutes, Mary Ellen emerged. "Do any of you know where I put my purse? I need my phone."

Larry found the purse next to where she'd been sitting on the porch. She dug into it and retrieved her phone. Larry and the girls were silent as they watched her turn it on and wait for it to reboot.

"Seven missed calls. Three from my brother, three from my sister, and one from the nursing home. I've been attached to my phone for three weeks, day and night. And when they really needed me, it was turned off. If this wasn't so awful, I might laugh at the irony."

"Do you know what happened?" he asked gently.

She struggled to compose herself. "Someone—either Maureen or Rosie or I—have been there for every meal these past weeks. She had to have her food puréed because of swallowing problems. I'm not sure what happened. Someone must've given her the wrong meal, or given her a bite or two and then left her. Maureen said that Frank walked in around five-thirty and found her unresponsive. The nurse tried to revive her and found food in her mouth. They rushed her to the hospital, but Maureen had just been told that she was gone. They think she aspirated a piece of food. It would never have happened if I'd been there."

Larry looked up at his daughters, who were both crying. "Dakota, would you please turn off the grill? If you girls are hungry, the salad is in the fridge. Let's give Mary Ellen some space, okay?" He gestured for them to leave the room.

Larry watched her cry for a few minutes before he went over and cradled her in his arms. "It's not your fault. We can't protect the people we love from every possible contingency. Your mother knows you love her. You did your best. When my mother died, I tried to keep in mind how much she loved me. It's been seven years since I lost her, and what I remember most is the love. That never dies. It will stay with you for the rest of your life."

She sobbed harder. Finally, she pushed herself from him. "I just can't believe she's gone, Larry. The last thing I did before she had the stroke was hurt her. I can't get that out of my mind. My selfishness probably caused that stroke, and now my neglect caused her death."

"What possible good can it be for anyone—your mother, yourself, or your family—to think like that? You made choices that felt right to you. If your mother had a problem with those choices, that was her challenge. I'm sure that ultimately, she would have wanted you to be happy and loved, don't you think?"

She nodded.

"Try to remember how much she loved you. And how much you love her. That's all that matters in the end."

She stood and walked toward Larry's study. "I'm going to call Maureen, and then I'm going to go back to Worcester. Thank you for everything. You've been a wonderful friend." She went into the study and shut the door.

Twenty-three

FIVE DAYS LATER, at three-thirty in the afternoon, Mary Ellen entered the funeral parlor with Maureen and Frank and their families. The rooms were hushed, their footsteps cushioned by thick carpets. Jack Rafferty, the funeral director, greeted them, and offered his condolences. Maureen held Mary Ellen's hand tightly as they headed up to the open casket. The scent of roses emanated from two magnificent arrangements that stood on pedestal tables that flanked the casket. Mary Ellen had already shed an ocean of tears in the past days, but now she was dry-eyed as she gazed at her mother lying there on a bed of pale blue satin. The undertaker had done a good job. Agnes's steel gray hair was fixed exactly as she liked it, the crown curled, sides combed back from her made-up face. She had on her favorite royal blue blouse, her gold crucifix necklace resting on her bosom.

"She looks good, don't you think?" Maureen whispered.

"She looks dead," Mary Ellen replied. She hadn't seen her mother since she left her with Maureen and Teddy at the nursing home. Agnes's waxy appearance brought home to Mary Ellen that her mother was no longer alive. Her spirit was elsewhere, she hoped, but she would never again hug or criticize her, make her laugh or drive her crazy with her melodrama.

She touched her mother's cold hand and bent over to kiss her cheek before walking over to take her place in the line of chairs at the side of the room. She wanted to be calm as she received friends and relatives who would be coming to pay their respects.

After spending a few moments in front of the casket, Lou joined her. He was wiping away his tears; Mary Ellen hugged him.

"Man, I can't believe she's gone," he said. "She was so alive. I'm still in shock. I wasn't crazy about the idea of living with her while you were in China, but you know, I feel like I got to know her pretty well. She was so good to me."

Mary Ellen nodded. "She loved you, Lou. You were her first grandchild, and she was so proud of you."

Lou nodded his head and quietly sobbed. She handed him a tissue and stroked his back.

Jack Rafferty came into the room and asked if they were ready to receive people. "Line up however you're comfortable, and then I'll let them in," he said.

Mary Ellen was in the first chair near the casket, but she moved down so they'd be lined up from oldest to youngest—Frank and Rosie, Maureen and Joe, then Mary Ellen. Lou took his young cousins to sit in the rows of folding chairs that faced the front.

Mary Ellen took a deep breath. She'd been through this before when her father died ten years ago, but this felt different. Her mother had been with her then.

Michael was among the first to arrive. He spent a few minutes in front of the casket and then shook hands with the family. When he reached Mary Ellen, he put his arms around her and held her for a moment before stepping back. "I am so deeply sorry, Mary Ellen. Your mother was a lovely woman, and I'm so glad I met her. This must be very hard for you."

His gentle words made her cry, and she wrapped her arms around him while trying to master her emotions. "Thank you, Michael. My mother thought the world of you. Thank you for being here." She managed to smile and stepped out of their hug. "Lou is over there with Teddy and Joanna if you'd like to say hello," she said as she nodded toward them.

"I will," he replied. "I'm going to stay for a little while; I hope we can talk again if you're able."

"I hope so, too," she answered, squeezing his hand.

Childhood friends of each of the siblings arrived to pay their respects. Irish cousins, some quite old, shuffled behind aluminum walkers and shared their memories of "little Agnes," making Mary Ellen laugh. People continued to file in, standing patiently in line to kneel before the casket and say a prayer.

"Look at all these people," she said to her sister. "Ma really had a lot of friends. People loved her."

"And listen to the noise in this room," Maureen replied. Laughter rose as people greeted one another and shared stories about Agnes, the loudest of which were Betty, Nora, and Ellie, her bevy of Irish beauties. "It's a real Irish wake. All we're missing is the whiskey."

"Unfortunately. I could use a shot. My legs feel like lead."

"Why don't you take a break and go talk to Michael and the kids? Frank and I will greet people."

Just then Mary Ellen spotted Danny and Kate. She went over and received their welcome hugs.

"How are you holding up?" Kate asked.

"I'm okay. Being with all these people helps." She smiled. "Michael Wong is here. Let's go say hello."

Michael had been entertaining Teddy and Joanna by pulling quarters from their ears, to the children's delight. When he saw the O'Days, he stood up and shook their hands and said how good it was to see them again. He offered Mary Ellen his seat; she took it gratefully.

"Why did I wear heels?" she asked. "My arches are killing me."

"Well, they go well with your outfit," Kate said, scanning the fitted black suit Mary Ellen was wearing. "You look really thin. How much weight have you lost?"

"Not much. Black is great camouflage."

"It's very becoming," Michael added. "Very elegant. I think your mother would approve."

She chuckled. "Yes, she was always trying to get me to dress up. Here I am, and it's too late for her to see me."

"Actually, I think she's here," Michael said, looking around the room. "I can picture her walking through the crowd, listening in to the conversations, smiling with pleasure, and feeling the love."

Mary Ellen teared up. She nodded in agreement. "Yes, I think her spirit is here. And she's enjoying her wake." She put her shoes back on. "I should get back to the receiving line. I hope you'll all stay for a while."

Kate and Danny joined the line to offer Frank and Maureen their condolences, while Michael stayed with Lou and the children.

When Kate reached Mary Ellen she said, "He is very sweet, isn't he?"

Mary Ellen nodded. She'd been touched by Michael's thoughtful words. It was both perceptive and comforting of him to point out her mother's presence in the room.

But as Kate walked away, Mary Ellen felt someone else's eyes on her; she looked across the room to see Larry gazing at her while waiting for Dakota to sign the guestbook. It was the first time she'd seen him since the night her mother died. She left her place in line to greet him and his daughter.

He hugged her, and pain rushed into her chest as she remembered that night at his house when she got the call that her mother was gone. She stepped away and turned to Dakota.

"I am so sorry for you," her young friend said as she hugged her. "This is all so sad."

Mary Ellen nodded and found her voice. "I want to introduce you to my family." She led them over to Frank and Rosie. Her brother eyed Larry carefully as he shook his hand. His face flickered with conflicting emotions, and Mary Ellen suspected that he blamed both her and Larry for her mother's stroke.

Fortunately, warm, loving Rosie reached over to shake his hand and then gave Dakota a hug. "It's so nice to finally meet you, Dakota. My son described you as absolutely gorgeous, and he was right."

Mary Ellen felt a wash of gratitude for her sister-in-law, whose kindness to others always eased tense situations. She must have developed the skill in response to her husband, who, Mary Ellen thought, often put his foot in his mouth. She was grateful that whatever he was thinking, he was holding it in right now.

She introduced them to Maureen and Joe and sensed that they were also cool to Larry, but warm to his daughter. It made sense, she supposed. Larry was at the heart of all the drama. But he was innocent, wasn't he?

She stayed in the receiving line while the Bishops went to chat with Kate and Danny. She noticed Larry and Michael step away from the others and speak to one another. Then she was distracted by one of her mother's friends, and when she looked again, Michael was nowhere in sight. A sick feeling swelled inside her stomach. Had he left without saying goodbye?

By six-thirty, Mary Ellen felt as if she were sleepwalking. There were no new mourners to greet. People stood in small groups, chatting quietly. Joe had taken the kids home; they'd been well behaved, and Maureen didn't want to push her luck.

Mary Ellen slipped out of her heels and tucked them under a chair. Dakota and Lou sat close together in conversation.

Larry sat alone in the back of the room, eyes closed, head leaning back against the wall. Mary Ellen sat down next to him.

"You look as wiped out as I feel," she said.

"I am tired," he admitted. "And you still have the funeral to get through tomorrow."

"Well, it's all been planned. It's going to be beautiful. My friend Ben is going to sing the Gounod *Ave Maria*, which is my mother's favorite, and Maureen and Lou are reading her favorite scriptures. I'm not taking an active role. I only have to show up." She paused. "Do you know why Michael left so suddenly? I saw the two of you talking, and then he was gone. What was that all about?"

"He asked me if you and I were seeing each other romantically."

"I see. What did you say to him?"

"I said that I'd very much like that, but that you needed to make that decision."

"And what did he say to that?"

"He looked over at you, watched you for a few minutes, and thanked me. Then he said goodbye to everyone and walked out."

Mary Ellen closed her eyes. She hoped this didn't mean that Michael was gone for good. She did have decisions to make, ones that her mother could no longer influence. This was her life. But she was not going to make any decisions tonight.

She took a few breaths before turning back to Larry. "I need to go be with my family now."

"Anna-Mei is coming with Dakota and me to the funeral tomorrow."

"Oh, Larry, she doesn't have to come. None of you do. You didn't know my mother, so I know you'll be coming for me, but that's not necessary. I know you care. I appreciate you being here tonight, but please don't put yourself through that tomorrow."

"Don't be silly. I want to come."

"Look, you folks are going through your own trying time right now. I'd like you to do something fun with your daughters tomorrow. Go for a hike, take them somewhere nice for lunch, or walk on the beach somewhere. I'll know you're thinking of me and that's enough."

"I think maybe I've taken on some of your guilt."

"This isn't yours to feel guilty about, Larry. I chose my actions, and whether they caused the stroke or not, nothing can be done to change anything. I'm trying to put that behind me, and I hope you will, too."

She saw the funeral director come in the door and check his watch. It was time for the wake to end. She reached over and took Larry's hand.

"Thank you for being here tonight and for being a good friend through all of this. I wish you and your girls healing and peace in whatever is to come for you." She kissed his cheek and walked away.

She walked over to where Dakota was sitting and said goodbye to her before she went back to the casket and knelt, looking at her mother's face. As she closed her eyes to pray, she became aware of someone kneeling beside her. She glanced over and saw her brother's sorrowful face.

"Mary Ellen," he whispered. "I'm sorry I didn't do what I was supposed to do the night Ma died. I should have been there earlier. I could have prevented her death. There I was blaming you for causing the stroke, and I'm the one who really killed her. I'm sorry I blamed you, and I'm sorry I was irresponsible that night. You must hate me."

She took his hand. "No, Frank. I don't hate you, and I've never blamed you. It happened. Ma's gone and we can't change that, but we can love and forgive each other. Let's do that, okay? That's what Ma would want more than anything."

They cried together as they embraced on the kneeler until Mary Ellen lost her balance and almost tipped over and fell onto the floor. Frank caught her and they laughed as they wiped away their tears. Rosie and Maureen had been watching; they didn't know what the conversation had been, but they joined in the ending embrace. They each kissed Agnes goodbye and walked out together. In the parking lot, Frank stopped.

"I'm not sure you girls know this, but Ma asked me to be the executor of her estate. I have a copy of the will at home. There's probably another copy wherever she kept her important papers. We need to get together soon to read it."

"Have you read it?" Mary Ellen asked. She felt a twinge of fear in her gut.

"No. Let's do it together. Maybe after the funeral?"

"Frank, let's get through that first, okay?" Maureen answered after she must have seen the dismay on her sister's face. "We can talk about it tomorrow."

Mary Ellen gave Frank, Rosie, and Lou another long hug. Maureen needed a ride home, but Mary Ellen asked if she would drive her car. She needed to let her tears come. Who knew there were so many kinds of tears? Tears of sorrow for her mother, of gratitude to her brother, of uncertainty for her future, and, she realized with surprise, tears of relief that, in an instant, she'd made the decision to leave Larry behind.

Twenty-Four

MARY ELLEN MANAGED TO DELAY the reading of the will until the Sunday after the funeral. She needed time to rest and to grieve in private. Who knew how long she would continue to live in the only home she'd ever known? She was certain that her mother would have looked out for her; she just had no idea how it would play out. They'd never spoken of her death. To Mary Ellen, it had been something that was far off in the future. But if her mother had prepared a will, she had been looking into that future with a more realistic eye.

She expected her brother and sister to arrive at one. She wanted to meet at the kitchen table, the site of so many family meetings. The kitchen was where she felt closest to her mother, the place where she'd last heard her voice the morning of the stroke. In that room she could recall her mother's face, the scent of her lily of the valley perfume, the sound of her voice. She put a fresh box of tissues on the table, doubting she'd get through this without tears.

Last night she'd searched her mother's room and found an unlocked metal box on a shelf in her closet. It contained a stack of large envelopes labeled in her mother's florid handwriting. She placed the box in the middle of the table.

Then she heard a tap at the apartment door, followed by the click of a key in the lock. She stood up to greet her family.

"We let ourselves in so you wouldn't have to come downstairs," Frank said as he entered with Maureen. "Where do you want to sit? Living room?"

"Let's sit in the kitchen," Mary Ellen answered, leading the way. "What's in the bag?"

Frank put a brown paper sack on the table and reached in. "Guinness," he said. "Two for each of us. Cold."

Mary Ellen laughed. "And here I was thinking about whether I should make coffee or tea. Speaking of surprises, I found this box in Ma's closet." She gestured to it as the others took a seat. "It's full of envelopes, but I haven't opened any of them yet. A copy of the will is probably there."

Frank pulled the box over and looked inside. "Damn, she was organized, wasn't she?" He pulled out a stack of envelopes and began to shuffle through them. "The deed to the house—good to have—her insurance papers, receipts for home improvements and repairs, investments." Then he held one up. "Here it is—the last will and testament of Agnes Elizabeth Shea Kelleher."

Mary Ellen closed her eyes.

They sat, silent, for a moment.

Then Frank cleared his throat. He placed the envelope in front of his sisters and pulled another envelope—the last one—from the box. He read their mother's handwriting on the front. "To my children, Frank, Maureen, and Mary Ellen, to be opened after my death."

"I had no idea she was this prepared," Mary Ellen said, shaking her head. "But it's so Ma, isn't it? The melodramatic touch."

"I figured she was up to something when she asked me to drive her to her lawyer's office while you were in China," Maureen said. "She said she needed to check her investments. She was there for well over an hour."

"Do you think she disinherited me? She was really upset about me going on that trip."

"Doubtful. But there's only one way to find out. You two share one copy of the will, and I'll read from the one she left with me," Frank said.

They read silently, Frank more quickly than his sisters.

"I don't speak legalese," Mary Ellen asked after she'd read half a page. "Can either of you interpret?"

"It looks to me like she wants us to sell this house and split the proceeds three ways," Maureen said. "But am I reading this right, Frank? Mary Ellen can live in the house until she turns forty, and we can't sell it until then?"

"She wanted to make sure I was officially an old maid before she kicked me out."

Frank cleared his throat again. "We can sell the house only if you don't want to keep living here, but if you want to stay it can only be for five years. There are investments, too. Those will also be split three ways. It'll take me a while to go through them, but from a quick glance, I'd say we're looking at over a hundred thousand apiece."

"Wow. I had no idea," Maureen said soberly.

"Dad started a retirement fund for them years ago. The money was to take care of them in their old age," Frank said.

"I didn't know she had this kind of money," Mary Ellen said. "She was always saying she couldn't spend money on one thing or another. Why didn't she spend it on herself?"

"She wanted it to last. But I'm guessing that she also wanted to make sure there was something to leave to her children and grandchildren. That would be like her, wouldn't it?" Frank asked.

Mary Ellen shook her head, smiling sadly. "She was the most generous, loving, *aggravating* mother a girl could have."

"Shall we read the letter?" Frank didn't wait for an answer but slid his finger under the seal of the last envelope. He pulled out a sheet of paper and three separate envelopes, each bearing the name of one of Agnes's children. "I guess we each have our own." He opened the sheet of paper and began to read.

My dearest children,

All my life I assumed I would live forever. I know that sounds crazy, but I just couldn't imagine this world turning without me. I've been to enough wakes and funerals in my life to know it couldn't be so, but still. In the past year I've started to feel my age. Not just the creaky bones and body aches, but I've found I just can't handle the stresses of life very well. I get dizzy a lot. I wake up with my heart pounding, and I can't get back to sleep. I'm more tired than I used to be. I've told my doctor, but she just puts me on different pills. Your father knew he wasn't going to live forever, and he was the kind of man who made sure his family would be taken care of when he was gone. He had a good life insurance policy and put money aside for our retirement. The poor guy only got a few good years after he retired before he got cancer. I was luckier, and I've gotten to see the ripe old age of 75. Now it's my turn to make sure things are in place so you can live good lives after I'm gone.

You three are my pride and joy. Your lives have given me purpose. You have all been very good to me. Now I ask you to be good to each other. Love each other, stay close, and make sure everyone has what they need. I love you very much.

—Ma

Mary Ellen and Maureen each grabbed a tissue and Maureen slid the box across the table to Frank. The letter had brought a fresh wave of sorrow to Mary Ellen. She wondered how she'd be able to read the one that was addressed only to her.

After Frank had wiped his eyes and blown his nose he said, "Hoo, boy. This is hard, isn't it?"

"I feel like she's sitting right here with us, and I want so much to be able to give her a hug and tell her I love her," Maureen said.

Mary Ellen was silent as her tears fell. She nodded in agreement.

"I don't think I can sit here to read my letter," Frank said. "What do you say we each find a private space and read our own? We can meet back here and share anything we want to share, but I think Ma meant these to be for our eyes alone."

"I'd like to sit in Ma's room, if that's okay," Mary Ellen said, reaching slowly for the envelope with her name on it.

"I'll go out on the front porch," Frank said. "I used to sit out there with her on summer nights when I'd come to visit."

"I'll sit in her chair in the living room," Maureen said. "Let's take all the time we need, okay?"

Mary Ellen stepped into her mother's small room off the kitchen. It still smelled of her perfume. She sat down on the bed and pulled a crocheted afghan across her lap. She closed her eyes and pictured her mother's face, her dark brown eyes shining with love for her daughter. She took a deep breath before opening the envelope and then began to read.

> *Mary Ellen—my baby girl, my roommate, my pride and joy,*
>
> *First of all, I want to say how sorry I am to have died. If you are reading this, then I am gone—dead and buried in St. John's Cemetery next to your father. It's hard for me to even*

imagine it, but I know it's going to happen eventually. You are in China right now. I didn't want you to go, and I'm worried sick about you while at the same time I admire your courage and the strength of your will. You didn't let me talk you out of going. That upset me at the time, but thinking about my own death made me realize that this is actually a good thing. When I'm gone, you will have to live your own life and make your own choices about everything. Depending on when I go, you may have an excellent inheritance, one that will help you settle into a new home and fund some pretty nice trips.

Did I ever tell you that when I was eighteen, I almost eloped with a man who ran the merry-go-round for a traveling carnival? My brothers got wind of it and stepped in before I could even pack a bag. Thank God for them. They put the fear of God into me, and I played it safe after that. It couldn't have had a happy ending for me, I'm sure. But once in a while I imagine that I pulled it off and lost my virginity to the dark-haired, sexy Charlie. I taught you to be well behaved and careful, but I think there's a little bit of that wild girl in you. You have an adventurous spirit. You've also played it safe so far, but I have a feeling that this trip to China will show you the way to go. You're either going to start taking more chances, or you're going to continue as is. My will gives you five more years to figure that out. That should be enough time. Far be it from me to ask you to leave the only place you've called home. So, if you're reading this before you turn forty, know that you've got some time.

You are a kind, generous, smart, and loving woman, Mary Ellen. I thank God for you every single day. Somewhere out there is a good man who will see those qualities in you if you let him. You're not too old to start a family, but let's face it, you've got to get going on that soon.

I pray that you will always remember me and keep me in your heart. I want you to be happy, healthy, and loved throughout your life, and someday I'll be there to greet you on the other side. Words aren't enough to tell you how much I love you.

—Ma

Mary Ellen read the letter three times. Her mother once wanted to run away with a carnival worker? She laughed out loud through her tears. In the days before her mother's death, she'd felt so misunderstood by her. Now she realized that her mother had understood her perfectly and truly wanted the best for her. She'd seen the goodness and sincerity of unattached Michael and had wanted to use everything in her power to push them together. She knew that getting involved with a man who was not yet divorced from his wife of twenty years was probably not the best idea. But Mary Ellen had pushed against her, wanting to do it her own way, choosing the opposite of what was most likely the smoothest course to love. Why did she seem to be her own worst enemy?

She could hear her brother and sister talking softly in the kitchen and went out to join them. "I think it's time for a Guinness," she said.

Frank grabbed one from the fridge and poured it into a waiting glass. Mary Ellen took a grateful sip. "Did either of you know that Ma tried to elope with a carnival worker when she was eighteen?"

"What are you talking about?" Maureen asked.

Frank looked at her, no doubt wondering if this was a strange joke.

She read the full paragraph to them and waited for their reaction.

"Let me see that," Maureen said, reaching for the letter. "Losing her virginity to the dark-haired, sexy Charlie? I cannot believe she wrote that. When I was dating Joe, she practically ordered me to wear a chastity belt."

Frank shook his head repeatedly. "Ugh. I don't want either of those images stuck in my head. Thank goodness for her brothers. Big bros save the day, don't they?"

"Sounds to me like they threw cold water on her adventurous spirit forever," Mary Ellen said. "Funny she would bring up this deep, dark secret at the end of her life. Why do you think she told me?"

"I think she was encouraging you. I think she was saying, 'move on, sell the house, create a life of creativity and joy,'" Maureen said. "I mean, no pressure if you're not ready to go. But five years is a long time to hang around here, trying to figure out what to do with your life."

"Neither of you needs to worry about that. I was already in the process of moving downstairs. With the money from my share of the house I can put a down payment on something I really want. All the things I've been dreaming of—a quiet street, a cat, a garden." She paused. "But maybe it's too soon. Don't they say you should wait a year after someone dies to make changes?"

"I think that applies to a spouse," her brother said. "And you already had plans in the making, so I think it'll be fine. Shall I call a realtor to come take a look and see how much they think this old place is worth? Don't worry, I won't call Nancy Shugrue."

"Frank," Maureen said with a tone of warning. "I don't know what Ma wrote in your letter, but she said she trusted me to make sure that Mary Ellen had all the time and support she needed. Please let her decide when she's ready."

"Oh, I'm not pushing," he protested. "I just want to get the ball rolling. These things can take time. Ma said the same thing to me, by the way. I mean, after she told me what a fantastic son I was."

His sisters laughed, and Mary Ellen threw a crumpled napkin across the table at him.

"Look. School starts tomorrow. It's just meetings for the first two days, but the kids arrive on Wednesday. Kate and Ben and some of the other teachers got my room pretty much set up for me. I don't technically have to start this week because of bereavement days, but I think I'd rather be there for the first day of school with my kids. I need to get back to being busy now. So Frank, go ahead and get a realtor to look at the house. Give me a few weeks to get into the swing of things at school, and then we can talk about when to put it on the market. I'll stay put right here until it sells."

"Are you sure about this, Mary Ellen?" her sister asked. "Don't you want to take some time to think it through, make sure you're ready?"

"I'm positive. Ma's right. This feels like a natural next step. I'm sorry that she had to die for me to finally know it. I hope she forgives me."

"There's nothing to forgive." Maureen put her arms around her sister and held her close.

The phone rang, and Frank picked it up. He listened for a moment. "No, you've got the right number, Michael. Nice to hear your voice. Mary Ellen's right here."

Mary Ellen extricated herself from the embrace and reached for the phone. "Hello?" She listened with a smile and said, "Of course. Come over as soon as you can. Maureen and Frank are just leaving. Do you remember how to get here?"

She handed the phone to Frank to hang up for her. Then she sat down, looking slightly dazed.

"What's up?" Maureen asked.

"Michael," she answered. "He's been thinking about me since the wake. He drove all the way to Worcester, trying to get up the nerve to call me. He wants to see me."

"So why do you look shell-shocked?" Frank asked.

"Michael left the wake without saying goodbye, and he didn't come to the funeral. I wasn't sure I'd hear from him ever again. But he'll be here in fifteen minutes. He wants to see me, to talk to me."

"That's good, isn't it?" Maureen asked.

"It's just that the timing is kind of amazing. I just read a letter from Ma telling me to let myself be open to someone who sees my good qualities, and now Michael is arriving on my doorstep."

"Yup, Ma's feeling pretty smug right now, wherever she is," Frank said. "Well, let's go, Maureen. Love is in the air, and far be it from me to stand in the way."

"Just remember, Mary Ellen," her sister warned. "Ma is gone. This is your life. You do what you think and feel is best. Maybe Michael is your guy, maybe not. Pay attention."

Mary Ellen stood up. "Thanks for the reminder. I will pay attention. But in the meantime, I'm going to go splash cold water on my face and brush my hair, so I don't look like a grief-stricken wretch when I welcome him."

"You're beautiful, Mary Ellen," Frank said. "You've already got color back in your cheeks and a sparkle in your eye since you talked to him. You're going to be fine."

She hugged them both one more time and watched them leave. She felt so grateful for them, so grateful for her mother's letter. She knew that her love for them, and theirs for her, would bind them forever.

From the kitchen window she saw Michael's car pull up. She walked slowly downstairs, preparing herself to meet him with an open heart. *It doesn't take a doctorate from Harvard to see what a good catch he is*, she heard her mother say. She opened the door to the man who wore a hopeful smile and carried a huge armful of garden flowers. He opened his mouth to speak, but Mary Ellen silenced him with a kiss. She wasn't sure of anything except that love would take her where she needed to go, and for now, that was enough.

Acknowledgements

MANY PEOPLE INSPIRED THIS STORY: my mother and her sisters; my three sisters; and Cathy, Brian, Olivia, Bryan, and Jackie, with whom I traveled to China in 2010.

I had many readers over the years of writing this novel. Ed Londergan and Jack McClintock of the Quaboag Writer's Collaborative offered insights during the pandemic. Barbara Ramian, Amy Paul, and Phyllis LaMontagne gave valuable feedback as I got closer to finishing. Kasey Rogers and Virginia Heslinga have supported and encouraged my writing for many years. To everyone who read my work at various stages of its development—and there were many—thank you for your time.

My parents enthusiastically supported me in my musical and literary pursuits. I wish they were alive to read this novel.

Finally, Bryan, Tom, and Jackie—you've cheered me on and supported me for almost thirty years. Your love and support give me strength for everything I do.